Praise for the Graves Glen Series

"A spooky romantic comedy treat that had me sighing at one page, laughing out loud at the next. *The Ex Hex* is the perfect book for fall."

—Tessa Bailey, *New York Times* bestselling author

"Sterling casts a spell on her readers with this romantic comedy. . . . A cute and laughable holiday read to get you through the harsh winter weather."

—*USA Today* on *The Ex Hex*

"Filled with delightful witchiness and humor, this playful romantic comedy from Sterling explores second chances and self-discovery. . . . Comedic chaos rules the day, with plenty of laughs overlaying just a touch of introspection as the exes realize how much they still mean to each other. The result is a fluffy Halloween treat."

—*Publishers Weekly* on *The Ex Hex*

"Sterling writes a fun, sexy romantic comedy with a compelling plot, fantastic worldbuilding, twists that give the story depth, and engaging primary and secondary characters. The novel wraps up plenty of loose ends, but readers will be eager for sequels."

—*Library Journal* on *The Ex Hex*

"*The Kiss Curse* is sexy and fun, fast pac⟨ed⟩ ⟨. . .⟩ ⟨In Sterling's⟩ supernatural realm, down-to-earth m⟨a⟩ ⟨. . .⟩ feats of wizardry. She peppers in sm⟨. . .⟩

details, and every sentence is packed with substantive description and imagination. This kiss is definitely worth the curse, a sexy rom-com with just the right amount of sorcery."

—*BookPage* (starred review)

"Sterling's novel is ultimately crisp and sweet, like biting into the perfect caramel apple, and makes for an equally delicious autumn treat that will sweep readers up into a world of whimsical magic. A wickedly funny rom-com about the power of second chances, family, and love."

—*Kirkus Reviews* on *The Ex Hex*

"Erin Sterling delivers another bewitching romance set in the delightful fictional hamlet of Graves Glen, Georgia. . . . Reading *The Kiss Curse* will definitely have you in a magical mood. The sinister plots and sizzling chemistry make for an alchemical combination that once again produces gold."

—Book of the Month Club

THE
WEDDING
WITCH

Also by Erin Sterling

The Ex Hex
The Kiss Curse

THE
WEDDING
WITCH

a novel

ERIN STERLING

AVON

An Imprint of HarperCollinsPublishers

HarperCollins books may be purchased for educational, business, or sales promotional use. For information, please email the Special Markets Department at SPsales@harpercollins.com.

FIRST EDITION

Interior text design by Diahann Sturge-Campbell

Illustrations © createvil; Rogatnev/Stock.Adobe.com

Library of Congress Cataloging-in-Publication Data has been applied for.

ISBN 978-0-06-329759-3 (trade paperback)
ISBN 978-0-06-341116-6 (hardcover library edition)

24 25 26 27 28 LBC 5 4 3 2 1

For Tessa and Holly

PROLOGUE

Last Christmas Eve
Queen's Head Pub, London

Elves really were dickheads.

Not the one currently grinning at Bowen from the chalkboard near the pub's entrance, a wee little guy sketched out in red and white, grinning dementedly next to the evening's special of venison lasagna and something called MERRY YULE NOG!

That fella, with his jaunty cap and overly big eyes, seemed like he might need to lay off the caffeine a bit, but tonight Bowen's grudge was against *real* elves. The wankers with their long white robes, mysterious mountain homes in the wilder parts of Scandinavia, and nearly indecipherable language that he had just spent the better part of a *bloody week* trying to read, only to realize what he'd spent hours poring over in a dusty back room of the British Library was actually a recipe for *fucking mead,* something that didn't seem to require more than a hundred pages of text, and *yet.*

Bastards had better be glad they all fucked off about five hundred years ago, he thought darkly as he sipped his pint and watched passersby hurry down slick streets as Christmas lights twinkled overhead and cars threw up sheets of freezing water.

Over the pub's speakers, a singer warbled about chestnuts and open fires just as a group of shoppers burst through the front door, laughing and talking all at once, and Bowen felt his shoulders creeping up closer to his ears.

A week in the city was about six and a half days too long for Bowen's taste, but he had one more little bit of business in London tonight before he could head back to his house—well, "hut" was a better word—in the mountains of Wales. It would be freezing and dark and lonely, and he would be far, far more comfortable.

Of course, now that this elf thing had turned out to be such a waste of time, he'd have to go back to the drawing board on Declan's spell, but that would be all right. He was always happier when he was working anyway.

Thinking of work had Bowen glancing back at his phone: 4:58 P.M.

They were supposed to be here at five, but you never knew with these types. Bowen had dealt with more than one "Acquirer" in his day—humans who sold magical artifacts. It was a shady business, deeply secretive by requirement, and too many of them didn't take the time to actually learn about what it was they were selling. Bowen had once bought a crystal goblet from an Acquirer. It had been crafted sometime in the thirteenth century, and it had the ability to poison any drink within a fifty-foot radius.

The idiot had been keeping it with his coffee mugs.

So no, Bowen didn't have the highest opinions of humans who meddled in things they didn't understand, but he couldn't deny that they were useful. Unlike witches, they weren't tempted to keep the things they acquired, and there was no history with these kinds of people, no tangled family feud from centuries back that could lead to issues.

And the one he was meeting tonight, this "TLB Acquisitions, Ltd.," had been *especially good*. Thanks to their work, for the past year or so, Bowen had gotten his hands on a grimoire no one had seen since 1832, a tarot deck that had once belonged to the sorcerer John Dee, and an album that could cause an outbreak of St. Vitus's dance.

All of it done quickly, discreetly, and, yes, fucking *expensively,* but worth it as far as Bowen was concerned.

Which was why he'd asked for a meeting with T from TLB. Thankfully, it turned out they'd both be in London at the same time, and now, as the clock ticked over to five, he glanced toward the door.

As though Bowen's thought had summoned him, a man strode through the door, jangling a bell overhead. He was wearing a smart suit, his bald head gleaming under the lights as he shook off an umbrella there in the vestibule. With his shiny shoes and rimless glasses, he looked like a banker, which meant he was almost certainly an Acquirer.

They all looked like that.

Bowen lifted his chin, but the man only glanced briefly at him before his face broke out into a wide smile as he waved at someone off to Bowen's right and hurried to a table of other similarly dressed men.

Bowen watched him pass with a frown, then heard the bell sound again and looked back to the door just as a small figure that seemed to be made entirely of white fur came barreling in. A gust of wet sleet rattled on the slate floor before the door slammed closed again, and the human-sheepdog hybrid shook itself slightly as it reached up to unwind a tartan scarf from around its head.

Soft brown hair spilled out over the white fur, and the woman turned, her eyes searching.

They landed on him.

And . . .

Fuck.

It was like a battering ram to the chest.

A tankard to the temple.

A . . . Christ, he couldn't come up with any more similes, because this absolute vision in fake fur was now *smiling at him* and *walking to his table, St. Bugi's balls and all his other bits.*

As she approached, he could see that her eyes were the same rich brown as her hair, and she had dimples in each cheek, deep ones, and Bowen was suddenly very glad he'd decided to grow a beard all those years ago, because he was pretty sure he was blushing.

Blushing—kill him now.

His thighs bumped the table in his hurry to stand as she

approached, but she didn't seem to notice, offering him a gloved hand that he took without thinking.

"Bowen," she said, and how did she know his name?

Had he died? Was this pub heaven? No, he'd done studies of the afterlife in various cultures, and he didn't think he'd ever heard it described as a pub anywhere, and she had an American accent, which seemed odd for an angel in a Welshman's heaven, but surely such things are possible, and—

"Tamsyn Bligh," she went on. "So nice to finally see the face behind the emails!"

Then her eyes moved over him, and she frowned a little.

"Well, the *beard* behind the emails," she said, and he knew he was supposed to laugh at that, or at least acknowledge that it was a joke, but his brain was still hung up on *emails* and *Tamsyn,* and . . .

This was T.

This was the Acquirer he'd been working with for over a year now.

And he was . . . holding her hand.

Giving it a quick shake, Bowen nodded and stepped back a little, gesturing to the table. "Right. Um. Have a seat."

"Thank you," she said, and he pulled out her chair for her, catching a whiff of rich, citrusy perfume as she sat down.

The pub suddenly felt too warm, too crowded, and he heard himself say, "Let me grab you a drink," before turning and heading to the bar, nearly smacking into a man wearing a very loud Rudolph the Red-Nosed Reindeer jumper and singing along to "Rockin' Around the Christmas Tree."

The jumper may have been to blame for what happened next.

That and the panic he felt when the bartender looked at him expectantly, and Bowen realized that he *probably* should've asked her what she actually wanted to drink instead of flailing off toward the bar like an absolute tit.

He could've gotten her a pint.

A glass of wine.

Even a plain old gin and tonic.

Instead, he had pointed at the little easel on the bar reading RUDOLPH'S ROSÉ, £7 and said, "I'll have that."

A few minutes later, he was back at the table, and Tamsyn turned slightly in her chair, a smile already on her face.

It faded as she looked at what he was holding.

"The, um, the . . . glitter wasn't advertised," he told her as she took the drink with wide eyes.

"And the light-up curly straw?"

"No."

"The fact that it looks like blood?"

"No. Or the, uh . . . the tree."

Picking the huge sprig of rosemary out of her drink, Tamsyn gave the tumbler an experimental sniff before taking a sip.

Terrible as the thing looked, it must not have tasted bad, because Tamsyn drank again and then gave a shrug. "If you can't drink a tacky holiday cocktail on Christmas Eve, when can you?"

Bowen had just slid back into his seat, but now he frowned, looking outside. It was still sleeting, but he could see the little shop on the corner had already closed for the night, and there was a family making their way past the pub dressed in various patterns of Christmassy tartan, the father carrying a bottle of wine underneath one arm as he laughed at something the mother was saying.

Tamsyn set her drink down and leaned forward, folding her arms on the table. "Did you not know it was Christmas Eve?"

Bowen absolutely had not, but after Rudolph the Nightmare Rosé, he needed to cling to a little bit of dignity here.

"Witch," he reminded her. "We celebrate Yule, and that was a few days ago."

Not that he had celebrated it. He'd been too busy with the elves—*bastards*—and their mead, after all. In fact, Bowen wasn't sure he could remember the last time he'd participated in Yule. Ten years ago, maybe? Before everything with Declan. Before he'd made fixing this fuck-up his life's work.

Which was why he'd made this meeting with T.

With *Tamsyn*.

Who was now watching him with those bright eyes and a slightly quizzical smile, like she was trying to work him out. She'd taken off her coat and gloves while he'd been fetching that abomination currently sparkling and blinking in front of her, and the deep green turtleneck she was wearing brought out golden lights in her dark hair.

Her name suited her, pretty and soft, but there was something about it that was ringing a faint bell. Had she used it in any of their emails? She couldn't have, or he wouldn't have been so surprised she wasn't a bloke. Maybe he'd read it somewhere else or heard another witch mention her.

"I have to say," she said, resting her cheek on one hand, "I was really surprised you'd want to work with me, much less want to have drinks with me."

"Why?"

She blinked at him. "Because . . . you're Bowen Penhallow?"

Bowen grunted in the affirmative, and she looked even more confused.

"And . . . your family hates me?"

Now Bowen frowned. "What?" Like any magical family, the Penhallows had grudges and feuds that went back centuries, but Bowen couldn't remember anyone named "Bligh" ever being a part of those. Unless . . .

"Do you mean my da? Simon Penhallow? Because he hates everyone."

Including all three of his sons at the moment, he added silently. Bowen hadn't spoken to Simon in over a year, and the saddest part of that was how sad Bowen *wasn't* about it. It wouldn't have surprised him one bit to learn his father had started some kind of magical beef with an Acquirer, especially one as talented as Tamsyn.

But she just shook her head. "Rhys, actually."

"Rhys doesn't hate *anyone*," Bowen replied automatically, but then a thought occurred to him, one that made his stomach drop and his hands go a bit sweaty on his pint glass. "Are you . . . did the two of you . . . ?"

Of the three Penhallow brothers, Rhys was the youngest and—much as Bowen and their oldest brother, Wells, hated to

admit it—the only actual charmer in the family. Bowen definitely couldn't blame Rhys for being interested in a woman as
gorgeous as Tamsyn, but after the Katie Evans War back in '07
(and also '09 and then again in 2013, which put an end to it until
hostilities unexpectedly resumed in 2016), the brothers had all
agreed never to date the others' exes.

Not that this was a date, of course. It was a business meeting,
which was why it was absolutely fucking ridiculous for him to
feel this disappointed at the idea that she might have dated Rhys.

Even worse, though, was how thrilled—how bloody *elated*—he
felt at the look of horror that crossed her face at the very idea of
her and Rhys.

"Oh my god, *no,*" she said quickly, shaking her head. "No, no,
no, he was very much attached when I met him."

Sighing, Tamsyn took another sip of her drink, and Bowen
got the impression that she was steeling herself.

"I *might,*" she said, tilting her head to one side, "have been trying
to acquire a certain . . . *item,* using . . . less than aboveboard means,
let's say."

And now he remembered why her name had sounded so familiar.
Rhiannon's tits.

"Tamsyn Bligh," he said, nodding. "Pretended to work for the
College of Witchery in Graves Glen, gave Rhys and Vivienne a
Eurydice Candle to—"

"To capture a ghost so that I could sell a possessed candle to
a very lucrative client, yup!" she finished up brightly, like if she
said it nicely enough, it wouldn't sound that bad. "But then the

ghost was way more dark energy than I was prepared for, your brother and his girlfriend had to save my ass, and I left Georgia a reformed woman. And now I am the very professional, very not-shady Acquirer you see before you now!"

Holding both hands out to the side, Tamsyn wiggled her fingers with an implied *Ta-da!*

"Huh" was all Bowen found he could say. And then: "She's his wife now. Vivienne. Not his girlfriend."

"Congrats to them. I'll send a gravy boat. Now"—Tamsyn placed both hands flat on the table, patting out a quick rhythm— "It's Christmas Eve in London, and you've brought me out in the freezing rain for what, exactly? I assume a job?"

Bowen took another sip of his Stella, trying to get his thoughts in order. From the moment she'd walked in, he'd been playing catch-up, and if he wasn't careful, he was going to say this all wrong.

"I want you for me."

Fuck fuck fucking fuck, mate.

"I want you *to work* for me," he clarified as Tamsyn's eyebrows vanished beneath her heavy bangs, her lips slightly parted. "As an Acquirer, obviously, that's . . . that's the job I'd be hiring you for. The job that you do already. Only you'd do it for *me,* as in there are certain things I need—magical things, nothing weird. Well, weird because they're magic, but nothing *dangerous,* and you could . . . acquire them. How you do now, but . . . different? Not different in the means you'd use, that is, but—"

"You'd like to offer me an exclusive contract to acquire magical artifacts for you and only you," she interrupted, and Bowen closed his eyes briefly, blowing out a deep breath.

"Yes. That."

She studied him in silence for a few beats, long enough for Bowen to wonder how many Rudolph's Rosés he'd have to drink before the memory of these last few minutes was permanently swept away. Five? Half a dozen? Maybe he'd try ten just to be safe.

"Why?" she asked, and when he didn't answer right away, she gave another careless shrug. "I just mean I've been acquiring for you for over a year now on an as-needed basis. What's changed?"

What had changed was that Bowen had the sense he was running out of time. Ten years now he'd been trying to find a spell that would save Declan, and he was no closer than he was the day he started. He couldn't waste time running down every piece of every spell that *might* work, and no other Acquirer he'd ever worked with had been as good at the gig as Tamsyn was.

But no one knew what it was Bowen had been up to for the last decade, and he wasn't ready to start sharing now.

"Does it matter so long as my checks clear?" he asked, and Tamsyn rocked back in her chair, grinning.

"Now you're speaking my language, Bo. Can I call you Bo?"

"Please don't," he said, to which she chuckled, folding her arms over her chest.

"Fine. *Bowen*. How much?" she asked, and Bowen sat up straight, relief coursing through him.

This part, he'd been ready for.

He said a number.

She said a different, bigger number.

He said a number smaller than that, but bigger than the first offer, and after a few more back and forths, they settled on a price that made them both happy, even if Bowen's savings account would undoubtedly be wincing.

It would be worth it, though.

The sleet had let up some, and both their glasses were empty as Tamsyn reached for her coat. Bowen stood up, too, grabbing his beat-up leather jacket from the back of his chair. The pub wasn't nearly as crowded now, so there was no need, really, for him to put his hand lightly on her lower back as they maneuvered their way to the door, but Bowen found he was doing it anyway. She was close enough to him that if he lowered his head just the smallest bit, he could smell her hair.

Luckily, even a man who'd spent most of the last decade alone on a Welsh mountainside was more civilized than that.

Barely.

As they reached the vestibule, Tamsyn suddenly turned, looking up at him. Once again, Bowen got the sense that she was trying to figure him out, her brain whirring behind those big brown eyes.

"So that's that?" she said, fluffing her hair out from under the collar of her coat and hitting him with another wave of that perfume that somehow smelled like Christmas. Warm, spicy. Like clove and orange. "No paperwork? No contracts? We just shake hands like gentlemen, and boom, I work for you?"

"Long and short of it, yeah," Bowen said, sliding his hand out of his pocket and offering it to her.

But Tamsyn didn't take it. She just stood there in her fuzzy coat as rain pattered on the glass panes in the door, and the plinking synthesizers of "Last Christmas" started up over the speakers.

"What?" he asked, his voice gruff even as he looked a little more closely at his hand. He'd washed up before sitting down, but the kind of magical substances he worked with didn't always go away with a little soap and water. But there was no stain of ichor on his palm, no stubborn dusting of powdered dragon scales (worse than glitter, that shite was), and therefore no reason he could think of for her not to shake his hand.

And then she said, "Once we shake on it, it's official, right? We're coworkers?"

Still confused, Bowen frowned even harder. "Aye," he confirmed with a nod, and she matched it with a nod of her own.

"Right then. Better do this first."

With that, she reached out, fisted her hand in the front of his jumper, and yanked his mouth down to hers.

Bowen had a moment—just the briefest spark of a second— to think, *What—?*

Then no more thoughts at all.

Just taste. Her mouth, sweet and cold from the wine.

Scent. That perfume, but also a deeper, softer scent that he knew was just her skin, the way her sheets would smell.

Feel. Christ, the *feel* of her. Her lips pliant, mouth wet; her tongue against his with no shame, no hesitation. Like they weren't in the shadowy alcove of a pub, but in her bedroom, alone and far from any eyes.

Somehow Bowen's hand had fallen to the curve of her hip, his fingers digging into the denim of her jeans as he held her close to him and kissed her back just as thoroughly. He was dimly aware of someone giving an approving whistle, but that was impossible, because there was no one else here, no one else in the whole world, no doubt, except him and this woman.

And then it was over.

He felt the cold air slide back between them as she stepped out of his arms, her face flushed, her lips almost obscenely wet, and those big dark eyes of hers glassy with desire.

Bowen's chest was heaving, his hand still out, fingers curled in the space between them, and Tamsyn gave a shaky laugh as she smoothed her hair back from her face.

"Personal rule," she told him. "Never get involved with a co-worker. *But.* Also a personal rule: Never let a good mistletoe moment pass by."

She pointed above them, and Bowen saw the gathered cluster of green leaves, white berries, gold ribbon.

He was still dazedly staring at it when Tamsyn grabbed his hand and gave it a firm shake.

"See you later, boss," she said, and with a jingle of the bell and a gust of cold air, she was gone.

January

From: BGPCymru@gmail.com
To: BlighAcquisitionsLLC@aol.com
Subject: (none)

T—

Attaching description/last known location of 13th century goblet mentioned in last email. Supposed to be a necromancy thing, probably bollocks, but keep an eye out.

B

From: BlighAcquisitionsLLC@aol.com
To: BGPCymru@gmail.com
Subject: RE: (none)

B—

"Probably" bollocks? PROBABLY? When it comes to necromancy, I feel like that "probably" is doing a lot of work, my friend! Pay and a half. For hazards.

T

From: BGPCymru@gmail.com

To: BlighAcquisitionsLLC@aol.com

Subject: RE: RE: (none)

We didn't negotiate hazard pay.

From: BlighAcquisitionsLLC@aol.com

To: BGPCymru@gmail.com

Subject: RE: RE: RE: (none)

Okay, then this is me doing that! Because "zombies" are a hazard, I feel we can both agree. Any items related to necromancy are double my usual fee. (See, this is the negotiating, because before I said "pay and a half," but then *you* wanted to argue about it, so now I'm going even higher, and it's *not* going to be easy to talk me down, just so you know. ☺)

From: BGPCymru@gmail.com

To: BlighAcquisitionsLLC@aol.com

Subject: RE: RE: RE: RE: (none)

Fine.

From: BlighAcquisitionsLLC@aol.com

To: BGPCymru@gmail.com

Subject: RE: RE: RE: RE: RE: (none)

Bowen, please stop sending me these long, flowery messages, I don't have time to read all that, SHEESH!

From: BGPCymru@gmail.com

To: BlighAcquisitionsLLC@aol.com

Subject: RE: RE: RE: RE: RE: RE: (none)

Taking the piss out of me is fun, I know, but it doesn't pay double. Finding that goblet will, so maybe get started on that.

From: BlighAcquisitionsLLC@aol.com

To: BGPCymru@gmail.com

Subject: RE: RE: RE: RE: RE: RE: RE: (none)

Oh, Bowen.

Bowen, Bowen, Bowen.

My good buddy Bo.

Didn't I tell you I was the best? And don't you think the best can make fun of you *and* find the goblet? Because while I've been engaged in this extremely tense salary negotiation with you, I have *also* been emailing my buddy Hollis, because I was pretty sure I'd seen this goblet in his collection, and sure enough, it is! Hollis is wrapping that bad boy in bubble wrap as we speak, and I should have it to you next week.

Now admit I fucking rock, and remember my 30% finder's fee!

Xoxo!
Tamsyn

From: BGPCymru@gmail.com
To: BlighAcquisitionsLLC@aol.com
Subject: RE: RE: RE: RE: RE: RE: RE: RE: (none)

Christ Almighty, Tamsyn, you're a bloody wonder. Bit terrifying, but a wonder all the same.

Cheers. (And double your fee is 20%, but nice try.)

B

May

Remember how I get hazard pay for necromancy stuff? Well, I have an addition—gonna need at least quadruple pay for anything involving slime.

Do I even want to know?

You definitely don't, but I'm going to tell you anyway. (Also, did you know sea monsters are real? Okay, not MONSTER monsters, these were just weird little specimens in jars. Or rather they WERE in jars, until yours truly was reaching for your stupid cauldron.)

Did you get the cauldron?

Awww, Bo!! Your concern for my well-being is so touching! Now I'm really sad I put back that "World's Best Boss" mug I almost got you at the airport!

I'll pay your dry-cleaning bill.

And I'm sorry you got slimed.

Although I know Dr. Lewis's collection pretty well, and those aren't sea monsters. They're attempts at re-creating dragons on a small scale using lizards.

Obviously not a successful experiment in the end.

Anyway.

(Not slime is the point I'm making, more a mix of saline and I think amniotic fluid.)

(Not magic slime, just normal human organic stuff.)

(If that makes you feel better?)

Hello?

> Sorry. Everything about that series of text messages sent me into some kind of fugue state.

> I am a different person now than I was before I read any of that. I was so much younger just two minutes ago. So innocent. So unknowing.

Ha-ha.

I love texting with you, Bowen, truly. It's either like talking to a GPS or it's full-on campfire shit, nothing in between.

"The artifact is located in the northeast quadrant of the home."

"DID YOU KNOW THESE MAGICAL THUMBSCREWS ONCE WENT ON A THUMBSCREWING RAMPAGE IN 15TH CENTURY BELGIUM?"

Really wish you would've rephrased "thumbscrewing."

Big words from Mr. It'll Surely Make Tamsyn Feel Better to Learn She Is Currently Covered in Amniotic Fluid and the Remnants of Frankenstein Lizards.

When you put it like that, I can see where I fucked up.

THANK YOU.

(Still not going back for that mug.)

November

TamOShanter: Why are you awake and online at 3 in the morning?

BGPCymru: Working

TamOShanter: I figured that. On what?

BGPCymru: Spellwork. Boring, trust me.

BGPCymru: What time is it where you are?

TamOShanter: I'm home right now, so a little after ten p.m.

BGPCymru: You have a home?

BGPCymru: Sorry, that sounded rude. I just meant that I always picture you in motion.

BGPCymru: Traveling, I don't picture you moving.

BGPCymru: Like your body, I don't picture that.

TamOShanter: Exactly what every girl longs to hear!

TamOShanter: And I know you're over there typing out a long response to this that is just digging the hole deeper and deeper, so let me spare you from that and tell you that I knew what you meant, I am absolutely BEGGING YOU not to explain any more.

TamOShanter: And home is South Carolina, btw. Low Country. Not far from Charleston. I bought a plot of land and an Airstream trailer a while back.

TamOShanter: Honestly, you'd probably love it. I can go days without seeing another person out here.

BGPCymru: I've gone months without seeing someone up here.

TamOShanter: Ooooh, are we having a Lonely Loser-Off? Because I will cede that title to you, friend. No one hermits better than you.

BGPCymru: Thank you.

BGPCymru: I think.

TamOShanter: I actually was thinking of you just last week. I was in London and dropped into the Queen's Head.

TamOShanter: Sadly no Rudolph Rosé until next month, but they assure me they've got an even twirlier straw this year!

TamOShanter: Just in case you didn't have plans on Christmas Eve—sorry, YULE—this year.

TamOShanter: I mean, it did take me three days and about a thousand teeth-brushings to make my teeth *not* pink after drinking that thing last year, but if we wanted to make liver poisoning an annual tradition, I'm available!

BGPCymru: I'll be in Graves Glen this year.

BGPCymru: Taran's first Yule.

TamOShanter: Oh, right! The new addition! How is your nephew?

BGPCymru: From the pictures Vivienne sends, bald. Happy. Really interested in eating his hands.

TamOShanter: Please tell me you're bringing him a developmentally appropriate gift and not, like, an elk horn dagger for scrying or something.

BGPCymru: You couldn't use a dagger for scrying, and in any case, a witch doesn't get his first elk horn until he's thirteen.

BGPCymru: (That was a joke.)

BGPCymru: (There's no age limit on elk horn.)

BGPCymru: Anyway, not sure how long I'll be there. I think they'd like me to stay for most of December, but that feels like . . . a lot.

TamOShanter: Bowen, two hours in another person's company is probably "a lot" for you. A month with family? Family with a BABY??? You will need an entire TANK of Rudolph Rosé by Christmas Eve.

BGPCymru: Too fucking right. All right then, sorted. I've got a Traveling Stone, so getting there from Graves Glen won't be hard. Christmas Eve, the Queen's Head. You and me. Twirly straws.

TamOShanter: Red dye 40 and glitter.

BGPCymru: Pink teeth and liver failure.

TamOShanter: Mistletoe and bad choices.

    BGPCymru . . .

    BGPCymru . . .

    BGPCymru is typing

    BGPCymru . . .

    BGPCymru is typing

BGPCymru: Was that a bad choice?

BGPCymru: The mistletoe?

TamOShanter: Ohhhh, it is too late to be having this conversation, Bowen. That way lies danger.

BGPCymru: You're right. Sorry.

BGPCymru: Honestly, I should get some sleep. Words are starting to blur, and I'm clearly at the talking bullshit stage.

TamOShanter: And I have a hot date with several Real Housewives currently saved on my DVR.

BGPCymru: Clearly time to go to bed because every bit of that sentence sounds like a hallucination to me.

TamOShanter: Ha-ha. Okay, off you go! Have fun in Georgia, and see you Christmas Eve.

BGPCymru: See you then.

BGPCymru: Oh, and check your email tomorrow, I might have a lead on a dagger I need you to track down for me.

TamOShanter: Classic Friday at the office! Will do. Night, boss.

BGPCymru: Night, Tam (still not your boss).

BGPCymru: (And I didn't think it was a bad choice, by the way. The mistletoe.)

TamOShanter: (Neither did I.)

CHAPTER 1

This December

"Santa hat."

"Absolutely not."

"Santa. Hat."

"Just repeating the words is not an effective argument, you know."

"A hat in the style of Santa."

"Rhys, I will chuck you straight out of that window if you come any closer to me with that abomination."

Bowen had been in Graves Glen for—he checked his watch—about twenty minutes now, and this was the third argument his brothers had had. The first had been over peppermint lattes (Rhys was in favor, Wells was not). The second had been about . . . well, Bowen hadn't really been paying attention until Wells and Rhys had gotten pissed off enough to lapse into Welsh, and by that point, it had mostly just been insults.

Now Rhys stood on the other side of the counter at Penhallow's, the magical shop Wells ran in Graves Glen, dangling a red-and-white hat at his eldest brother with a decidedly demented gleam in his eye, and Bowen wondered if he should get involved.

Of course, the last time he'd done that—the Yule Brawl of '02—he'd ended up with a dislocated elbow, bright green hair, and the unfortunate "talent" of only being able to speak in iambic pentameter. It had taken their father nearly a week to find a reversal for that spell, and even now, Shakespeare made Bowen shudder, so yeah, probably best to sit this one out.

Luckily, there was another Penhallow happy to put a stop to this nonsense.

Just as Rhys went to lean in a little closer, hat still dangling from one crooked finger, it was snatched out of his hand by the baby strapped into some kind of contraption on Rhys's chest, and as the three brothers watched, Rhys's son, Taran, attempted to shove the entire thing into his mouth.

"Oh, no, *fy machgen,* let's not do that," Rhys said, tugging the hat from his son as Wells chuckled.

"See? The boy is clearly on my side."

"He is not," Rhys said, putting the now slightly mangled and damp hat on the counter. "He just doesn't want us arguing on Bowen's first day back. A peacekeeper, my son. A pacifist. Isn't that right, Taran?"

At the sound of his name, the baby tilted his head back, giving a gummy smile to his father before releasing what, to Bowen's ears, sounded an awful lot like a banshee's cry and flailing out with one adorably small hand to try to grab a handful of wands from the ceramic vase on Penhallow's counter.

Both Wells and Rhys made nearly identical shouts of alarm as they reached out to steady the vase, but a few wands escaped anyway, rolling to where Bowen sat perched on the arm of a velvet wingback chair.

He leaned down to pick them up, but before he could, one slowly floated up from the floor, wobbling a little before clattering back down.

Taran gave another happy shriek, kicking his little feet and waving his arms, and Bowen got up and walked over to Rhys, crouching down to look in his nephew's eyes.

They were the same clear hazel as Vivienne's, but the expression in them was pure Rhys Penhallow, and Bowen frowned as he straightened up.

"One of you was really enough," he said, nodding toward the baby strapped to Rhys's chest. "Not sure I'm up for going through this again."

"First of all," Rhys said, wrapping one arm around Taran's middle, "I was a *delight* as a child. All my teachers said so."

"You know the words 'handful' and 'chaos personified' and 'perhaps actual demon, has your family been dabbling in sorcery?' do not mean the same thing as 'delightful,' don't you?" Wells mused.

He'd turned away, pulling a massive black ledger out from under the counter, so he didn't see the deeply offended glare Rhys shot his way.

"And 'pleasure to have in class' is what they say when you're a stuck-up swot who will never know the touch of a woman, but you don't see me pointing that out to you, do you?" Rhys replied.

"Stuck up, yes," Gwyn, Wells's girlfriend, chimed in, clomping up the stairs from the storage room, a cardboard box cradled in her arms. "And I don't know what a 'swot' is, but that does kind of sound like Esquire, so I'll allow it. However!"

She dropped the box on the counter next to Wells, its contents rattling as she leaned over to throw an arm around his neck, pulling him close even as he began to write in the ledger.

"Trust me, he knows this *particular* woman's touch very, *very* well."

Wells smirked, finally lifting his gaze from the book. "Thank you, my darling," he said, turning to press a kiss to Gwyn's temple.

Rhys's hands hovered around Taran's head, landing briefly over his ears before settling over the baby's eyes instead, and Bowen grunted in amusement.

"See what you did, being a smart-arse?" he asked Rhys. "Now we have to think about Wells shagging, and that's on you."

Rhys's hands flew back to Taran's ears, the baby giggling and kicking his feet again. "Yes, I realize that backfired on me, now let's all just stop talking about it before Taran's first word is 'shagging' and Vivienne curses me yet again. Justly this time."

"It was pretty justly the first time," Gwyn said just as Wells muttered, "You honestly did deserve that," and Bowen added, "Complete wanker behavior."

Rhys straightened up to his full height, looking as dignified as a man could with a small child wearing a onesie proclaiming "Daddy's Li'l Turkey!" strapped to his chest. "You are all horrible influences on my son, and I can no longer risk his potential moral degeneracy by staying in your company. Come, Taran. Let's go see if the nice ladies at the Coffee Cauldron have one of those cake pops for you to mangle."

With that, he left the shop, the bell overhead jangling.

"I don't think I'm ever going to get used to Rhys being someone's father," Bowen said, watching his brother walk past Penhallow's window, one hand still firmly on his son's stomach, his dark hair flopping over his forehead as he leaned down to press a kiss to Taran's head. It was strange, the way that casual, affectionate gesture made Bowen's chest feel a little tight.

"The hell of it is," Wells said with a sigh, "he's really bloody good at it. No idea how he picked it up so naturally."

Bowen glanced over at his older brother. The estrangement from Simon Penhallow had been necessary for all three brothers, but Bowen knew Wells had taken it the hardest. Of course, Wells had been the most hurt by their father's scheming in the end.

Wells must've been thinking the same thing, because he sighed and seemed to shake himself a bit before saying, "Anyway, his propensity for chaos aside, Taran is a delightful child. Thank Rhiannon for those Jones genes, I suppose."

"Aww, babe, you think I'm delightful?" Gwyn replied, then pointed at Bowen. "You are my witness, Bowen. He said it."

Smiling slightly, Bowen lifted his hand in acknowledgment. "I was also witness to how absolutely shattered he was when he thought he'd fucked it all up with you, if you want to hear that story. Again."

"You know I do," Gwyn said with a wink, and the tops of Wells's ears went slightly red. "Anyway," she went on, "Esquire is right about Taran being delightful. I've asked Vivi to start bringing him into Something Wicked whenever she can, because he may be only ten months old, but that kid is a natural born salesperson. He'll point at something in the store and start cooing over it, and the next thing you know, everyone wants whatever it is he liked. It's like . . ."

"Magic?" Bowen supplied, his eyebrows raised, and Gwyn's smile faded.

"Shit. I'm letting a baby ensorcell my customers, aren't I?" Then she shrugged. "Oh, well. He usually likes the cheapest stuff in the store anyway."

"So when you two have kids, are you going to make them split their time between the stores?" Bowen asked, but Gwyn shook her head.

"Oh, kids are not for us," she said. "We already decided that. A of all, we have the Baby Witches, and that's all the parenting we can handle."

Bowen was fairly certain the "Baby Witches" Gwyn and Wells so often referred to were all people in their twenties, but he wisely held his tongue as Gwyn went on. "And B, Sir Purrcival has very strong opinions about babies, turns out. The first time Taran tried to pet him, he used words we didn't even think he *knew*."

"Right, but that cat can't live—" Bowen started to say, only to immediately swallow the rest of that sentence when Gwyn—

and Wells, to Bowen's surprise—shot him a glare that should've incinerated him on the spot. "—that cat . . . can't live . . . with a-a baby," Bowen managed to get out. "That's what I was going to say. Just agreeing with you. One hundred percent."

Gwyn gave a firm nod. "That's what I *assumed* you were saying. But just in case it wasn't, your punishment is to wear this to family dinner tonight."

Reaching into the box she'd brought up from the storage room, Gwyn pulled out a bright red sweatshirt and tossed it at him.

Unfolding it, Bowen stared at the demonic face sneering back at him, bright green script underneath its curling tongue reading "Christmas Really Krampuses My Yule."

Bowen grunted.

"In retrospect," Wells said with a frown, "it was a mistake to let the Baby Witches design a holiday shirt for the stores."

"It's possible we've neglected pun skills when it comes to their education," Gwyn agreed, then put her hands on her hips and fixed Bowen with a determined look. "But you're still wearing it."

She snapped her fingers, and Bowen felt a draft of cold air before looking down to see that somehow, the perfectly normal black jumper he'd been wearing was now on the floor, and the forked-tongue Krampus was snarling up at him from his chest.

"At least it's comfortable," he grumbled, and then, almost without thinking, reached into his back pocket and pulled out his phone. Snapping a quick picture of himself in the sweatshirt, he was halfway through his text to Tamsyn when he realized the store had gone uncomfortably quiet.

Looking up, Bowen found Wells and Gwyn both staring at him like he'd grown an extra head. Worse, actually, because that had happened to Bowen when he was thirteen, thanks to one of Rhys's pranks, and Wells had looked significantly less disturbed then than he was now.

"What?" he asked.

"Did you . . . Bowen, did you just take a selfie?" Wells asked, and Gwyn grabbed her boyfriend's arm, her eyes wide.

"Wells, he took a selfie of himself *wearing a stupid novelty sweatshirt*. Who are you sending that to? Are you putting it online? Do you know how online works? Is there, like, a secret Facebook for witchy mountain men? Or! *Oh!*"

Practically levitating, Gwyn pointed a finger at Bowen, who could feel blood start creeping up his face.

"That is for a *woman*. You are *sending that to someone* because you *like her*."

"It's not like that," Bowen heard himself say, but Gwyn was on a roll now.

"Or a guy! I guess it could be a guy, I've never even asked you about that kind of thing, Bowen, because frankly I was more concerned with whether or not you were a werewolf than who it is you bang. Which"—she wrinkled her brow—"are you? A werewolf? You can tell me now, we're family."

"I'm not," Bowen replied. "They're not actually re—"

"Okay," Gwyn went on, waving that away. "Good to know. But point is, you are sending that to *someone* because you are *into them*."

"I'm sending it to a mate," Bowen corrected. "As a joke."

"Nope," Gwyn said, shaking her head. "You angled that phone, Bowen. You almost smiled. I saw it. Or at least I think I did, the beard really remains insane, dude."

Scratching at that beard, Bowen studied the selfie on his screen, the still unsent text to Tamsyn underneath.

Since you like making fun of me so much, some new material.

Fuck, he *had* angled the phone, and yeah, definitely a hint of teeth there.

He'd just delete it. Bad enough to have a crush on someone who'd flat-out said she wouldn't get involved with him so long as they were working together. Even worse, bringing up the mistletoe the other night.

But it had been late and he'd been lonely, and seeing her message pop up in his chat had made him so bloody happy for some reason.

Talking to her always did that. Even when he was fucking it up, even when he was wishing there was some way to *un*say the stupid shit that tended to fall out of his mouth, any conversation with her tended to be the highlight of his day.

Which was . . . pathetic.

The past year had been good. They were a solid team. And that's all they were, all they *should* be. He was a fucking mess and in no shape to offer anything to anyone. She was smart and beautiful and sharp as a fucking obsidian blade. Best to leave her to find someone who actually knew how to be a person.

A human.

Bowen knew all of that.

But he still hit send.

CHAPTER 2

It wasn't easy sending a text with one hand while you held an Etruscan knife that some fifteenth-century witch had used to castrate a demon in the other, but Tamsyn had always prided herself on her ability to multitask.

And besides, a rare Bowen Penhallow selfie deserved an immediate reply, even if a girl *had* just pulled into her driveway after a very long flight and several hours of hellish traffic.

Love it, she typed as she headed toward her front door, gravel crunching under her boots, but that better not be my Christmas bonus!

Yule bonus, came the immediate reply, followed by one word:

Knife?

Smirking, Tamsyn lifted the knife and the phone at the same time, snapping a quick selfie complete with duck lips and an awkward peace sign around the hilt of the dagger.

She was about to slide her phone into her back pocket when it buzzed again with Bowen's reply.

Good lass.

The evening air was chilly, but the heat that rushed through Tamsyn at those two little words made her feel like she was glowing, a bright beacon of lust in the December twilight.

"Like a horny Christmas star," she muttered to herself as she slid her phone into her back pocket before unlocking the front door of the Airstream trailer she'd been calling home for the past year.

She'd lived in better places, but she'd also lived in worse, and as she made her way into the kitchen—which meant taking four steps from the front door—Tamsyn bent down to plug in the little Christmas lights she'd strung up before leaving for Italy.

They sprang to tacky, multicolored life, and Tamsyn smiled before setting the dagger down on the counter and opening the cabinet on her left.

Pushing past plastic cups and plates, she reached for the false back of the cabinet and traced her fingers over the rune Bowen had taught her to make for just this purpose.

It was weird, using magic when you weren't actually magic yourself, and Tamsyn still hadn't gotten used to it, that little zip of heat, the way her hand always tingled for a few seconds afterward.

The back of the cabinet popped open, revealing stacks of bills in various currencies, a leather folder that contained multiple IDs and passports, and a handful of magical coins she'd picked up on a job four years ago and hadn't worked out what to do with yet.

Tamsyn gently set the knife down inside her safe, then pushed the hidden door back into place and traced the rune again, this time in reverse. Another tingle rushed up her arm, stronger this time, and she flexed her fingers absently as she looked around her.

The Christmas lights cheered the place up, and the velvet pillows, brightly colored throws, and various non-magical knick-knacks she'd picked up from her travels—a framed piece of folk art from Iceland, a teak candleholder from Bali, a mirror she'd bought in a Paris thrift shop for three euros—made things homey, but it still had the same vaguely neglected air every house, apartment, duplex, or camper van she'd ever lived in seemed to develop, something she decided she didn't want to think about too hard at the moment.

Right now, what Tamsyn needed was a hot shower, soft pants, and about three hours of mindless scrolling on her phone before she slept for the next twelve hours.

"And food," she said out loud, turning back to the kitchen cabinets.

Unfortunately, her cupboards had been fairly bare before she'd left on this last-minute trip to Italy, and while Bowen had certainly worked some magic on this place for her remotely, he had not, it seemed, given her Magically Replenishing Groceries.

"Now *that* would be a Yule bonus," Tamsyn said, pulling out a plastic container of microwavable noodles.

While those heated up, she grabbed a quick shower in the trailer's minuscule bathroom before putting on a pair of sweatpants and an oversize T-shirt she'd gotten from Gwyn Jones's store, Something Wicked. Tamsyn was pretty sure Bowen's brother's girlfriend would turn her into a newt on the spot if she ever stepped foot in the store these days, but when she'd done that job in Graves Glen a few years ago, she'd stopped in a few times.

Her favorite purchase was a heavy piece of amethyst that she always threw in her carry-on bag, but this shirt with its grinning black cat and the words "Maybe *You're* Bad Luck, Ever Think About That?" underneath was a close second.

Although she might need that Krampus sweatshirt Bowen had been modeling in his selfie just for the *WTF?* of it all.

Pulling out her phone, Tamsyn opened his text and looked at the picture he'd sent again.

His dark curly hair was overly long, brushing his shoulders now, and his beard was thick as ever, but she could see the hint of a smile, and there was something in his expression, a warmth that Tamsyn felt even through the screen.

Groaning at herself, Tamsyn shook her head and closed the text app, connecting her phone to the Bluetooth speaker on the counter and pulling up her holiday playlist. Christmas carols were exactly what she needed to jolt her out of this swooning teenager thing, and while she grabbed her dinner from the microwave, the Ronettes sang their perky hearts out about sleigh rides and ring-tingle-tingling.

Tamsyn sang along, fishing a clean fork out of the silverware caddy by her sink, and then she carried her dinner and her laptop to the kitchen table, settling in on the leather banquette seat before looking around her.

The lights twinkled, the little Christmas tree she'd picked up last week stood proudly in its corner, and the music was so festive Tamsyn half expected Santa himself to come bursting through the front door. And with Bowen occupied with family stuff for Yule, she was technically on Christmas vacation now.

Practically a whole month to herself to . . .

Sit alone and eat Cup O' Noodles.

Except it wasn't even Cup O' Noodles. It was the off-brand one she'd grabbed the last time she'd remembered to go to the store.

Lifting the steaming bowl, Tamsyn inspected the looping yellow font spelling out "Noodz 4 U" and shook her head with a sigh.

"This is a new low, kid," she muttered, before blowing over the steaming contents and shrugging. "Still gonna eat it, but just need to acknowledge this moment."

Not for the first time, it occurred to Tamsyn that maybe she needed a pet. Or at least a houseplant, something she could say she was talking to instead of just talking to herself like that.

But she traveled so much, and that wasn't fair to a pet. Or to a plant, to be honest.

"Nope, just me and the Noodz," she said out loud now, and even the Ronettes sounded a little sorry for her as they launched into "Winter Wonderland."

It was stupid, though, this little spike of self-pity. She didn't have to sit here with microwave dinners and cheap Christmas decorations. Her parents had a condo in Florida they'd bought last year, and her brother and his husband always did a huge dinner on Christmas Eve. Tamsyn knew she'd be welcomed at either—both!—with open arms if that's what she wanted to do. Her family may have never really understood her, never gotten her restlessness and itchy feet, but they loved her in their way, and she definitely owed everyone a visit.

So yeah.

That's what she'd do first thing tomorrow. Call Mom, call Michael, spend the holidays like a normal person sipping eggnog, and watching bad movies, and eating her weight in sausage balls and fruitcake.

She was absolutely going to do that. One hundred percent.

Tamsyn was still telling herself that as she opened her laptop and, with a few clicks, found herself back in her old hunting grounds.

For something that existed on a server so hard to access it made the dark web seem positively fluorescent, the site looked surprisingly innocuous, the listings similar to what you'd see on a normal auction house website. Pictures, descriptions, soothingly bland language.

The difference was, where those other auction houses were selling paintings, pieces of furniture, or jewelry, this nameless site was selling . . . well, paintings, pieces of furniture, and jewelry, but a lot of it could kill you.

Tonight, however, there wasn't much on offer, or at least nothing Tamsyn thought Bowen might be interested in. Mostly crystals, one creepy-looking journal, and a pair of cuff links that were allegedly made from—

"Oh, *ew*," Tamsyn said, pushing her noodles away.

She kept scrolling, but nothing else caught her eye, and she was about to close her laptop when she found her cursor hovering over one of the tabs at the top of the site.

The one that said *Requested*.

She hadn't clicked on that in nearly a year, not since she started working for Bowen. That was the deal they'd made, after all, that she was acquiring for him exclusively, and she'd stuck to that even if Bowen didn't pay as much as some of her other clients had.

But then Bowen had never asked her to get anything truly dangerous, and some of the requests that came in weren't so much "acquisitions" as they were "suicide missions."

Tamsyn pulled her lower lip between her teeth, one foot tapping underneath the table.

"It's just looking," she reminded herself. "You're not going to take anything. You're just gonna see if there's anything interesting. Or something Bowen might need to know about. You're being . . . dedicated. Proactive. Working well with others."

That was the thing about talking to yourself—nobody around to call you on your bullshit.

So she clicked.

The first few listings were nothing special. As always, there was some dork offering to pay millions for the Philosopher's Stone, and someone else was asking for something from Salem, even though there hadn't even been real witches there, according to Bowen.

Still, Tamsyn kept clicking, drawing one foot up onto the

bench, her arm wrapped around her knee as she scrolled with the other hand, and her playlist switched to Dolly Parton mourning her "Hard Candy Christmas." She was just about to call it a night when she saw the brooch.

It caught her eye because, unlike most of the illustrations accompanying the listings, there was a color photograph, not a sketch from some ancient tome, and the jewels sparkled, a spiky cluster of gold and emeralds and rubies that wouldn't have looked amiss on top of a Christmas tree.

The description was brief.

Y Seren: Brooch consisting of emeralds, rubies, Welsh gold. Currently in possession of Carys Meredith, Tywyll House, Wales. Piece MUST BE ACQUIRED by 12/24 of the current year. Due to high-risk nature of retrieving brooch from home and accelerated timeline for delivery, compensatory pay offered beginning at US$1M.

"Holy Noodz," Tamsyn muttered.

She'd had well-paying gigs before, but a job that *started* at a million? That was a first. And she wasn't sure she'd ever seen a listing with so few details. Nothing about what the thing even *did*. Which, in Tamsyn's experience, meant that either it was a complete dud—just a piece of jewelry someone had decided *must* have magical powers—or it was something genuinely powerful.

For a second, she thought about calling Bowen. Or at least texting him since talking to him on the phone was usually a nightmare. Not only did his service suck up there on that mountain of his, but the man was truly terrible at calls in general. Tamsyn felt like she asked "Are you still there?" at least fifteen times per call, and sometimes he wasn't—that shitty service—but more often than not, he had just gone completely silent because Such Was Bowen Penhallow.

So yeah, if she was going to get in touch and ask him about this, definitely going the "written communication" route.

Reaching across the table, Tamsyn grabbed her phone, but once it was in her hand, she hesitated.

That's right, Bowen wasn't in Wales right now. He was in Graves Glen.

Where he would be until Christmas Eve.

Her eyes went back to the brooch.

"This is bad," she said out loud because it was clearly something she needed to hear. "What you're thinking? It's bad."

Or was it?

No, it was, definitely.

"One last job" was *such* a cliché, and Tamsyn was pretty sure it was also the kind of thing that inevitably got you killed.

"Because of the irony," she said around a mouthful of noodles. One benefit to living alone and talking to yourself was that you didn't have to worry about table manners.

Still, her free hand kept drumming on the keyboard, her eyes fixed on that brooch.

Even in this old, low-quality picture, the emeralds and rubies sparkled, and while Tamsyn understood the monetary value of the piece, she was having trouble working out what was magical about it. The buyer wasn't saying, that was for sure.

Everything about this was fishy as hell, she knew that. And she also knew she'd made a deal with Bowen to tell him about any artifacts that might be dangerous, to give him a chance to buy them first.

But . . .

This was a million dollars.

Bowen wasn't going to pay her that. Bowen almost certainly didn't *have* that, no matter how fancy his dad had been.

And it was a real test of her skills, the kind of job she'd once run straight toward until tangling with that ghost in Graves Glen a couple of years ago. Wouldn't it be fun to see if she still had what it took to pull this kind of thing off?

A challenging magical heist.

A million bucks.

And then . . . maybe an end to this line of work?

The thought sprang into her head like it had always been there, and Tamsyn sat very still, surprised at herself.

Is that why this acquisition appealed to her? Not only was a million dollars a pretty solid freaking foundation for a new life, but if she could lift something like this from a private house, she could say she'd gone out at the top of her field.

She'd have something to show for the last decade of lying and stealing and sneaking and occasional arson. Something more than an Airstream in a field and an expired jar of minced garlic in her fridge.

And then she could . . .

Tamsyn wrinkled her nose.

What would she even *do* if she wasn't doing this?

For just a second, Tamsyn's brain conjured up an image: Bowen's cabin, his unruly dark hair falling over his eyes as he leaned over his work on that big, scarred table she'd seen in video calls. He was wearing one of those thick sweaters she liked so much, and in this vision, she was wearing one, too. One of his, the hem brushing her bare thighs as she stood at the stove and cooked . . .

Okay, so her brain conjured up yet another package of Noodz 4 U, but if—*when*—she had time to cook, she'd definitely learn some recipes. Fancy ones, Ina Garten style.

"And you will *not* be cooking them for Bowen Penhallow," she told herself firmly as she mentally put some pants on the version of her in his cabin.

She let herself do this too often, slip into some daydream where she and Bowen were a lot more friendly and a lot more naked, and every time she did, Tamsyn swore she'd stop, swore she'd keep Bowen in that box she'd labeled "Just a (Weird and Also Very Hot) Friend, NO SEXY THOUGHTS ALLOWED."

And yet here he was, out of that box, and her thoughts were very sexy indeed.

Until she pictured what he'd say if she took this job.

Now the version of Bowen in her head wasn't looking at her with that warm fondness she sometimes caught in his gaze, and he definitely wasn't watching her with the hungry heat she'd just been imagining.

He was scowling and worried and pissed off. He'd hate everything about her taking this job. Too many unknowns, too many risks.

But Bowen was in Graves Glen.

Making bad decisions during the holidays was nothing new for Tamsyn. She had three tragic haircuts, two ex-boyfriends, and one holiday photo from her teenage years where she was wearing a sweater that read "Fa La La La Fuck It" while *standing next to her grandmother*—all offering proof that Tamsyn + December + Too Much Free Time = Disaster.

"This is so stupid," she muttered, her finger hovering over the discreet button reading *Accept Request*. "It's dangerous," she added, raising her voice. "And complicated! This is going to take *prep*. It's going to take *resources*. You can't go racing off to someone's house to lift a brooch by Christmas Eve. You are an *adult* who knows better. You . . ."

Trailing off, Tamsyn gave her better angels one more chance to save her, but maybe they were taking a holiday break, too, because her hand was moving, her finger was clicking, and now the screen simply read, *Request Engaged, TLB Acquisitions*.

Tamsyn sat there, mouth dry, heart pounding, and head so light she was almost giddy.

She was going to Wales. She was getting into this house and making off with a very expensive-looking piece of jewelry, and she was going to do it all by Christmas Eve.

Fa la la la fuck it.

Chapter 3

B owen wondered if he'd been on his mountain so long that he'd forgotten just how loud family gatherings were in general, or if his family in *particular* was just That Loud.

He suspected it was the latter.

Of course, not all families had a talking cat adding his own voice to the cacophony.

"Treats?" the little beastie asked as Gwyn stepped out of the kitchen with yet another bottle of wine, just as Taran banged his wee fists on the table with an echoed "TREEEEEEEEEE!"

"Wonderful," Vivienne said, shifting the baby on her lap and shooting a wry look at Gwyn. "He's learning to talk from the cat."

"Sir Purrcival has a better vocabulary than Rhys, so you should be thankful," Gwyn said, handing the wine to Wells to open.

"When that cat starts using words like 'peripatetic' just because he's going on a walk, let me know," Vivi replied, and Rhys leaned over to kiss his wife's offered cheek.

"Thank you, my darling," Rhys said, before shooting Gwyn a two-fingered salute. She only laughed merrily, flipping him off right back, but Wells glared at his brother and raised his voice to intone, "We are in *my house,* Rhys, and—"

"Actually, this is Da's house, you just live in it, which is a *bit* sad for a man your age."

"SAAAAA!" Taran screamed, and Rhys nodded at him.

"Just so."

They were in the dining room of the house Simon had built high on the hill—Bowen couldn't call anything around here a *mountain* no matter what the locals said—in Graves Glen, a house Gwyn and Wells had taken over and, in the words of Gwyn, "majorly de-creepified."

Bowen had only vague memories of this place before, but he had to admit it was nice now, warm and cozy. Lived in. Gwyn's touch was everywhere, from the brightly patterned seats of the dining room chairs to the whimsical mirror shaped like a crescent moon, but Bowen could see Wells here, too: the faux-horn candelabra (now moved safely out of Taran's reach), the hand-tooled leather placemats.

It had been a house, but now it was a home, and Bowen was happy for his brother.

For both of them.

But the longer he'd sat there tonight, listening to them tease and banter, argue and laugh, the hollower his gut had become.

Bowen thought he'd done a pretty good job of hiding it, but then Vivi turned to him, the baby still in her arms, now happily absorbed in tugging at the ends of her long hair, and asked, "Is everything all right?"

He glanced at his brothers, but they were now engaged in a debate over where to find the best Yule log, and Gwyn had turned to talk to her mother, Elaine, who sat at the head of the table, a piece of holly stuck behind one ear as she swirled her wine in its glass.

"Fine," he told her, but his brother had married a damn smart woman, and she wasn't so easily put off.

"I know you look . . . well, you look . . . like that," she said, waving at his face, "a lot, but it just seemed like something was bothering you."

What was bothering him was a strange mix of guilt—Declan would never have this, would never sit at a table with his family again, and whose fault was that?—and something else, something he was less used to.

Loneliness.

He was lonely, even as they included him, even as they pulled him into their arguments and their conversations, because he could feel how easy this was for all of them, how natural. How apart from it he was.

By choice, but it ached all the same.

Clearing his throat, Bowen answered her, but addressed the rest of them at the same time. "I, um . . . I know we'd talked about me staying through the new year."

That brought Rhys and Wells's discussion to a halt, and everyone turned to look at him now, causing a dull flush to creep up Bowen's neck.

Folding her arms over her chest, Gwyn fixed him with a steady look. "Not just talked about, Bowen. *Planned*. First big Jones-Penhallow Yule celebration. All of us together for nearly the whole month. Cutting down the Yule log, wassail . . . Esquire here even agreed to wear the holly crown!"

She elbowed Wells in the ribs, sloshing his wine.

"I did," he confirmed. "Once I had an assurance of no photographs."

Bowen nodded. "Right. Right . . . I . . . Right."

"And they made you a wee, sad little hut out back!" Rhys added. "So you'd feel at home."

Christ, he hated when it was two against one.

"It's just . . . I'm working on something right now," he said, telling a partial truth at least. "And I can't spare a full month away from it."

"You can work on it here," Gwyn said, and Wells nodded.

"Plenty of space upstairs, and as Rhys noted, we made you a hovel in the woods, since that's more what you're used to."

"And between the college, Aunt Elaine, and the store, I'm sure you'd have anything you'd need to do your weird magic science," Vivi said, brightening.

Taran babbled something at him, too, then gave him another one of those gummy smiles before trying to eat Vivi's hair.

"Of course," Elaine said, "if you'll tell me what kind of work you're doing, I'd be happy to help."

"Ooh!" Gwyn sat up straight in her chair. "*And* you're welcome to anything in Something Wicked, too, but I feel like your kind of magic probably doesn't call for sage and lavender bath salts."

"Right," Wells said with a clap of his hands. "So that's sorted then, yes? You're staying."

St. Bugi's balls, he hadn't reckoned with the combined force of these people.

But then Bowen could be stubborn, too.

In his way.

"I'll stick around for a few days," he said. "But that's all I can promise."

It's all I can give.

BOWEN HAD JUST thrown another log on the fire when the ghost appeared.

It was, he had to admit, the perfect setting for a spirit— December night, howling storm outside, remote Welsh mountainside, man brooding in the general direction of a fireplace—but he shrieked like a wee girl all the same.

"Calm yerself, Bo, Christ. It's just me," Declan said, raising one translucent hand as Bowen stood by the fire and tried to stop his heart beating out of his chest.

"You oughta get chains like that fella in *A Christmas Carol*," Bowen told him with a scowl. "Or a bell. Like a cat."

His former classmate and best friend flipped him off, bluish fingers wavering in the firelight. "Wanker."

"Arsehole," Bowen replied, then sighed. "Don't tell anyone I made that noise when you appeared."

"Oh, because that was gonna be a big topic of conversation for me and all my ghosty buddies at the lunch table, sure," Declan replied with a wry grin.

It made Bowen's chest hurt, that grin.

That was one of the first things he'd come to like about Declan, all those years ago, the way he smiled like the whole world was a big joke, and weren't the two of you lucky to be in on it?

It had reminded Bowen of Rhys a bit, and maybe that's why he'd become friends with his roommate at Penhaven College so quickly.

Graves Glen might be a lovely place now, but all those years ago, it had seemed like millions of miles from home, the mild winters and hot, humid summers of Georgia so different from his wild Welsh homeland.

But then he'd met Declan, a Scottish lad from Edinburgh who was as passionate about ancient sorcery as he was his beloved Midlothian Hearts football team, and they'd become best mates almost immediately. No one was smarter when it came to magic than Declan, no one quicker to pick up a spell or know exactly what book in exactly what part of the shadowy, cluttered library would have the ritual they were looking for.

No one had been more willing to embrace the wilder side of magic, either.

Bowen had told himself a thousand times that what had happened wasn't his fault. Hell, Declan had said the same.

But it had been Bowen who'd found that spell.

The log on the fire popped, releasing a shower of sparks, and

Bowen stepped back a bit, dusting his hands on the back of his jeans as he studied the spirit that had once been his friend.

"Haven't seen you for a bit," Bowen said. That wasn't unusual—he'd once gone nearly a whole year without seeing the spirit, and he'd hoped maybe that meant whatever it was tying Declan's spirit to the earth had finally been severed, but no such luck. "Where'd you get yourself off to now?"

Declan went a bit "thin," as Bowen always thought of it. His form didn't seem quite as substantial, the bookshelf behind him now very visible, his football jersey barely readable.

Then the room got a little colder, and Declan started coming in clearer again, still translucent, but a little more solid, and for the first time, Bowen realized he was holding something in his hand.

An envelope.

Bowen took it from Declan's outstretched fingers and frowned at the heavy weight of it in his hand.

"Wedding invitation," Declan said, but Bowen was less concerned with the *what* of the thing and more the *how*. As in—

"How the hell did you manage to get this thing here?"

Ghosts could move objects, but rarely did they have enough power to transport something.

"That's why I haven't been around for the past few months," he said, nodding at the envelope. "That showed up at my mum's house back in July. It's taken me this long to get it here, and now time is pressing, mate."

Bowen pulled out the card inside and squinted at the elaborate calligraphy. "Morgana's tits, I can barely read this."

"Don't worry," Declan said with a gusty sigh. "I've had time to memorize it. It says that Sir and Lady Meredith have the pleasure of inviting you to the wedding of their daughter, Carys, to a Mr. David Thorsby on December twenty-fourth."

"Carys Meredith," Bowen said, throwing Declan a sharp look.

The ghost threw up his glowing hands. "Yes, *that* Carys."

"Your fiancée," Bowen went on, and Declan scowled, folding his arms over his chest.

"Former fiancée. This *David* apparently now holds the title."

Given that Declan made the name "David" sound like a communicable disease, Bowen refrained from pointing out that it wasn't like Declan was exactly able to take a wife, so maybe moving on had been good for Carys.

Bowen had never met her, but he remembered her picture in its place of honor on Dec's desk in the room they'd shared. She was pretty in a delicate sort of way, her hair so blond it was nearly white, but her eyes were dark brown, and in the picture Declan had, she'd been laughing at the camera, her head tilted back, her arms thrown wide.

Declan had been mad about her, and Bowen had always wondered what she'd been told about what happened to her fiancé.

What she must have thought.

"It's not just a wedding," Declan went on, pointing at the

invitation. "Whole long weekend sort of thing. A Yule celebration mixed in. Carys's family always was a little over the top, to be honest."

Shaking the card at Dec, Bowen asked, "And it's next week?"

Declan gave a grim nod. "Told you, I've been trying to get this bloody thing to you since *July*. I almost thought I wouldn't make it."

"Hmmph," Bowen snorted, thinking that over as he thwacked the card against his palm. "You know—"

"I could've come to you, told you about the wedding, and then had you magic up an invitation, or possibly contact my parents and get it yourself, yes, these were all things that occurred to me the second you picked the fooking thing up, thank you, Bowen."

That was a thing with ghosts—they got so fixated on whatever quest it was that was keeping them tied to the mortal plane that they sometimes forgot the way the human world worked. It was both endearing and a little sad, and not for the first time, Bowen wished that he'd been a little bit more forceful trying to talk Declan out of that bloody stupid spell.

Still, it was done now, wasn't it?

"Why bring it to me at all?" he asked, and Declan gave him a look that Bowen remembered very well from their university days. It was the one that said, *How can one man be this thick?*

"Because I want you to go," he said.

Bowen could actually feel his frown deepen. If Tamsyn were here right now, she'd probably already be doing an exaggerated impression of it.

"You . . . want me to go," he echoed, "to your ex-fiancée's wedding."

Declan nodded, his hair—which had been bright red when he was alive, but was now more of a sort of grayish blue—flopping over one eye. "Mmm-hmm. I need you to whip up a really nasty curse. Right at the vows, stand up and proclaim it, maybe add some thunder and lightning for effect? Ooh, can you do, like, a scary black cloud thing, too? You know, just to really sell it."

Bowen stared at his friend for a couple of beats as the fire crackled away and sleet rattled against the door.

Then, slowly: "You're fucking with me."

Declan's eyes went a little wider as he crossed his arms over his chest. "Huh. Usually takes you a little longer to figure that out."

"I've had more practice lately," he muttered, Tamsyn's dark eyes, bright with amusement, suddenly springing to mind.

He should introduce her to Declan one of these days. They'd like each other, Bowen was sure of that. But then explaining Dec to Tamsyn would mean explaining his own role in how all this had happened, and Christ, wouldn't that be a mess?

"Seriously, though," Declan said, dropping his chin and looking at Bowen from underneath a curtain of that floppy hair. "I can't go myself. That house is magicked to hell and back, and anything that feels off to it gets spit right back out. Don't ask me how I know. Okay," he went on, holding up a hand. "I know because I've been trying to haunt the damn place for the last decade, and every time I get within a few feet of the house, I'm poofed right out to somewhere miles away. The Merediths apparently don't fuck around."

Bowen nodded, but his mind was already moving.

"Meredith," he echoed, and then he walked past Dec to the bookcase at the back of the room, the biggest one just by the door to his bedroom. Reaching up, Bowen pulled down a book that was so heavy he actually winced as the full weight of it landed in his arms.

It was a massive tome, the cover a cracked and fading black leather, the gilding starting to peel from the edges of its pages. It was the sort of thing that, had it been a prop in a movie, he would've had to blow dust off so that the audience knew just how ancient it was, but no books ever gathered dust in Bowen Penhallow's home. He'd looked something up in this one just the other day, as a matter of fact, thanks to a late-night phone call from Rhys, who had suddenly worried that Taran's middle name, "Emyr," had belonged to one of their less savory ancestors.

It hadn't, thankfully, and Bowen flipped backward, past the section on the Penhallows, the Parrys, the Owens, the Neagles, until he finally came to the elaborate script proclaiming "MEREDITH."

He could feel a cold breeze at his back and knew Declan had stepped closer, reading over Bowen's shoulder.

"I knew her family were Posh Witches, but I didn't know they were posh enough to be in your book," he said, his breath icy on Bowen's neck.

"Not just posh," Bowen told him, his eyes scanning the names.

"Powerful. This Meredith right here? Powys in 1283?" Bowen tapped the name. "Hanged, disemboweled, burned, then decapitated."

"And he didn't die?" Declan asked.

Bowen shook his head. "No, all those things killed him. Well, I suppose just one of them killed him. The others probably just hurt a lot."

"And this . . . denotes 'powerful' . . . how, exactly?"

Bowen reached over Declan's ghostly arm to pull his notebook and pen closer, inadvertently dragging them through Declan, who yelped with offense.

"Sorry," Bowen said, distracted, and as he began to write, Declan snorted.

"No, you're not," he replied, and if Bowen hadn't already been absorbed in his work, he might've smiled.

"Doesn't hurt you anyway," he reminded Declan, who lifted his chin and floated to the other side of the table.

"Right, but it's *rude*. Now explain to me what you meant about Carys's great-great-times-a-bloody-million-grandfather being powerful."

"The English did all those things to him because he was dabbling in dark magic," Bowen said, still taking down names, dates. He could remember things he'd read pretty easily, but if he wrote it down, he never forgot it.

"Okay, but it was 1283," Declan said. "'Dark magic' could've meant . . . I don't know. Taking a bath. Not wanting a leech applied to his cock."

"That's ignorance speaking, Declan. The Middle Ages were not nearly as filthy and backward as people think. In fact, did you know that entire idea about them having bad teeth is false? They didn't have sugar, so—"

"Mate," Declan said, holding up one hand, and Bowen scowled but tucked that particular diatribe away for another time.

People always gave him so much shit for not talking that much, but then when he *did* want to talk about something he was interested in, it was all glazed eyes and "mate."

"To the point, dark magic in this case was truly dark magic. Necromancy, that sort of thing."

Declan perked up a bit, and the hope in his eyes was enough to make Bowen's stomach churn. "Necromancy. Like bringing the dead back to life."

"You're not dead, Dec," Bowen reminded him, his voice as gentle as he could make it. "Not really."

The sound Declan made was too dark to be called a laugh, but it was close. "Not dead, not alive, a ghost, but no body moldering away anywhere . . . Yes, Bowen, we've been over this. And I wasn't asking you to go because I hoped it was the answer to"—Declan looked down at his wavering form and gestured to it—"whatever the hell this is."

Turning to face Bowen more fully, Declan reached out, laying his hands on Bowen's shoulders. Bowen could feel the cold, but there was no weight there, no real touch.

"If I'd married Carys, you would've been my best man, right? Now, I can't watch the woman I love get married, but you can.

For me. It's the closest thing I can think of to being there myself."

It had been a while since Bowen had felt like this. The tight throat, the sudden stinging in his eyes. Not since that last night he'd talked to Da, probably, that cold evening last year when Bowen had made sure Simon Penhallow knew that all three of his sons were done with him and his scheming for good.

It had been the right thing to do, but fuck, it had been hard. Almost as hard as staring into Declan's pleading face now.

"Dec," Bowen said softly, "I can't just . . . invitation or no, pretty sure they'll remember they didn't invite me."

"Your family is ancient and powerful," Declan reminded him. "Just as much as the Merediths. No one is going to question you showing up with an invite. Carys will probably assume This David's family invited you. And This David will think it was Carys's terrifying grandmother. But not a one of them is going to tell a Penhallow he can't be there."

Declan had a point. Welsh witch families were strange in that way, a tangled mess of marriages and blood feuds and ancient treaties, and Bowen's family was one of the most influential there was. He could just channel Wells a bit, be an imperious dickhead, and everyone would assume he belonged there.

In a remote castle for a whole bloody weekend with a bunch of witches he didn't know.

At Yule.

Again, Tamsyn's face came to mind. They were supposed to meet in London on the twenty-fourth. The pub, the Reindeer Rosé.

The mistletoe.

"Please, Bo," Declan implored again. "I know I've lost her and that she's gone, but if you could watch the wedding, if you could just tell me about it . . . if I could know you were there and that there was at least one person in that room who was thinking of me, maybe it wouldn't hurt this much."

And that was a bloody knife to the heart, wasn't it?

He had taken so much from Declan, still hadn't figured out the way to make it right, and here was this one thing—a small favor in light of it all—that Declan was asking him to do.

"Look," Dec said, flashing him that grin again. "It's going to be cold and uncomfortable, and you'll probably be miserable, but—"

"But how is that any different from every day of my life," Bowen finished dryly, and Declan laughed, another rush of cold air settling on Bowen's skin.

"Pretty much," he confirmed. "Although you'll probably like Tywyll House. Creepy as fook, full of all sorts of old magical shit. Think of it as a working vacation."

There was something about that name—Tywyll House—that rang a faint bell in the back of Bowen's mind. Something that seemed important.

Something he should know.

But then there was another gust of wind howling down the chimney, the fire flaring briefly, and the thought—and Declan—vanished.

CHAPTER 4

Tamsyn was no stranger to creepy places.

Occupational hazard, really, and one she'd encountered more and more frequently since she started working for Bowen. She'd been in old dungeons and more gloomy basements than she could count, and on one memorable occasion, she'd ended up stuck in something called an "oubliette" for a couple of hours, so yeah, when it came to The Spooky, she was a seasoned pro.

But as she stared up at the iron gates of Tywyll House, Tamsyn had to admit this was a new level of creepy.

"Advanced Creepy," she muttered to herself, ducking down to peer at the top of the gates through her fogged-up windshield. "Graduate Level Eerie."

It had taken her ages just to find the place, the map of the area she'd acquired being a good sixty years out of date. But then from her research, it was no surprise that the Merediths had made their ancestral manse this hard to find.

If Tamsyn had thought Bowen's family history was complicated, it was nothing compared with these witches', and she'd had a long flight to London plus a train ride to North Wales to do her homework.

She knew that the Merediths had been in Wales since there *was* a Wales, basically, and that they had a tendency to get killed in a variety of horrifying ways. She knew that the current head of the family, Madoc Meredith, had one child, a daughter named Carys, and that his wife, Amelia, had fucked off to Italy a few years ago.

She knew that Tywyll House had started its life as a kind of fortress in the fourteenth century before gradually being added on to over the next five hundred years, so it was less a house, more a hodgepodge of styles with at least twenty-five bedrooms and who knew how many other rooms.

She even knew that there were, according to legend, at least three ghosts haunting the castle, one of whom was apparently missing a head.

What she didn't know was where the brooch she'd been sent to acquire was.

Or what it did.

Or why someone would pay over a million dollars to get it.

"Details," Tamsyn said out loud to herself now, as she tugged on the ends of the blond wig she was wearing.

Did the job technically require a disguise?

Probably not.

Had she missed this part of things, playing a role, getting a costume, committing to the bit?

She really, *really* had.

"You're stalling, Bligh," she said, still looking up at the gates. They were open, the word "Tywyll" curling through the iron, rusted in parts, and a strong gust of wind sent one listing drunkenly to the right.

Taking a deep breath, Tamsyn gently pressed on the gas and steered her rental car through the opening.

In the spring, the long winding drive up to the house was probably charming. The trees would be bursting with leaves, their branches creating a fragrant green tunnel that would reveal the occasional glimpse of bright blue sky. There would be birds singing and . . . and bees buzzing, probably, and maybe the gentle babble of a brook nearby.

That was the image Tamsyn kept firmly in mind as she drove, because otherwise, she would have to acknowledge that she appeared to be driving directly into an old horror movie.

No blue sky today, just a turbulent gray that suggested rain later this evening. No leaves, either, just row after row of wet black branches reaching skeletal fingers up to the clouds, and as another gust of wind buffeted the car, Tamsyn clutched the wheel more tightly and gritted her teeth.

"A million dollars," she reminded herself, once again checking her reflection in the rearview mirror.

She'd pulled out an old identity for this gig, one she hadn't used in at least five years, but Anna Ripley felt right for this particular crowd. Asymmetrical platinum bob, oversize glasses with red acrylic frames, statement jewelry. A little eccentric, but artsy. Anna Ripley was a gallery owner, after all, an acquaintance of Carys's mother—they'd met at that charming little studio in Venice, just off the Campo Sant'Angelo, remember?

Her mysterious employer had gotten her the invitation, but this—the story, the disguise, the persuasive power of her charm—*this* was Tamsyn's gift.

It was honestly kind of shocking how quickly people went along with something as long as you were casual and confident and had done your homework.

Tamsyn had initially thought of pretending to be a college friend of Carys's, but then she homed in on Amelia instead. Flighty, always seeking out new people, new experiences. Tons of pictures of her in various society columns flitting all around the world, always surrounded by a sea of faces, always a glass of champagne near at hand. She wouldn't remember meeting "Anna Ripley," but she wouldn't be able to say for sure that she hadn't, and her upper-crust manners would prevent her from doing anything as awkward as demanding proof, especially when Tamsyn would be coming with invitation in hand.

"Because I'm the fucking best," Tamsyn reminded herself, smiling a little even as the road got a little darker, the trees closer together.

It was fun, getting to stretch this particular muscle again, and if she felt just the tiniest bit guilty about it . . .

Her eyes briefly flicked from the road to her bag.

Bowen had texted the other day. Not with a job, just a terse message about not being able to meet on Christmas Eve after all and that he'd talk to her in the new year.

Stupid to feel disappointed about it, especially since she'd been about to cancel on *him* thanks to this job, but when it came to Bowen Penhallow, Tamsyn was beginning to think she'd always be a little stupid.

Maybe that's why she'd wanted to do this job: a reminder of who she was, of what she could do, that had nothing to do with Bowen. That she'd be fine once he inevitably didn't need her anymore and moved on to some new magical fixation up there in his weird little hut.

The road twisted and turned along with Tamsyn's thoughts, and she winced as she drove over a root big enough to scrape the rental's undercarriage. She'd driven long enough that she was beginning to wonder if the house was even there when she took another turn, and it was suddenly rising up before her.

It was . . . enormous. Crenellations and towers reached up to the gray sky, and the door—if it could even be called that—was two massive slabs of oak studded with iron bolts and rivets. Mist drifted over the ground, and honest-to-god *torches* flickered in iron cages affixed to the exterior walls.

It looked foreboding. Haunted. Terrifying.

And she was spending the next three nights in it.

A million dollars, she repeated in her head as she parked the car and stepped out into the damp, cold afternoon.

Think of it like a challenge. Like one of those reality shows where you do scary shit, but at the end of it, you win a Toyota Tercel or something.

Right.

She could do that.

Tamsyn grabbed her leather purse and the old-fashioned suit-case she'd thought someone like Anna Ripley would own and took a few slow steps toward the . . . okay, it called itself a house, but really "castle" was a better word. If a dragon were curled around one of those towers, it would look right at home.

There was a creaking noise so loud the trees seemed to shiver with it, and the massive doors slowly swung open to reveal a man in a dark green wool suit, the fine rain that had started glistening on his bald head as he stepped forward to greet her.

"Welcome!" he boomed out, a bright smile on his face as he held out a hand to her, and Tamsyn took it without thinking.

Immediately, her fingers were engulfed by his massive palm, and he pumped her arm hard enough to almost wrench it from the socket.

"Anna—" she began, but he was already nodding and pulling her inside with a hearty pat on her back.

"Yes, yes, wedding guest, last to arrive, my dear, but no matter, no matter. Beastly weather, I'm afraid, Wales in December and all that, never have understood why Carys wanted to get married at Yule, but there's no arguing with a bride, is there?"

He laughed then, the sound echoing in the cavernous front hallway, bouncing off the stone floor and the dull row of suits of armor that marched down a long, wide hallway toward a roaring fire at the far end of the room.

A chill had settled into her bones from the second she'd stepped out of the car, and Tamsyn made to move toward the fire only to have her host steer her to the right instead, down another dark hallway and past a massive staircase that rose up into gloomy darkness.

"We'll get you to the kitchen and get some tea in you, eh? Always the best thing, I find, on days like this. Tea and perhaps a bit of whisky?" The man grinned at Tamsyn, then placed a thick finger over his lips. "Our secret," he whispered. Or at least Tamsyn thought he was *trying* to whisper. She wasn't sure he was capable of anything quieter than a shout, honestly.

"That would be—" she said, but then he was moving her along again, his hand firm on her elbow.

"Yes, yes, tea and then perhaps a lie-down, and you'll be right as rain. I'd recommend a hot bath as well, but with this many bloody people in the house, I can't promise our ancient pipes are up to the task of anything more than a *lukewarm* bath, really, and that can be worse than no bath at all, can't it? Yes, indeed, it can, as I always used to say to my father, but he'd say, 'Madoc, my boy, our ancestors bathed in freezing rivers and streams, so cold water flows in Meredith veins, you ponce,' which wasn't a very *kind* thing for a father to say . . ."

He continued prattling on, but Tamsyn could barely hear him over the ringing of alarm bells starting up in her head.

This was Sir Madoc Meredith, head of the family, host of this entire wedding weekend, father of the bride, and a man who, according to what research she'd been able to do in the few weeks she'd had before showing up here, was one of the most powerful witches in the world.

And something had him scared to death.

She'd seen it in that brief moment when he'd looked over at her, joking about the whisky. He'd been smiling, but above those bright teeth, his blue eyes had been wide, blinking too fast, and the finger he'd lifted to his mouth had been trembling.

And there was the way he'd practically yanked her down this hall, glancing over his shoulder every few moments even as he'd kept up his steady stream of chatter. His hand, still holding her elbow, was so cold she could feel it through her sweater, and even in the dim light of the hallway, Tamsyn could see that his skin was vaguely gray.

Something was wrong here.

Badly wrong.

Fuck a duck, Tamsyn thought, even as she smiled at Madoc Meredith.

She was good at this part of the job: reading people, picking up on what they were feeling even if they were trying to hide it. It was a vital skill to have in this line of work, one that had saved her ass more than once over the years, and every cell in her body was currently screaming at her to leave, to say she'd left something in the car, then get in it and peel out of here as fast as she could. Forget the brooch, forget the job, because anything that had this powerful a witch this terrified was not something she wanted to tangle with.

From somewhere in the distance, Tamsyn heard a crash. It sounded like metal hitting stone, and she remembered that long line of suits of armor in the front hallway. But no, whatever it was, it was farther away than that, the sound muffled.

Sir Madoc jumped as though it had been a gunshot right

next to his ear, then reached into his jacket to pull out a mono-grammed handkerchief. He used it to mop his brow even though the hallway was so cold Tamsyn could see her breath.

"Is everything all righ—" she said, but then he looked past her, his expression brightening a little.

"Ah! Here's another of our guests for you to meet!"

Tamsyn was way more interested in just what the hell was going on in this house than she was in meeting some fancy witch, but she plastered a smile on her face all the same as she turned around.

The hallway was dim, watery gray light from the windows set high above their heads casting strange shadows, the electric sconces on the wall barely penetrating the gloom.

But Tamsyn didn't need a lot of light. She would have known that walk—that pose with the hands in his back pockets, his shoulders slightly hunched—anywhere.

Oh, no was the only clear thought in her head.

Well, not exactly true. There were other thoughts currently slam dancing around in there, including *Fuck my liiiiiife* and *Of all the gin joints or whatever that quote is—maybe I should watch more old movies?* and *Oh my god, he actually owns clothes that* aren't *sweaters, boots, and jeans, but that's actually a bad thing because I had gotten* almost *immune to those, and now I have to learn how to deal with him all dressed up without wanting to climb him like a tree, and am I that strong? Is ANY WOMAN THAT—*

"Our last guest to arrive, meet our *first* guest to arrive," Sir Madoc said, and keeping that fake smile plastered to her face, Tamsyn offered her hand to a glowering Bowen Penhallow.

CHAPTER 5

B owen had spent enough years studying magic to know that there were larger forces operating in the universe. He'd seen them up close, after all, and studied them, tried to learn their secrets. He might not understand them all, but there was no doubt that he *believed*.

And now, as he watched a blond Tamsyn turn around and give him her fakest smile, he *also* believed that those same forces clearly hated his fucking guts.

"Bowen Penhallow," Sir Madoc boomed as Tamsyn slipped her hand into Bowen's, "may I introduce . . ." The older man frowned, his vaguely purple face darkening a bit. "Sorry, love, what was your name again?"

"Anna Ripley," Tamsyn said smoothly, still shaking Bowen's hand. Her palm was ice-cold against his, and Bowen wondered if that was from nerves or if it was just that the Merediths clearly thought things like "heating" were for lesser mortals.

"Anna," Bowen echoed slowly as he studied her face.

Tamsyn's brown hair was concealed beneath a bright blond

bob, and while her eyes were just as warm and as dark as ever, they were now behind a pair of large glasses with bright red frames. Her shoes were red, too, bloodred, the heels so high and so thin that he wondered that she hadn't already pitched face-first onto the stone floor. They made her tall enough to almost look him dead in the eye, and as Bowen watched her now, he thought her gaze was communicating something like *Please don't cock this up for me, mate.*

Only . . . more American, obviously.

"Excellent, excellent," Sir Madoc blustered, gesturing for both of them to continue down the hallway to a small kitchen.

This was clearly the older part of the house, the wood-beamed ceiling low, the brick around the fireplace charred with centuries of soot, but it was cozy in its way. A fire crackled in the hearth, and there was a steaming pot of tea on the rough wooden table in the center of the room along with a few mismatched china cups.

Sir Madoc walked over to them now, pouring two cups before producing a flask from his jacket and adding a healthy dollop to each. He went to cap the flask, then paused, and as Bowen and Tamsyn stood there just inside the doorway, Sir Madoc tilted the entire container up and drained it.

"Ah," he said, placing the empty flask back in his jacket. "That's more like it. Now, if you two will excuse me, much to do, much to do, but please, enjoy your tea. Cocktails will be served in the library at seven, followed by dinner at eight. Miss Ripley, I'll have your things sent to the Blue Room, I think. No. No, Yellow. Yes, Yellow Room, much nicer views, closer to the gardens."

Walking back toward them, Sir Madoc gave both Tamsyn and Bowen hearty claps on the shoulder, and then he was gone, the gloom of the hallway seeming to swallow him up.

Leaving Tamsyn and Bowen alone.

For a moment, they both just stood there, the only sounds the shifting of the logs in the fireplace and the wind whistling through the eaves.

Tamsyn broke first, sighing as she walked over to the table in those high, high heels, each step clicking loudly in the quiet room.

"I need to be fortified to have this conversation," she said, picking up the cup and sitting down on one of the stools circling the table.

Bowen sat as well, the fragile cup warm in his hand as he took a sip. The splash of whisky Sir Madoc had poured in started a pleasant simmer in his veins. Tamsyn was watching him warily, but Bowen let the silence spool out a bit before finally saying, "You look . . . different."

Tamsyn turned her head so sharply that the edges of that very geometrical haircut swung like pendulums over her shoulders.

"That's it?" she said, raising her eyebrows beneath the platinum bangs. "You find me here, obviously on a job, and all you have to say is 'you look different'?"

"Not all I have to say, just the first thing," Bowen countered. "The second is pretty obvious, I'd think."

"What am I doing here?" she guessed, propping her cheek on

her hand, and Bowen reminded himself that he was annoyed with her and that was *not* bloody fucking adorable.

"Pretty much, yeah."

She heaved another sigh, ruffling her bangs. "Do you want the short version or the long version?"

"The true one. Be honest with me," he said, lowering his head to look into her eyes.

Tamsyn seemed to deflate, slightly, her fist sliding away from her cheek. "It's very uncool that you do that," she told him. "The whole ... earnest thing. With the eyes and the voice and the ..." She waved a hand over her face. Bowen had no idea what she meant by that, but ignored it as she said, "I'm here on behalf of a client, obviously."

"I'm your only client now," he replied.

She was too good and too quick to give away much, but Bowen saw it, the brief flash of guilt in her eyes, the lower lip caught between her teeth for an instant.

"Tam—" he began, and she rolled her eyes, throwing up her hands with a clatter of gold bangles.

"You are my only client in the sense that I only *currently* work for you, but I worked with a *lot* of people before I met you, Bowen, and sometimes a girl likes to flex her skills a bit, is all. I was on the site that I use to find artifacts—"

"There's a website for that?"

She held up one hand, and for the first time Bowen noticed her nails were the same scarlet as her outfit. "There's a website for everything. Unfortunately. Anyway, I saw something interesting. I decided that since you didn't need me in December, I might as well take a little freelance work, and said freelance work involves *this* walking nightmare of a place."

Bowen grunted and drained the rest of his tea.

As he sat the empty cup back on the table, he reminded himself that feeling angry was normal. What Tamsyn did, acquiring magical artifacts for the highest bidder, was dangerous. It made things harder for all witches, and he was a witch, right?

So yes, perfectly fine to feel irritated. Frustrated.

Natural to be curious, too. What on earth might be in this house that someone would pay Tamsyn's prices to get it?

And he *was* curious, just like he was angry and frustrated.

But the worst part, the thing that bothered him the most, was the feeling underneath those other, perfectly rational ones.

He was hurt.

Why hadn't she told him she was going to take another job? No, she didn't owe it to him as a coworker, maybe, but as a friend—

Bowen slammed the door shut on that line of thinking.

Not helpful right now.

"So you went back on our deal," he said, folding his arms over his chest. "Unless 'exclusive' means something else to non-witches?"

The corners of her mouth turned down, eyes blinking behind those huge glasses. "No," she said. "Or . . . well, not exactly. This is a one-time thing, Bowen. One last job."

"That cliché?"

Her scowl deepened. "A cliché for a *reason*. Because it's enough money not to ever have to do any other kinds of jobs again. It's a No More Noodz job, Bowen."

Bowen had . . . questions, lots of them, but for now, he focused on the simplest one: "How much money?"

He could actually see her thinking about lying to him. Something in the way her gaze slid away just for a heartbeat and the sudden tapping of her heel against the rung of the stool.

But then she shook her head and laid both hands flat on the tabletop, a cabochon ruby winking at him. "Starts at a million."

"Dollars?"

"Yup."

"Huh."

More than he'd thought. More than he'd ever would've guessed, if he were honest.

And that worried him. People didn't go around offering that kind of cash for a ceremonial goblet or a bit of bewitched crystal. Whatever Tamsyn was here to get, it had to have serious magic attached to it.

Tamsyn must've picked up what he was thinking from his expression, because she leaned forward and lowered her voice to a whisper: "It's a piece of jewelry. Some ugly brooch called Y Seren."

"The Star," Bowen translated, and she nodded, pulling her phone out of the little handbag still dangling on her shoulder.

"See?" she said, showing him the screen.

The brooch was definitely ugly, a gaudy cluster of rubies, emeralds, and diamonds, and Bowen was slightly relieved that he'd never heard of the thing before, never seen it. He'd spent his life eyeballs-deep in the arcane—if this thing were dangerous, surely he would know about it.

"What, no gruff warning?" Tamsyn asked, pulling the phone back. "No long and gruesome legend about how this brooch actually melts eyeballs and flays skin or something?"

"I've never heard of it," Bowen replied, scratching the side of his neck. While he'd kept his beard, he'd cleaned it up a little for this wedding, something Tamsyn only just seemed to be noticing.

He didn't miss it, the way her eyes moved over his face now, just like he hadn't missed the little flare of . . . something in her gaze that hadn't just been panic when she'd turned around and seen him standing there in the hallway.

For the first time, it occurred to him that he and Tamsyn would be in this house for the next few days, tucked into this dark and gloomy castle in the Welsh countryside. There would be roaring fires, and walks through the woods, and probably more fucking mistletoe, and yeah, Bowen suddenly realized he had a lot more to worry about on this trip than Tamsyn attempting to steal a piece of jewelry.

Clearing his throat, Bowen sat up straighter, his hands clasped in front of him. "You'll need my help," he told her. "Getting that thing. If it belongs to the Merediths, then they've probably done Rhiannon only knows what kind of magic on it."

Tamsyn frowned but didn't object.

At least not out loud.

Instead, she asked, "Are you friends with them? Is that why you're here?"

"Never met them," Bowen said with a shrug, and the silence stretched out between them for several loud ticks of the clock.

"Soooo . . ." Tamsyn drawled, propping her chin in her hand. "No more to that, then? No explanation, no backstory, for what you're doing here?"

He thought about telling her the truth, thought about mentioning Declan and the whole mess, but instead he heard himself say, "Representing my family. Old witch family shite, basically."

Tamsyn nodded, those crazy earrings of hers swaying again, and opened her mouth to reply, but before she could, there was a distant howling from somewhere in the house that had her bolting up in her seat, her face going a little pale.

The sound rose: a thin, keening noise that could've been mistaken for the wind if it didn't make your blood freeze and every hair on your body stand on end.

Then it suddenly stopped, and the silence was somehow even eerier than the noise had been.

"What . . ." Tamsyn started, then stopped, swallowed hard, and began again. "What was that?"

Bowen had asked himself that same thing when he'd heard the wailing noise not ten minutes after he'd arrived. He'd also wondered why the third-floor hallway was so cold you could see your breath.

By the time he'd seen an antique vase rise about an inch or so off a rosewood end table in the library, he'd understood.

"Ghost," he told Tamsyn now, and she turned those wide brown eyes back on him, her lips parting.

Sighing, Bowen sunk lower on his stool. "So we have a wedding to witness, a brooch to steal, and on top of that, place is haunted as fuck."

CHAPTER 6

Sir Madoc had been wrong about the water at Tywyll House—it was plenty hot, steaming up the bathroom and turning Tamsyn's skin rosy as she lay in a claw-footed tub that was bigger than the Ford Fiesta that had been her first car.

Too bad she was pretty sure *lava* wouldn't be warm enough to chase the chill out of her bones.

It wasn't just the house itself or the frigid and wet December evening, although those things definitely hadn't helped. It was Bowen's words there in the kitchen—*place is haunted as fuck*—that were making her shiver even as sweat beaded her forehead.

"You are a Bad Bitch," she reminded herself, sinking a little deeper into the water. "You're not gonna *say* the *I ain't afraid of no ghosts* thing, but you're going to *think* it. Except you just said it because you're talking to yourself again, which is definitely a sign that you are not feeling your Baddest and Bitchiest."

It was just that . . . well, ghosts freaked her out. She'd never actually *seen* one, but she'd felt one, and that had been enough to last her a lifetime. Even now, she could remember the heaviness that had settled over her room at the B-and-B where she'd been hiding out after getting the Eurydice Candle from Vivienne Jones. There hadn't been any floating spirit or strange noises, just that feeling like the air itself was pressing down on her and a frigid iciness that had slithered through multiple layers of clothing.

If someone had asked her to describe the presence she'd lived with for a couple of days, all Tamsyn would've been able to come up with was that it felt *wrong,* and the whole thing had scared her so badly that she'd sworn off any acquiring for months after.

Tywyll House didn't feel like that, exactly, but she knew Bowen was right: there was *something* here, and suddenly a million bucks didn't seem worth it.

From somewhere deep in the house, a clock chimed, and sighing, Tamsyn glanced over at her phone, precariously perched on the windowsill just above the tub. Quarter past six.

She hauled herself out of the tub, picking up a slightly scratchy towel folded on the corner of the sink, and started getting ready for what she already suspected would be a *very* long night.

Bowen hadn't provided any more explanations past *Hey, this house is haunted,* because why would Bowen ever explain *anything,* and as she situated her wig back on top of her head, Tamsyn tried to remind herself that whatever—whoever—was haunting this place wasn't going to have any beef with her. Weren't these the kinds of houses that had family ghosts? Dead Auntie Clara, or whoever the spirit was wandering these halls, wasn't going to go after some random American lady staying here only for a few nights. She was no doubt too busy trying to tell her descendants where the hidden treasure was or who had murdered her, something like that.

"That's how ghosts work, right?" she said aloud as she fished an eyeliner pencil out of her makeup bag.

Tamsyn was halfway through her second smoky eye when she paused, the eyeliner wobbling.

"Unless the ghost is attached to the brooch," she muttered, her stomach suddenly twisting.

A ghost *definitely* would go after someone lifting family heirlooms.

"Shit."

Tossing down the pencil with a clatter, Tamsyn braced both hands on the sink and stared hard at herself in the mirror.

"How badly do you want that money?" she asked her reflection, and after a beat, she nodded. "Right, really badly. Okay, Bligh, big-girl panties and all that. Besides, you'll have Bowen with you."

God, it was annoying how warm that thought immediately made her. Just like it was annoying how, after the panic had lifted, she'd been glad to see him.

No, not glad. *Happy.* It had made her happy to see him there in the hallway in this weird-ass house, handsome and familiar and . . . solid.

Safe.

Like how she felt when she came back from a job and saw the soft glow of the lamp through the windows of her Airstream. Happy, relieved, at peace . . .

And the thing was, she was pretty sure he'd been happy to see her, too. Irritated, for sure, and definitely not thrilled about what she was doing here, but Tamsyn had still seen it, the softness in his gaze as they'd sat there across the table from each other.

But none of that mattered because: A) Tamsyn didn't mix business with pleasure, and B) even if she *did* decide to Risk It All where Bowen was concerned, she wasn't sure he'd be able to do the same. Bowen was brilliant and hot and—in his gruff way— kind, but he was also closed up, walled off, keeping secrets she didn't fully understand.

Once a girl hit thirty, any idea of *I can fix him* had to go out the window, and that rule was even more sacred to Tamsyn than not hooking up with a coworker.

She finished up her makeup before moving into the bed- room, the space a good deal chillier than the balmy warmth of the bathroom, her bare feet sinking into deep gold carpet. Sir Madoc had called this the Yellow Room, and he had not been lying. The massive canopy bed that dominated the room was covered in yellow-and-cream-striped fabric, and the wall- paper was a dizzying riot of yellow roses and daisies. Even the two wingback chairs situated in front of the fireplace were the burnished color of old coins, and if she hadn't been so nervous about the job—and freaked out about how haunted this place apparently was—Tamsyn would've been thrilled to have such a lush and luxurious room for a whole long weekend.

As it was, she got dressed in a hurry, wanting to spend as little time alone in the room as possible.

She'd dipped into her savings putting together a wardrobe for this job, telling herself it would be worth it once she was a million bucks richer, and as she appraised her reflection in the full-length mirror in one corner, Tamsyn had to admit the indulgence had been worth it. For tonight's dinner, she was wearing a black velvet jumpsuit, the sleeves long and loose, the neckline plunging. She'd paired it with ropes and ropes of pearls in all different lengths and another pair of sky-high stilettos, plus black-rimmed cat-eye glasses.

"It's a look," Tamsyn said as she turned one way and then the other, the subtle diamanté buckle at her waist catching the lamplight.

Smoothing her hands over her hips, she gave herself one final nod of approval, and was just turning away from the mirror when a movement over her right shoulder froze her in her tracks.

At first, she thought it was just a trick of the light or some flaw in the mirror, but no, there was definitely . . . *something*. Almost like a haze hovering just there near the footboard of the bed, curling like smoke several feet off the ground.

Tamsyn's reflection was pale and wide-eyed, and she suddenly realized the temperature had dropped in the room, her breath coming out in faint white clouds.

You're okay, she wanted to say to herself, but her mouth was too dry, her heart pounding so hard she was surprised it wasn't rattling her pearls.

The haze was still churning in the mirror, not getting bigger, but not dissipating, either, and Tamsyn made herself turn around, stumbling a little as her heel caught in the plush carpet.

But when she looked at the bed, at the very spot where she'd seen whatever it was floating around, there was nothing there.

And when she turned back to the mirror, all she saw was herself—or Anna Ripley—staring back at her.

CHRIST, BUT WITCHES are annoying.

Not the most charitable thought, Bowen could acknowledge, and probably fairly daft given that he himself was a witch, but after just fifteen minutes of making small talk in Tywyll House's library, he suddenly understood those fuckers with their pitchforks and their burning stakes a little bit better now.

"And so *your* grandfather Harri was actually the third cousin of *my* grandfather Corwin. Now, Corwin was known to be one of the more powerful witches of his generation, as I'm sure you know," the man standing next to Bowen went on, his warm, whisky-scented breath wafting over Bowen, who hid his grimace with a sip of his own drink. "And I don't believe Harri ever did all that much, which is why we were all so surprised when your father turned out to be so talented in magics. But your grandmother Elspeth, now *she . . .*"

The man continued to rattle on about the Penhallow family lineage, entranced enough with his monologue that he didn't seem to notice that Bowen wasn't paying attention. But to be fair, if this man—what was his name again? Something poncey. Peregrine, maybe?—knew as much as he claimed to about the Penhallows, then he would've known that Bowen knew every bit of his family history, had had it drilled into him by Simon

Penhallow until Bowen could recite every ancestor since the ninth bloody century.

Still, he had to admit that Declan had been right—Bowen's last name was all the currency he needed in this place, granting automatic acceptance, no questions asked, even though there weren't that many guests actually staying at the house for the entire weekend. Most, Sir Madoc had told him, would be arriving just for the event itself on Sunday, but about twenty or so people were currently milling around the library.

Tamsyn wasn't one of them, and Bowen's eyes darted toward the library door for what felt like the thousandth time that evening.

He'd thought about stopping by her room to escort her downstairs, but that had seemed . . . presumptuous. And he was already uncomfortable enough, wearing a fucking *tuxedo*. Could've been worse, of course. The Merediths could've been sticklers for tradition like Bowen's father and made everyone wear formal robes. The penguin suit was not his favorite, but it was a damn sight better than those stuffy gowns with their flowing sleeves that always seemed to end up in the soup or dragged through sauce on a plate.

Besides, Tamsyn mocked him enough as it was. If she knew about the robes? St. Bugi's balls, he'd never live it down.

"And that is why *my* aunt Griselda stopped speaking to *your* aunt Bronwyn!" The man finished up with a hearty laugh, slapping Bowen on the shoulder so hard that the ice rattled in Bowen's now-empty glass.

Bowen gave him a tight smile and then lifted his glass, nodding toward the liquor cart set up near the fireplace. "Need a refill," he said, and the man laughed again, holding up both hands.

"Say no more, say no more, I think I may—oh, now hang on a tick." The man looked past Bowen, his jovial expression shifting into something sly. "Who on earth is *that* glorious creature?"

Bowen knew it would be Tamsyn before he even glanced over his shoulder, but that didn't lessen the impact of seeing her there in the doorway in something black and slinky, pearls glowing against her tanned skin, and a neckline so low that his hands almost ached to slide inside of it. She'd be warm and soft, and her lips would part when his knuckles brushed—

"Finally, a fuckable woman who *isn't* the bride," the man said, his smile turning predatory, and Bowen was amazed the glass in his hand didn't shatter into a thousand pieces.

He didn't realize he'd made a noise until the man—not Peregrine, Bowen suddenly remembered, *Perseus,* fucking wanker—blanched slightly, his eyes blinking rapidly. "What?" he asked, then gave a nervous chuckle and took another sip of his whisky. "You already called dibs on her or something?"

"Or something," Bowen growled, before crossing the room to Tamsyn.

She smiled when she first saw him, but the closer he got, the more her smile faded so that by the time he was standing in front of her, she was looking at him with the same wary mix of alarm and confusion Bowen felt the first time she tried to explain what a Real Housewife was to him.

"There you are," he said, and before he could let himself over-think it, he slid an arm around her waist, pulling her in close. She was as warm and soft as he'd imagined, smelled just as fucking delicious as she had that first night they'd met, and Bowen couldn't resist letting his lips graze her skin just the littlest bit as he leaned down to murmur, "Sorry, but—"

"That red-faced guy currently sweating alcohol and staring daggers at us said something pervy about me, and you're letting him think I'm yours because even though it's the twenty-first century, men are still Like That?" she replied sweetly, her expression loving as she reached up to pat his cheek, and Bowen grunted in assent.

She gave a low, throaty chuckle that went straight to his cock, and Bowen's hand reflexively tightened on her hip.

To distract himself, he asked, "What took you so long? Was beginning to think you might skip cocktail hour altogether."

Her expression clouded over, a wrinkle appearing between her brows as she shook her head. "Something weird—" she started to say, but before she could finish, there was a crash from just outside the library door, a sound so loud that Bowen's brain struggled to even make sense of it.

And then someone started to scream.

CHAPTER 7

I t was probably a sign of just how messed up things already were at Tywyll House that Tamsyn's first thought upon hearing the scream was *Oh, yay, that sounds like a person!*

"And that's a good thing?" Bowen asked, frowning down at her as some of the crowd began to move toward the big double doors.

Okay, so apparently that hadn't been so much a "first thought" as a "first thing out of her mouth," but those things were frequently the same, so she shouldn't be surprised.

"It's better than the ghost," she murmured in reply as they let themselves be carried along with everyone else out into the hallway, Tamsyn practically glued against Bowen's side. Her mind was still trying to process the sight of Bowen in a tuxedo, his unruly hair actually tamed into soft waves, his trimmed beard enhancing the line of his jaw and the firmness of his lips, so maybe it was a good thing they had this little screamy distraction, because otherwise, she might have been tempted to do something insane like lick his face or propose.

Tamsyn wondered if he was fighting similar urges where she was concerned, because she had definitely seen the way his fingers had flexed around his empty glass when he'd spotted her in the doorway, and she wasn't sure if he'd needed to hold her quite so tightly when he'd appeared at her side, wasn't sure that brush of lips against her temple had been strictly necessary.

Not that she'd complained.

Even now, as they spilled out into the huge foyer with the other guests, it felt natural to slip her arm through his, and she liked the way his elbow moved closer to his side, pulling her to him so that she had to rest her other hand on his biceps to steady herself, and . . .

Okay, whoa. Bowen had clearly been hiding a lot under those sweaters he wore, and Tamsyn felt like she probably deserved a medal—or, you know, a Fuck-Off Huge Magical Brooch—as a reward for resisting the temptation to squeeze that firm curve of muscle underneath her fingertips.

Bowen kept her close as he maneuvered them around a trio of women in gorgeous black evening gowns, and something crunched underneath Tamsyn's high heel.

Glancing down at the stone floor, she saw a chunk of glass there, and then another. And another. The whole floor seemed to be shimmering and crunching, and Tamsyn suddenly realized that the hallway was a lot darker than it had been just moments before.

"Chandelier," Bowen said, and yes, now that they'd moved closer to the front of the crowd, Tamsyn could see that it was indeed the massive crystal chandelier lying broken and crooked on the slate. That must have been the source of the crash.

As for the screaming . . .

It had stopped, but Tamsyn had a feeling it must've come from the ethereal-looking blonde in the white dress and tartan shawl currently shuddering just beside the staircase. One hand was clamped over her mouth, her gaze riveted on the broken chandelier, and Sir Madoc awkwardly patted her shoulder, while a tall black-haired man in a gorgeously tailored tux rested a hand on her lower back, his head low as he murmured in her ear.

Everyone was whispering now, the low voices surprisingly loud in the cavernous room, the soft sounds punctuated by the occasional whimper from the blonde, who kept looking back to the ruined chandelier.

They were close enough now that Tamsyn could make out Sir Madoc saying, "Darling, dearest girl, don't talk such nonsense. It's an old house, and you know as well as I do that not everything works as it should. Why, just the other day—actually, it was in October, now that I think about it, not *quite* the other day, but in any case, I was out in the—"

"This wasn't the house, Da!" the blonde said, her voice ringing out.

Ah, so this was the bride, then, Carys Meredith. Which must make the man beside her David Thorsby, the groom. They were a good-looking pair, her hair so fair it was almost white, him all dark and brooding, but Tamsyn noticed the way that Carys seemed to be almost leaning away from his touch and how David's jaw had clenched when she'd raised her voice.

"We've all been pretending this isn't happening, but it is," Carys continued, looking back and forth between her father and her fiancé. "It's him. He—he's here, and he's unhappy. He's *furious*. Otherwise why would he be doing all this?"

Next to her, Tamsyn felt Bowen tense up, and she looked over at him, confusion pulling her brows tight together. "What—" she started, but Carys went on, flinging out both arms, the shawl sliding from her shoulders.

"How much clearer can it be?" she asked, her voice almost pleading. "It's Declan. He's haunting me because he doesn't want me to get married."

Bowen took a deep breath, but Tamsyn wasn't looking at him anymore. She wasn't looking at the chandelier or scanning the room for any other possible Ghost Projectiles.

No, she was staring at the jewels pinned to the modest neckline of Carys's evening gown.

The hallway may have been a lot darker now that the chandelier was down, but even in the dim glow from the sconces and the distant fireplace, the rubies, emeralds, and diamonds at Carys's décolletage glittered.

Y Seren in the flesh, so to speak, but not locked in some jewelry box, not hidden away in a distant room where centuries of Meredith treasure gathered dust. Right here. In front of her.

On the bride.

Tamsyn jumped as Bowen's hand covered the one she still had settled just in the crook of his elbow. He squeezed, but she wasn't sure if that was a warning or just an acknowledgment that, yup, here was the thing she'd been planning to steal. Not some trinket the family never thought about, but clearly a treasured family heirloom, possibly something Carys was planning on wearing to the wedding itself.

Definitely the kind of thing someone was going to notice missing pretty damn quickly.

Tamsyn caught herself pulling her lower lip between her teeth, but no, that was the kind of thing Tamsyn Bligh did, *not* Anna Ripley, so she schooled her face into an expression she'd seen plenty of rich people wear over the years, one where you somehow looked both bored and hungry at the same time.

"Sweetheart, don't," David said, even as Sir Madoc pulled that handkerchief out of his pocket again and began mopping his brow despite the chill in the air.

"What other explanation is there?" Carys asked, ignoring the crowd. "We haven't had a ghost here in over fifty years. Now, right before I get married, we've g-got cold spots and . . . and paintings flying off of walls, and bloody chandeliers crashing down out of nowhere?" She shook her head, emeralds in her ears winking. "It's Declan, Da, I know it is."

"Your first fiancé? Well, even if it is, he's dead, my darling," David replied, his jaw a little tight even as he tried to smile down at Carys.

Tamsyn didn't like it, that little tic in the muscle of his jaw, the way his fingers were curling around Carys's arm, and Bowen must not have, either, because the hand still holding Tamsyn's clenched a little harder, and when she looked over at him, there was practically a storm cloud gathering over his head.

"Not loving David's energy," Tamsyn whispered to him, and Bowen made a sound nearly like a growl in reply before muttering something in Welsh.

Tamsyn didn't speak the language, but she *did* speak Bowen, and there was no doubt that whatever he had just called David was the kind of insult men used to fight duels over.

Lips still trembling, Carys wrapped her shawl back around herself, covering up Y Seren, and Sir Madoc gave her another one of those awkward pats before turning to the crowd and saying, "Apologies all, apologies, but a bit of drama always livens up a wedding, yes? Why don't we head on in to supper now, I'm sure we could all use some good food and some even better wine, yes, yes, just the thing, fix us all right up, come along, Carys, *fy ngeneth i.*"

"What did he just call her?" Tamsyn asked Bowen as the group began picking its way around the shattered glass on the floor and heading toward the formal dining room.

"My girl," Bowen replied, and Tamsyn had to work very hard to remind herself that he was just translating something an old man had said to his daughter, so there was exactly *zero* reason for her to be so turned on by those two words in Bowen's deep voice and lilting accent.

Zero. None.

And yet.

Ohhhh, and yet.

The group moved down another dimly lit hallway to a set of double doors opened to reveal a massive dining room. Huge portraits of glowering aristocrats covered the walls, and a row of candelabras marched down a long table, the candlelight playing on the pewter and china place settings. White and red flowers in tall vases filled the room with a smell that reminded Tamsyn unpleasantly of funerals, and as they all began to take their seats, she was glad to see there were no place cards beside the plates. That meant she wouldn't be stuck making small talk with Baron Already Way Too Drunk or Lord Looks Like He Has Wandering Hands. She could sit next to Bowen instead, and sitting next to him at a candlelit table while a winter storm raged outside made the thought of a ghostly spirit drifting around somewhere upstairs . . . Okay, look, even a hot man and a cozy setting straight out of a good Gothic novel couldn't make her feel better about the ghost, but it didn't *hurt*.

As a footman in slightly threadbare livery began pouring rich red wine into their glasses, Tamsyn leaned in closer to Bowen and whispered, "So do you think Carys is right? Is the ghost this dead fiancé of hers?"

She'd expected Bowen to do his normal grunting thing, but when she looked up at him, a muscle was flexing in his jaw and his fingers were curled tightly around the stem of his glass. "No," he said, his voice so tight she thought that bow tie of his might be strangling him.

Surprised, Tamsyn sat back, blinking. "How can you be so sure about that?" she asked, but before he could respond, the woman to her right said, "You're supposed to be talking to me, dear."

Tamsyn turned from Bowen to see a wizened old lady absolutely creaking under the weight of all the jewels she was wearing and frowning at her through a tiny pair of spectacles held just in front of her eyes.

"Oh," Tamsyn replied, startled. "Do we . . . do we know each other?"

"Every other guest is meant to speak to the person to their right first. After enough time has passed, our host will turn the table, and *then* you may speak to the man at your left."

The woman peered harder through her glasses, holding them closer to her face as she studied Bowen, who was currently glaring at a tureen of soup.

"I must say, though, I don't blame you for wanting to talk to a specimen like that over an old bat like me."

The woman gave a sharp laugh, causing several of the other diners to look over.

"Oh, eat your soup," the woman said with a wave of a jeweled hand. When everyone turned back to their meals, the woman once again leaned in close to Tamsyn and whispered, "They're all terrified of me. That's the one benefit to being old. Well, old and rich enough to buy and sell them all a thousand times over."

She gave another one of those cackles, and from his place at the head of the table, Sir Madoc called out, "Mother, you know how sound carries in this room."

"I do!" she cheerfully called back. "That's how I once caught your father shagging one of the maids in here back in . . . oh, '63 was it? Undoubtedly why his heart went out just a few years later. Well, that and my poisons."

She laughed again, and Sir Madoc went a red that was nearly purple, while Carys gave a faint "Granny, please."

The old woman only shrugged and then said to Tamsyn, "The part about the poisons was in jest, my dear, don't be alarmed."

Tamsyn *had* been giving her wineglass a closer look, but now she just smiled and said, "Good to know, Lady . . . I'm sorry, I'm not sure how to address you."

"Oh, it's a beastly name," the woman said, waving one hand as she took up her soupspoon with the other. "I was born Lady Angharad Carys Catrin Carew, then when I married Madoc's useless father, I became Lady Meredith, but now that I myself am a useless widow, I am the Dowager Lady Meredith, or sometimes Angharad, Lady Meredith. It's all a bit of a mouthful, really, so I usually ask people to call me Annie." She turned to Tamsyn with a bright smile. "You're welcome to. For one, you're American, so best to keep this all simple, and for another, it will greatly upset my son to hear guests calling me 'Annie' all weekend, and that brings its own degree of joy, as I'm sure you can imagine."

Well, there was no doubt where Sir Madoc got the talking gene from, but Tamsyn found she liked Annie here a lot more.

Plus—and to be fair, this did make Tamsyn feel like *kind* of an asshole—she might have valuable information about Y Seren.

"It's a lovely place, Tywyll House," Tamsyn said before taking her first sip of soup. It was cool and tasted like it had possibly been prepared next to a cucumber by a chef who had once heard of salt, but she made herself swallow anyway.

"Oh, it's ghastly," Annie said, still cheerful. "Whole west wing is crumbling to dust, there are bats in the turret, and just last week, our gardener dug up two skeletons in my rosebushes. I'd always said there was something wrong with that patch of earth, but no one bothered to listen."

The flavorless soup somehow went even more bland in Tamsyn's mouth before she managed to ask, "And do you think . . . do you think that might be why there's . . . well, the chandelier and the noises and all that?"

"The ghost?" Annie asked, then shook her head, teardrop diamonds in her ears swinging like pendulums. "Oh, no, I think our Carys has the right of that. It's that dead fiancé of hers, Declan McKenzie. Tywyll has had all kinds of ghosts over the years. I cannot *tell* you how many times I had to tell our Headless Lady to either put her ridiculous head back onto her ridiculous body or accept that never the twain shall meet again, because roaming around while holding it out in front of her like a plum pudding was a bit silly. That seemed to do the trick, and we didn't see her again. Now the Blue Boy, he was a little nicer, but we all could've done without the nasty vomiting business. How can one even vomit when one is noncorporeal?"

She shook her head, while Tamsyn accepted that she was never going to eat another bite of this soup. Pushing her bowl away, she asked Annie, "But this one seems different?"

"Hmm," Annie agreed. "Very different. All this moaning and knocking things over, very unlike the others. Ruder, if you ask me. And that fiancé of hers was Scottish, so."

She gave Tamsyn a significant look, but since Tamsyn had no idea what being Scottish had to do with any of this, she just smiled and nodded before asking, "And he died . . . recently?"

"A while back. Some sort of accident at school. All very mysterious, all very hush-hush. But she moved on, found David, who is very nice if slightly . . . Well, he's very nice. Human, unfortunately, but then so are you, aren't you, my dear?" When Tamsyn didn't reply right away, Annie reached over and patted her hand. "Oh, don't be alarmed, this group is a mix of witches and humans, although I think we outnumber you quite a bit. Who invited you?"

Tamsyn had had her whole plan of calling herself a friend of Carys's mother, Amelia, but thanks to Bowen's little display in the library, she now had an even better and more plausible excuse. "I'm here as Bowen Penhallow's guest," she said, turning slightly so that she could rest her hand on Bowen's arm.

He turned to her, flashing her a tight smile before leaning across her to say, "Nice to see you again, Lady Meredith."

"Bowen Penhallow. Didn't I catch you trying to use magic to steal apples from our orchard here at Tywyll one summer?"

This time, Bowen's smile was genuine, and Tamsyn was struck yet again by just how much younger that expression made him look, how warm his brown eyes looked in the candlelight. "That was actually my brother Rhys. He's still terrified of you."

Annie gave a pleased huff. "Excellent. Too handsome for his own good, that one. Although that appears to run in the family. If you'd shave that pelt from your face, I believe you'd give him a run for his money."

To Tamsyn's surprise—and utter delight—she could see Bowen going a little pink at those words.

Bowen Penhallow blushing. Wonders truly never ceased.

A clinking sound caught their attention, and Tamsyn glanced back up at the head of the table where Sir Madoc stood, crystal glass and butter knife in hand. His tufts of white hair seemed even . . . tuftier, and his face was still red, bald head shining with sweat. Still, he smiled down the table at everyone gathered there and boomed out, "Get thee a wife! So said the Bard himself, and who should we mere mortals be to quibble, eh?"

"Is the Bard a guy down at the local pub?" Tamsyn asked Bowen in a low whisper, and was gratified to see the way his lips quirked up just the littlest bit.

"Don't play the Dumb American, Tamsyn, doesn't suit you."

"Because I'm such a smart-ass?"

He looked back over his shoulder at her, their eyes holding just long enough for everything in Tamsyn's body to slow down and heat up all at once. "Because you're brilliant. Too clever for your own good."

Bowen's eyes flicked down, his gaze on her mouth, and Tamsyn felt that look like a touch.

Like a kiss.

"Too clever for my own good, too," he muttered, and then he

turned away again, leaving Tamsyn damn near breathless as Sir
Madoc continued speechifying about the marriage of true minds,
and love's endless bounty, and all kinds of words that were beautiful and important and legendary, and all Tamsyn could think
about was how there weren't any words to capture how she felt
when Bowen Penhallow called her *brilliant*.

"And so a toast!" Sir Madoc called out, raising his glass higher
before noticing that it was empty. With a muttered curse, he
gestured at a footman with his free hand, and the man—boy,
really—rushed forward with a bottle of champagne, topping
him off.

"A toast!" Sir Madoc repeated, and the rest of them stood as
well, everyone except Carys and David. "To my future son-in-law,
David, a gentleman of . . . of . . . great . . . temperament. And . . .
and manly attributes."

Clearing his throat, Sir Madoc turned to his other side. "And
to my beautiful daughter, Carys," he said, and now his expression
softened. For whatever Sir Madoc's faults, it was clear he loved
his daughter, and that made Tamsyn like him just the littlest bit
more. "The light of this family's life. Our most precious jewel."

Maybe everyone else missed the way Carys's fingers strayed to
Y Seren, still pinned to her dress, but Tamsyn didn't. Carys was
pale, and her plates had all been taken away untouched. In the
candlelight, the violet shadows under her eyes were even more
apparent, and when she raised her own glass, her hand was
trembling.

"To Papa," she said, and then she turned slightly, her glass now lifted toward David, who was smiling, but Tamsyn could see that his knuckles were white where they clutched the stem of his glass.

"And to David, the man I'll marry in just two short days," she added.

Not "To David, the man I love," Tamsyn thought. That wasn't a toast, that was just stating a fact. She might as well lift a glass herself and say, *To Bowen! A man with a lot of facial hair that I've had a not unconcerning amount of dirty dreams about.*

Still, Tamsyn lifted her glass like everyone else with a murmured "To David."

Maybe it was because she was still looking at Y Seren, or maybe it was because Tamsyn had just discovered a real soft spot for this girl who was so beautiful, so rich, and so obviously miserable that her eyes stayed on Carys, but Tamsyn was the first one to notice the way the bride's lower lip started trembling, how the champagne sloshed over the side of the glass as she raised it even higher and said, "And to Declan."

A low murmur started at the far end of the table, and David set his own glass down hard enough to make Tamsyn wince.

"If the world were a just place, he would be here tonight," Carys went on in a high but unwavering voice. "And he would be standing across from me at the altar in two days," she added, and now there weren't just murmurs but straight-up gasps.

"Carys!" Sir Madoc barked, but his daughter was already out of her seat, fast enough that the chair itself clattered to the parquet floor, and with a choked sob, Carys rushed from the room.

CHAPTER 8

Bowen knew multiple swear words in multiple languages, but he wasn't sure if any of them were strong enough to express how it felt watching the woman Declan had loved rush out of her bridal dinner in a flood of tears.

He could hear Sir Madoc calling after her, could see David rising to his feet as though he might run after her, and—worst of all—could feel Tamsyn's questioning eyes on him, but none of that mattered, because right now, Bowen was back in that attic at the very top of Penhaven College's library, and Declan was standing in front of him, alive, real, vivid. There was a chalk circle drawn on the floor in front of them and a crumpled piece of parchment in the center. Declan's eyes were so bright, unnaturally so, and Bowen had known then that he had to call a stop to this, that whatever magical knowledge could be gleaned from this was too much, too strong, but Declan was already saying the words—words Bowen had taught him—and there was a flash of light, and—

Tamsyn got up suddenly, her napkin landing in a heap near

her plate, and before Bowen had time to think, she was out the door and after Carys.

Luckily, he did have the perfect curse for this, one Tamsyn herself had said multiple times.

Fuck a duck.

Throwing back the last of his wine, Bowen rose from his seat, tossing his own napkin down, and Lady Meredith beamed at him from behind her pince-nez. "Ooh, very nice, do enjoy a bit of drama before dessert! Your lady friend goes in search of darling Carys, you go in search of your lady friend, and hopefully *someone* ends up rogered in the library. Oh, it's like the Yule Ball of '75 all over again!"

Bowen didn't know what that meant, and given that his father had referenced the Yule Ball of '75 multiple times, usually while a bit squiffy at the holidays, Bowen emphatically did *not* want to understand the reference.

Instead, he stalked off toward the double doors and out into the foyer, while behind him, he could hear Sir Madoc saying to David, "It's from her *mother,* you see, this penchant for theatrics. I met Amelia on a cruise down the Nile in the late eighties, and she was a performer, a *glorious* performer, but a performer nonetheless, so it's to be expected . . ."

The dining room had been dim, but the hallway was positively gloomy, all shadows and flickering sconces, and for a moment, Bowen froze, trying to figure out where they might have gotten off to.

Then he heard the distinctive click of those ridiculous shoes

Tamsyn was wearing somewhere off to his left, and he followed the sound down an increasingly dark hallway until he reached a set of French doors that led out onto the terrace. One door stood ajar, a cold wind blowing sleet onto the parquet.

Tamsyn was wearing a fucking velvet jumpsuit cut down to her navel, she didn't have a coat, there was no way she would've stepped outside into—

"Carys!"

Bowen heard her distinctive husky American voice, and something within him clenched even as he forced himself out onto the veranda despite his bloody impractical clothes and his even stupider shoes.

"Tamsyn!" he shouted, lifting a hand against the freezing rain that was rapidly becoming snow.

He saw her then in the light from the windows, standing on the brown lawn with her arms folded tight around her as she stared out at the tall, dark hedges in front of her. The blond wig she was wearing was definitely worse for wear and listing to one side as she threw one arm out in the direction of the garden maze. "She went in there!" she called back, and muttering every curse word he knew—yes, in all the languages—Bowen jogged down the few stone steps to where Tamsyn stood, shucking off his tuxedo jacket as he went.

The freezing rain bit into his shirt as he lowered his jacket around Tamsyn's shoulders, and she used both hands to pull it tighter around her. Her wig was sodden now, and without thinking, Bowen pushed it from her head, letting it land with a wet splat on the lawn.

"Which way did she go?" he asked over the wind, and Tamsyn lifted an arm toward the center of the hedges.

"She turned left once she hit the statue," she replied, and sure enough, there was a marble figure rising into the night, a woman with flowing hair and raised arms, a crown of crescent moons rising white against the black sky.

Hecate, goddess of witchcraft.

"It's so cold, and that dress was so thin," Tamsyn said. "She didn't even grab her shawl."

Bowen had lived over thirty years on this planet. Had wielded powers few had ever dared touched. Had dared things few had ever dreamed.

But he had never been in love. Never once until here, in this moment, standing in a freezing garden looking at a woman— a human—with wet hair streaming down her back, her skin pale and pebbled with gooseflesh. Someone who had come here to steal a jewel worth a life-changing amount of money, but who, when the woman wearing that jewel had vanished into a cold, harsh night, could only worry that that woman wasn't wearing a coat.

Christ, he loved her. Desperately, irrevocably.

Completely and totally.

He was still standing there, accepting that knowledge, when the love of his life slapped his chest with one wet hand and yelled, "Fucking *do something*, you dumbass!"

So he did.

"Carys!" he called, moving into the garden maze, shrubs leaving nearly frozen droplets on his sleeve. Behind him, he could hear Tamsyn also calling the bride's name, and the wind seemed to pick up, distorting the sounds, making every footfall louder than it was.

The rain was harder now, colder, and Bowen wiped it from his eyes as he squinted into the darkness, taking one turn, then another, Tamsyn right behind him.

Finally, he rounded a massive hedge and found himself in a clearing. There was another statue here, a slim marble figure that looked more modern than the ancient Greek goddess of witchcraft. From all the jewelry carved on the sculpture, he figured it might be Lady Angharad Meredith back in her debutante days, but he was more interested in the person kneeling in front of it.

Carys's white dress was sodden, and Bowen could see the pink of her scalp through her soaked hair. She was crying, and in her hands, he could make out the dim glitter of Y Seren.

She was muttering to herself in Welsh, but the rain and wind drowned out the words. That didn't mean Bowen couldn't feel them, though. Whatever she was saying, it wasn't gibberish or grief.

It was a prayer.

No, worse.

It was a spell.

"Carys!" he shouted, and she looked over at him, her face contorted with agony.

"You knew him!" she cried out, just as Tamsyn appeared at Bowen's side, out of breath and streaked with mud from the shins down. "You knew Declan. You were his friend, he loved you, and I . . ." Breaking off, she stared at the brooch in her hand. "I don't know how to do this without him."

"You do, though," Tamsyn said, stepping forward. Her heels sank into the mud, and she flailed one hand out. Bowen caught her easily, steadying her and moving forward as she did. "Carys, I didn't know Declan, and I'm sorry. It seems like you really loved him. But even if he's not here, you don't have to marry David. No one can make you! Hell, Bowen and I will drive you out of here right now. Right this second if that's what you want. Isn't that right, Bowen?"

She looked over at him, and Bowen could only nod, rainwater spilling down his beard and into the collar of his shirt.

"That's right, Carys!" he yelled. "We can leave right now if you want to. Declan wouldn't have wanted you to grieve like this. Or to marry someone if you didn't want to."

Carys stayed on her knees, her body curling further inward. "I can fix this!" she shouted over the storm. "I can undo it all!"

Confused, Bowen made a step forward, only to be brought up short by Tamsyn's hand on his arm.

"Look," she said, and even though she was barely whispering, he could hear her over the rain.

Carys was still kneeling, Y Seren clutched in both her hands, but as they watched, it began to glow.

The air around them felt electric, like anything he touched

right now would shock him, but Bowen still reached for Tamsyn's hand.

She took it, and sure enough, an electric pulse zinged through him, but he only held her tighter as the very ground started to shake.

"Take it back!" Carys cried, raising her head to the sky. She was still pale and fragile, but Bowen could feel the magic pulsing through her, and suddenly remembered just why it was that the Meredith family had been so feared for centuries.

"All of it!" Carys continued, holding the brooch to the turbulent skies. "Whatever can be undone, so be it!"

There was a crack of lightning, and next to him, Tamsyn yelped.

And then Bowen was . . . slipping.

Sliding.

Falling, even though Tamsyn's hand was still locked tight in his.

Falling, falling, falling . . .

CHAPTER 9

The first thing Tamsyn was aware of was the pain.

No, "pain" wasn't quite the right word. *Weight.* That was it. Like an elephant had just taken up residence not only on her chest, but her skull, her legs, even her hair. Her eyelids felt swollen, her heart beating sluggishly in her chest, and as she lay there on the damp earth, a memory popped into her head.

It wasn't one she chose to revisit often—honestly, if it was up to her, all memories of spring break should vanish from your brain once you hit about twenty-five—but that's what she felt like now. Like that night outside whatever club that had been in Panama City, Florida, one of her sorority sisters—Mamie, no, Amy; she always got them mixed up—placing a hand on her shoulder and saying, *Girl, you need to go home.*

I do, Tamsyn thought as she looked up at a dark sky. *I am a Girl, and I need to go home.*

"Tamsyn?"

She turned her head to the side, and oh, right. It wasn't Mamie or Amy lying on the ground next to her this time. It was Bowen.

Sweet, handsome, weird Bowen, who looked every bit as bad as she felt in this moment, but still managed to be the hottest man she'd ever seen.

"I'm the what?" he asked, and dammit, apparently she didn't feel too bad to *not* say things out loud.

"Nothing," she told him now, wincing as she raised herself into a sitting position. She was still in the garden, but it had stopped raining all of a sudden, and when Tamsyn glanced up, she didn't see the statue that Carys had been kneeling under.

Actually . . .

Tamsyn looked around even though moving her head that much hurt.

Not only did she not see the statue, but she didn't see Carys, either.

Bowen seemed to be realizing the same thing as he stood up, dusting off the back of his tuxedo pants and frowning up at the empty, dark sky.

"Rain's stopped," he observed, and now Tamsyn frowned, patting the grass around her.

"And the ground is dry," she said.

Bowen grunted.

Tamsyn went to stand, but her knees were still a little wobbly. Luckily Bowen was right there, a firm hand under her elbow as she staggered in her high heels, her stomach sinking.

Something was . . . wrong.

Bad wrong.

Magically wrong.

Bowen felt it, too. She could tell by the Advanced Level Three Frown he was currently wearing, the one that made him look like an old-timey sea captain scanning the horizon for land.

It was possible she'd incorporated that look into a fantasy or three, but now was not the time for Captain Bowen and the Pirate Queen. Now she needed to figure out just what the hell had happened.

And where the hell was Carys?

Furthermore, where the hell was Y Seren?

There was no moon tonight, but Tamsyn still searched the lawn for the telltale sparkle of the brooch.

As she crouched near one hedge, there was a sudden flash of movement just to her right, and she shot up, moving toward it as fast as her ridiculous shoes would allow, but Bowen beat her to it.

He reached into the hedge with one arm and yanked.

Tamsyn wasn't sure exactly what she'd expected to see him holding, but it was not a very small child in a kilt, frantically kicking his little brogue-clad feet in the air.

"I wasn't spying! I heard a noise, and people aren't meant to be in the garden, they're supposed to be having sherry in the drawing room. That's what Mother said, everyone to the drawing room for sherry! So if you're in the garden, you're not where you're supposed to be, and that's *naughty*. You are both *terribly naughty!*" the child went on, his voice nearly a shriek, his white-blond hair practically glowing even as he screwed his little face up in an expression of pure fury.

Bowen blinked at the child still dangling from his grasp,

dodging as the little boy tried to land a ferocious kick in the general direction of Bowen's crotch.

Tamsyn stepped closer, narrowing her eyes as she studied the child with his wild platinum curls, his little purple face with its round cheeks and almost bulbous blue eyes, and thought, impossibly—

"Madoc!"

A woman's voice rang out, and Tamsyn heard more footsteps, the rustle of material, and saw several bobbing lights heading in their direction. The child took their momentary distraction to swing another kick at Bowen, and while this one might not have found its *exact* mark, it did glance off his hip, making Bowen mutter something in Welsh before setting the kid back down.

"I am not a Cath Palug," the boy said, hands on his hips. "I am the master of this house. Or I will be once my father dies, not that I want that to happen soon, but when it does, I'm going to open up the oubliette in the house, and then ruffians like you will be sorry."

He paused, wiped at his nose.

"I'm also going to get a dog," he announced, and then there was a bright light as the most elegant woman Tamsyn had ever seen suddenly appeared out of the hedges, massive flashlight in hand.

"Oh, Madoc, for heaven's sake, are you threatening people with flaying again?"

"No, just an oubliette," Tamsyn supplied, even as her mind felt like it was sliding through Jell-O. "And a dog."

The woman rolled her eyes, reaching up with her free hand to pat at her elaborate blond updo. Despite the cold, she was wearing an off-the-shoulder taffeta dress that appeared to be deep green, a tartan belt nipping in her trim waist.

And there, pinned to her dress right over her heart, was Y Seren.

Tamsyn felt dizzy all of a sudden, that slippery, sliding feeling even stronger, because this small child still glaring up at Bowen was named Madoc, and Tamsyn could see the traces of the old man she'd met just this afternoon in this little boy.

And looking at the woman in front of her, Tamsyn somehow knew this was Lady Angharad Meredith—Annie—but a much younger version.

She looked at the group of people standing around in the hedge maze, all looking at her and Bowen with open curiosity, and she didn't recognize a single face except . . .

"Rhys," Bowen murmured, and it was that—seeing Bowen go pale and stagger back a step—*that* was when Tamsyn started to truly and thoroughly freak out.

Because one of the men in the group *did* look an awful lot like Bowen's youngest brother. Same dark hair and blue eyes, same slim build and striking height, but he was wearing glasses, and there was none of Rhys Penhallow's sparkle about him. If anything, the guy looked like *he'd* just been sentenced to life in an oubliette.

The man must not have heard Bowen, because he didn't reply, but Lady Meredith stepped forward. "Might I ask what you're doing here in our garden?"

Her voice was pleasant, but her eyes were steely, and Tamsyn reminded herself that even a nonagenarian Lady Meredith had been pretty formidable. In her prime? She was the kind of woman men probably went to war over.

Hell, Tamsyn was pretty sure she'd invade France if this lady asked her to.

"I'm Bowen Penhallow," Bowen said, and Tamsyn turned to him, eyebrows practically levitating in the air somewhere above her face, because did he really think just saying his name was enough to get them out of whatever weird thing this—

"Ah!" Lady Meredith clapped her hands together, smiling. "A Penhallow. Then you're here for the wedding."

If Tamsyn had been disoriented before, now she felt straight-up insane, and she looked at Bowen with a sound that was, unfortunately, a cross between a "Huh?" and a "What?" and somehow came out "Whuh-ugh?"

"I've told everyone not to use magic for travel when it comes to Tywyll because it's always such a mess, so no wonder you ended up in the garden, but never mind, here now, and not a moment too soon, eh, Harri?"

She looked back at the man who looked so much like Bowen's brother, but he only scowled, pushing his dark hair off his forehead with an impatient gesture. "I don't think some random cousin I've never even met can fix this, Annie," he said, and then looked back to Bowen and Tamsyn. "Shame you've come all this way, because the wedding is off. Elspeth's changed her mind."

With that, he turned and stalked off, several of the other men of the party trailing him. Tamsyn heard a muttered "Steady on, lad, steady on," while another man clapped Harri on the back so hard Harri nearly tripped.

"It's jitters, mate, nothing more. She'll come around, you'll see."

Lady Meredith watched them walk off, then sighed. "Oh, it's a good thing you're here, indeed, Mr. Penhallow. I'm afraid poor Harri is going to need all the help he can get. We all are. Now come along, Madoc, and stop digging in the dirt, you're *ruining* your clothes."

"Mrs. Beasley says no one can dig to the center of the earth, but if you have enough time and patience, I think you can," Madoc said, even as he dusted off his hands and went to his mother. "Of course, once you get close to the core, you'll need a space suit, but I can get one of those."

He turned and squinted at Tamsyn. "You sounded American. Do you have a space suit?"

Tamsyn actually did—an old job at Cape Kennedy, nothing she *ever* wanted to repeat—but she was saved from answering as Madoc placed a muddy hand in his mother's and said, "Perhaps I should build my own space suit. If I'm going to be the first Welshman to dig to the center of the earth, I shouldn't rely on foreign help."

"Too right, my love, too right," Lady Meredith said kindly, then looked back over her shoulder at Tamsyn and Bowen. "You and your wife are welcome at Tywyll, Mr. Penhallow. Wedding or no. I'll have a room prepared for you both, and"—her eyes drifted over Tamsyn's jumpsuit—"perhaps you'd like to change into something . . . warmer, and . . . less modern."

The group made its way back to the house, a line of flashlights and murmuring voices, and endless chatter from Madoc.

Tamsyn stood there next to Bowen, freezing, probably in shock, and not entirely sure she wasn't having some kind of psychotic break.

And yet her next words to Bowen were still "Did she call me your wife?"

"She did," he confirmed, but that didn't seem to rattle him nearly as much as it did Tamsyn.

And Lady Meredith was putting them in the same room.

A room that probably had only one bed.

A bed they'd share.

Bitch, you have apparently gone back in time. Maybe prioritize better when it comes to which thing should be freaking you out the most.

Crossing the few steps that separated them, Tamsyn stood in front of Bowen. "So we, um . . . we time traveled?"

"Seems like," he replied, still staring in the direction the party had gone.

"And that's little baby Sir Madoc. Only he's not a sir yet, obviously. And Annie! Oh my god, Annie was—*is*—a *dish*, good for her. And it's not raining! And Y Seren is here! And . . . okay, yeah, that's all I've got for 'Things About This That Are Good, Actually.' You?"

"I've heard of these kinds of spells," Bowen mused, stroking his beard idly. "Temporal displacement. It's hard as hell, though. Literally in some cases. Really dark magic to alter the course of time, and obviously a real fucking mess if you do anything wrong."

"Right, so I asked for things that were *good* about this situation, and you're just giving me things that are *bad,* and honestly that's less than ideal, Bo."

"Well, here's another bad thing," he replied with a sigh, then jerked his chin in the direction of the house. "That fellow. The one who looks like Rhys."

"The one who's a Penhallow," Tamsyn said with a nod. "A distant cousin?"

"My grandda," Bowen said darkly, and Tamsyn sucked in a breath.

"And your grandmother is . . . ?" she asked, but she already knew before Bowen said it.

"Elspeth," he confirmed. "The woman who just called off their wedding."

CHAPTER 10

It was an unusual feeling, Bowen thought, as he followed the group back toward Tywyll House, to truly have absolutely no fucking clue what to do next.

Bowen had always prided himself on finding solutions, Declan being the one, horrible exception to that rule. But that was what Bowen *did*. Figure it out. Why that magical ingredient, why that spell, which phase of the moon affected what element and how.

When it came to this, though? Finding himself hurled back to . . .

He ran the numbers in his head. His father had been born in 1960, and that had been three years after Bowen's grandparents had gotten married. He remembered seeing the nearly illegible purple ink in the family records.

Henry Penhallow and Elspeth Carew, December 24, 1957.
1957.

"So I'm going to go out on a limb here and guess you're just as confused about all of this as I am," Tamsyn said in a low voice as she came up beside him, her arm once again slipping naturally into his.

It felt good—natural—to pull her in closer, and with the warm weight of her at his side, his thoughts cleared a bit.

"We're at Tywyll House in December of 1957," he murmured in reply, ducking a particularly stabby-looking branch. "Right around Yule, clearly, and this should be my grandparents' wedding weekend, but . . ."

"But they've called it off," Tamsyn confirmed with a nod, then looked up at him, her dark eyes wide. "But maybe they don't! Is there any . . . I don't know, family lore? 'Remember how Nana told Pepaw to fuck off the night before the wedding, but then he . . . I don't know, did something romantic, and the wedding was back on?' Any fun family gossip like that?"

Bowen shook his head. "Not that I know of. And I didn't call them Nana and Pepaw." Stopping, he looked down at her. "In fact, I've never even heard the word 'Pepaw.' Is that really a thing?"

"Mmm-hmm," Tamsyn confirmed. "I have two."

"Huh." Shaking his head, Bowen continued on as the maze widened back out. "Well, they were *Taid* Penhallow and *Nain* Penhallow when I was growing up. I never actually met them. They died before I was born."

"Oh." Now it was Tamsyn's turn to come up short, and she tugged on his arm. "I'm sorry," she said, and Bowen shrugged, uncomfortable.

"Sailing accident," he said. "Da was only twenty. I always wondered if that's why he was such a . . . Well, anyway."

He had bigger problems to worry about than why his father was such a prick, but Tamsyn was still watching him with all those questions all over her face, and he heaved a sigh.

"I don't speak to my da," he told her. "Haven't for over a year or so now. It's complicated, but not nearly as complicated as *this* absolute mire of shite we've found ourselves in, so I'd rather not talk about it now."

Tamsyn didn't reply for a moment, looking down at the dark lawn before walking again, her arm still in his. "Man, 1950s you sure does talk a lot more," she observed, and Bowen frowned.

"Nervous response," he replied. "Not every day a bloke finds himself hurled nearly seventy years back in time."

"But you've heard of this kind of thing, right?" Tamsyn asked.

Sighing, Bowen said, "Read about it, yeah, but it's rare, and when it happens—"

"Don't," Tamsyn said, holding one hand up. "You're just going to say, 'And when it happens, the only way to get back is to carve out your own eyeballs and light them on fire,' or something similarly horrifying, and I don't need that negativity right now, Bowen."

"Fair," he acknowledged as the house came into view. It looked much the same as it did in the present day—that was a fun thing about old castles, the consistency—but it was lit up, light pouring from every window to leave bright, warm rectangles on the lawn. There were colored lights strung up on garlands just inside, he could see, and out on the terrace, the party was still milling around as several liveried footmen moved through the crowd. Some were holding heavy coats and distributing them to the guests, while the others circulated with silver trays of steaming mugs. As Bowen and Tamsyn approached the steps, Lady Meredith turned to them, gesturing with one arm as a footman helped her slide her coat onto the other.

"Ignominious arrival aside, you've really appeared at the perfect time!" she called down to them. "We were all just about to go cut down the Yule log before we realized Madoc had scampered off again. Honestly, Emerald, we told you you'd have to keep a sharp eye on the lad—slippery as an eel when he thinks no one is looking."

A young woman already bundled up in a coat several sizes too big for her was standing just to the left of Lady Meredith, a flashlight in one hand, an open book in the other. She lowered both to glare at little Madoc, who was currently holding two mugs of whatever it was the footmen had been passing around, his round face wreathed in steam, making him look like a particularly cherubic demon.

"I'm fifteen now, Auntie Angharad," the girl announced, lifting her chin haughtily. "I shouldn't have to look after that little creature anymore."

"Don't call your cousin a creature, Emerald," Lady Meredith replied with no real heat, and Madoc bared his teeth at Emerald, who stuck her tongue out in return.

Still more than a little dazed, Bowen accepted a black wool

coat from one footman and one of the steaming earthen mugs from another. It was some kind of tea, spiced with cinnamon, ginger, and a bit of orange peel, and as Bowen took a sip, he also got the warm, medicinal hit of gin. It felt good going down, chasing back some of the chill, and Bowen took another sip, the taste familiar. Other Yules, long ago. Him and his brothers trudging through snow for a Yule log, a thermos of this secreted away in Wells's bag . . .

No. That wasn't right. It hadn't been Wells with the thermos; it had been Simon. But Da hadn't come out with them for that kind of thing, had he? He would've been too busy with his books and his magic, and while they'd always had a Yule log, Simon hadn't gone with them to cut it.

At least that's what Bowen thought, but now he wasn't sure, and something about the memory made his chest ache.

"You okay?" Tamsyn asked in a quiet voice, and Bowen looked down at her with the tiniest smirk. "Fair enough, dumb question," she acknowledged, even as she shrugged on her own coat. Like Emerald's, it was a little too big, the sleeves covering her hands, the hem dragging on the ground, and when she accepted her own mug of spiked tea, her wrists looked fragile against those heavy wool cuffs.

Right, he was swooning over her *wrists* because he'd realized, about two seconds before they'd been forced through the space-time continuum into some kind of nightmare, that he was actually in love with her, and that was . . . a problem.

But then the terrace door swung open, and Bowen remembered he had bigger problems right now.

"I don't see why I should have to go," a woman said, marching out onto the stone patio. She was already wearing a coat, a red-and-green tartan creation with a bright red patent leather belt and a hood trimmed in white fur. The hood was down, revealing the woman's auburn hair and pale skin, her upturned nose and wide-set eyes. She was beautiful, heart-stoppingly so, and was probably used to men staring at her, but Bowen was staring for an entirely different reason.

His grandmother.

He'd seen pictures of her, but not many, and none of them had captured how lovely she was or just how much power radiated off her as a witch. The very air around her seemed to crackle, and as Harri appeared just behind her, his expression miserable, Bowen had a sudden pang of sympathy for his grandfather.

Real bollocks, being in love.

"It's tradition, Elle," Harri was saying now. "And even if there's not going to be a wedding, there's still a bloody Yule, isn't there?"

"Do *not* swear at me, Henry Penhallow!" Elspeth replied, and Tamsyn once again came close to Bowen's side.

"Your grandparents are kind of hot," she whispered.

"Stop it."

"No, they are, though," Tamsyn insisted as Harri and Elspeth continued to bicker in a way that made Bowen think of Wells and Gwyn. "Look at them. They're fighting, but they're also . . ."

She made a gesture with her hands that Bowen didn't quite understand, pressing her fingers together and wiggling them.

"They're also . . . worm people?" Bowen guessed, and Tamsyn swatted at his arm.

"They're *vibing*," she corrected him. "They're into each other even though . . . Yeah, she just threw a drink at him, and *yikes,* that stuff was hot—hope that one had cooled down a little?"

Bowen looked back to his grandparents, where Harri was now furiously wiping at his dinner jacket, and Elspeth was pointing one long red fingernail at him as she said, "You never learn not to call my bluff, not *once,* and we've known each other since we were five."

"Yes, and *one* of us has matured past that point," Harri sniped back, and Lady Meredith clapped her hands.

"All right, all right, enough of that," she said. "Wedding or no wedding, it's a new moon, Yule approaches, and we're cutting the log tonight. It's Madoc's first time being allowed to join us, so I want nothing to spoil that. And, Emerald, put down that silly book. You'll trip again, and you don't want to spend yet another Yule limping about and being tragic, do you?"

"Being here is tragedy enough," Emerald muttered, but she shoved the book into the pocket of her coat anyway. In the lights from the house, she looked younger than fifteen, her dark blond hair held back from her face with a green velvet band, and Bowen studied her, thinking there was something familiar about her, but nothing he could place.

"Pair up," Lady Meredith announced. "Madoc, go with Cousin Emerald."

Both children groaned but dutifully joined hands as the other adults began to pair off, too. A tall, older man with a head full of white hair offered his arm to Lady Meredith, and Bowen assumed this was her husband, Sir Caradoc.

Elspeth flounced away from Harri and, as Bowen watched with dawning horror, began making her way straight for him.

"And who are you?" she asked, a smile curling her full lips before her eyes slid to Tamsyn, who was still clutching Bowen's arm, thank St. Bugi's balls.

"He's my husband," Tamsyn said, drawing herself up as tall as she could, and Bowen knew it was part of their cover, knew it was the easiest way to keep the two of them together in this place, but that didn't mean his idiot heart didn't start pounding away in his chest at hearing Tamsyn call him that.

Elspeth gave a brief pout, but then shrugged, flipping the hood of her coat up over her hair. "Oh, well. Never really fancied a man with a beard anyway."

Harri was glaring absolute daggers at them even as Elspeth moved on to find some unattached man in the group, and Bowen tried to give his grandfather what he hoped was a reassuring, *Hey, mate, no interest in your girl on account of my heart being very taken by this woman at my side, and also because your girl is my grandmother, hope you understand!* sort of look.

He was fairly certain absolutely none of that translated, but at least Harri threw that baleful look in another direction, and Bowen sighed with relief even as Tamsyn tugged at his sleeve.

"What was it Carys said before all this happened?"

Bowen thought back to those last mad moments in the maze: the rain, the brooch, the sudden knowledge that he was in love with Tamsyn. There had been a lot going on. Was it any wonder he was struggling to remember what exactly Carys had shouted?

"'Take it back,'" he said, remembering. "She definitely shouted that. And something . . . 'whatever can be undone, undo it.'"

That had been it. So why had that sent them back here? Why this night, this year?

And if they were back here, then where the bloody hell was Carys?

Chapter 11

*B*ack to the Future.
Doctor Who.
The Time Machine.
Somewhere in Time.

No, dammit, that one was sad, and the entire point of listing all the time travel movies and TV shows Tamsyn had seen where things went *right* and ended *happily* was to keep her from absolutely *losing it* as she found herself walking through a dark, freezing forest in the year 1957 with absolutely no idea how she'd gotten to that year or—and this was the real kicker—exactly how she was going to get *back* to 2024.

This was the thing about hanging out with witches.

Sure, it was fun, and sometimes it was very lucrative, and some of those witches were . . .

Tamsyn allowed herself a sneaky peek at Bowen as they trudged along. She could just make out his profile, the beam of their flashlight—or *torch,* as everyone else was calling it—

concentrated on the ground. But even just his silhouette was enough to have her sighing.

So yeah. Exciting job, made good money, occasionally got to spend time with the hottest dude alive.

Flip side was apparently the chance of getting stuck several decades before you were even supposed to be born.

The night was cold and clear, and while there was no moon, the stars sparkled through the trees, brighter than Tamsyn had ever seen them, and that made her feel a little better. Those were the same stars she'd be seeing if she were back in her own time right now, and she lifted her hand just enough to give them the tiniest wave.

She didn't think Bowen had seen her, but then he pulled her in a little tighter against his side, his voice gruffer than normal when he said, "We'll fix this, I promise."

Tamsyn wasn't sure she believed him, but she believed *he* believed that, and that was comforting in its way.

"So do you think it's your grandparents?" she asked in a low voice, and even though she couldn't see his expression when he glanced down at her, she knew he was doing the Confusion Frown (not the Advanced One, though this was the one he used when she said something was "sus" or "that slaps").

"Why we're here," she explained. "Like, maybe we were sent back in time to be sure your grandparents get married and you get to be born. That seems like the kind of thing time travel would be useful for."

Bowen grunted, and Tamsyn assumed that was all the answer

she was going to get until he said, "But it was Carys's wish. Carys's spell. That's what sent us back here. That and Y Seren."

Shit, that was right. It's not like Tamsyn and Bowen had been trying to send themselves into the past. That had been all Carys, and she was nowhere to be seen.

But Y Seren was here, stuck on Lady Meredith's dress.

Tamsyn opened her mouth, but Bowen reached over and squeezed her hand even as he shook his head. "I know," he muttered. "If it got us here, it can get us home. I thought that, too. But maybe let's wait until we're alone to talk about it."

Alone.

Right, because they would be alone tonight.

In the same bedroom.

In the same bed.

Tamsyn was glad it was dark, because she could feel her face going hot despite the numbing cold, and to distract herself from the absolute riot of very, very dirty thoughts going on in her brain right now, she nodded at the flashlight.

"Why aren't you all just using magic? I've seen you do that before, conjure up glowing orbs and stuff."

"Witches are an odd bunch," he said with a sigh. "Some of them prefer the old-fashioned way; some think any magic that 'small' is . . . I don't know, disrespectful to the forces that be or summat."

Tamsyn smiled in the darkness. She always liked when he said that, *summat,* like he was a medieval blacksmith or something.

Ooh, Medieval Blacksmith might be a good one to add to the Fantasy Roster, now that she thought about it.

What did we just *say about dirty thoughts, huh?* Tamsyn chided herself just as the forest began to clear out a bit and the group came to a halt.

"Here we are!" Lady Meredith called out, and gestured at a tall tree standing just in front of them, its trunk so thick Tamsyn had no idea how anyone was going to saw into it.

But then no one seemed to have a saw, she realized as she looked around, and then Lady Meredith stepped forward, laying one hand on the tree. Her fingers glowed, and when she pulled her hand back, there was a perfect print there, outlined in golden light, and one by one, the other witches started moving forward and pressing their hands to the tree.

Bowen heaved another sigh, and Tamsyn looked up at him, worried. "Okay, so I can't do that," she reminded him. She was whispering, but Lady Meredith heard her anyway, turning and waving one elegant hand.

"Oh, are you human? No worries, darling, so is Lora." She pointed to a dark-haired woman stamping her feet against the cold. "And Emerald, of course," Lady Meredith added.

The teenager once again had her book out, and she stood slumped against a tree, her flashlight pointed at its pages. "My father was human," she called out to Tamsyn without looking away from her book, which Tamsyn now noticed was a tattered copy of *Rebecca*.

"Is that how it works?" Tamsyn asked Bowen. "One witch plus one human equals another human?"

"Depends," Bowen said. "I've done some research on magical genetics, but it really is random. There's been some research in Norway . . . no, Iceland . . . yes, Iceland. About climate maybe having an effect? Or moon phases, which seems more likely, and you . . . did not want to know *this* much about it, did you?"

"Are you kidding? Every day, I wake up and pray, 'Lord, please let someone give me an in-depth explanation of the effect of climate and the moon on magical witch babies.'"

Bowen smiled down at her, that fondness back in his gaze, and it felt so easy, so *right,* to reach up and rest a hand on his cheek, tweaking his beard as she added, "I never dared to dream I'd have my prayers answered *and* get bonus Scandinavian data."

"You're a pain in my arse, you know that?" Bowen replied, and Tamsyn grinned, her hand still on his cheek, her spirit entirely too light for someone trapped in the freaking 1950s, and then Elspeth loudly sighed and said, "You see, Harri? *That* is what two people in love look like."

Tamsyn dropped her hand so fast someone would've thought Bowen's face was suddenly on fire, and she went to step back, except, *oh right,* they were supposed to be *married,* so she probably wasn't supposed to basically shriek and leap ten feet away from him when someone suggested they looked in love.

Except . . . they hadn't been pretending in that moment. They had just been being themselves, and Elspeth had *still* thought

"I was planning on marrying you, Elle. I gave you my great-great-grandmother's ring made of gold mined from the mountain my family home sits on, the family home I was *planning* to gift to you as a wedding present, so I'm not sure how much more *in love* you expected me to appear."

"Oh, because that's what love is, isn't it?" Elspeth fired back. "Possessions. Traditions. Your bloody Penhallow lineage and finally getting a wife who could bring some power back into your bloodline."

"I never said that!" Harri shouted back, and Tamsyn inched closer to Bowen to whisper, "I feel like your chances of getting born are shrinking, not gonna lie."

"Hmmph" was Bowen's only reply.

Elspeth and Harri were still arguing even as they pressed their hands against the trunk of the tree, and after they stepped back, Bowen moved forward, his fingers spread wide as he laid them against the black bark.

Tamsyn waited for the glow to appear, but there was nothing, and Bowen frowned at his hand, pulling it back and flexing his fingers, then laying it back against the tree.

Still nothing.

"The fuck?" Tamsyn heard him mutter to himself, and Lady Meredith trilled out, "Language, Mr. Penhallow!"

"Apologies," Bowen said, turning away from the tree, but Lady Meredith only shrugged.

"I don't mind the odd bit of cursing myself, but one must set a good example for Madoc, isn't that right, dear?"

Madoc had already laid his small hand against the tree and was now patting his glowing handprint. "It's not even that bad a word, Mummy. It's Anglo-Saxon, and we are Anglo-Saxons, too, or we were before we were Welsh, so we can say fu—"

Bowen clapped his hand over the boy's mouth, giving a pained smile to Lady Meredith. "Again, apologies."

"Well, at least we didn't get him that parrot he wanted," Lady Meredith said, more to herself than anyone else, then she nodded at Bowen's hand, still covering Madoc's mouth.

"And as for your powers, I wouldn't fret. Happens to many men, so I hear!"

Tamsyn muffled a snort, and Bowen scowled while Lady Meredith turned back to the group with a clap of her hands. "The log is selected!" she cried, and as Tamsyn watched, the tree began to shiver and fade until it vanished from sight altogether.

Bowen had let go of Madoc and returned to her side. "It'll be back at the house," he told her, answering her unasked question, "already burning in the fireplace. Lot more convenient than cutting it down, hauling it back . . ."

"Makes sense," Tamsyn agreed, then added, "I mean, pretty much the only thing making sense at the moment, so I'm taking it."

They all started heading back toward the castle, Tamsyn's arm once again in Bowen's, and it should probably bother her just how easy that was getting for her, but it didn't.

What did bother her was the idea that Bowen's magic might be on the fritz. It was one thing to be stuck in another time with a witch. It was another if that witch couldn't access magic, a thing that seemed like it might be pretty damn useful in this situation.

"So your magic," she started, but Bowen just shook his head.

"It's nothing to worry about."

"Consider me not worried," Tamsyn lied.

Tywyll House was still lit up, and as Tamsyn stepped inside and handed her borrowed coat to a footman, she could feel the warmth of the house slipping into her, a big contrast from how the home had felt in the present.

In fact, everything looked different. It was still technically the same—same floors, same suits of armor and portraits of glowering ancestors—but something was different.

"It's not haunted now," Tamsyn said, and Sir Caradoc gave a booming laugh at that.

"Haunted?" he asked. "Oh, had you heard those rumors? No, no, there hasn't been a ghost at Tywyll House since . . . Darling, who was our last ghost?"

"The Blue Boy," she called back. "Sweet little fellow, but glad to see the back of him! And that was . . . oh, '51, I suppose? '52? Before him, there was the Headless Lady, but we haven't had any since."

Tamsyn wondered if she'd ever be in this world long enough to talk so casually about ghosts.

Down the hall, the Yule log was indeed roaring away, filling the whole downstairs with a pleasant warmth, and Tamsyn happily accepted another mug of tea as Emerald approached, her eyes wide.

"Your outfit is . . . it's very . . ."

Oh, right. Bowen's tux fit in just fine, but Tamsyn was wearing a jumpsuit with a way lower neckline than any of the other women were rocking this evening, and she smiled at Emerald with a shrug.

"This is how women dress in America," she said, hoping a teenage witch living in the wilds of Wales in the 1950s didn't have a lot of access to fashion magazines.

And she must not have, because Emerald just nodded slowly, her voice slightly awestruck. "America," she echoed, just as from somewhere in the house, a clock chimed.

"Goodness, it's already past midnight!" Lady Meredith exclaimed, checking a delicate diamond watch on her wrist. "I'm sure everyone wants to get to bed."

She threw a saucy look at Bowen and Tamsyn that had Tamsyn's stomach swooping.

"Especially you two lovebirds," Lady Meredith went on, and then winked. "Don't worry, I've got the perfect room for you. It's a bit small, but I don't think you'll mind snuggling in, will you?"

"I . . . snuggling is . . ." Bowen started, red creeping up his neck, and Tamsyn took his hand, squeezing it tightly.

"We don't mind at all, Lady Meredith," she said, and, gulping hard, followed her hostess up the stairs.

CHAPTER 12

Bowen wasn't sure what it said about him, both as a witch and as a man in his thirties, that with everything currently going on at Tywyll House—Yule, the now canceled wedding of his own fucking grandparents, a spell or more likely a curse that had sent him and the woman he had only recently realized he was in love with hurtling almost seventy years into the past—the thing that currently had him staring at the ceiling, worry churning in his gut, was that at any moment, Tamsyn was going to walk out of the bathroom in this suite they now shared, and he was going to be alone with her.

In a bedroom.

With only one bed.

At night.

With her in . . .

Well, he wasn't sure. Lady Meredith had had a bunch of clothing sent up for both of them after he'd made up a story about their luggage clearly not surviving their magical transit. Bowen was currently wearing a monogrammed set of black pajamas, an elegant "CMG" stitched in gold thread over his heart, which made him feel a bit like he was in a play or something. One of those old farces where bedroom doors kept opening and closing, and the hero kept ending up in the bed of the wrong woman.

What had Lady Meredith given Tamsyn to wear? What did women even wear to go to bed in 1957? Hell, Bowen wasn't *that* up to date on what women wore to bed now, so was it any surprise he didn't have a great handle on vintage nightwear?

The water was still running in the bathroom, and he wondered if Tamsyn was in there wondering what *he* was wearing.

Christ, she was going to piss herself laughing once she saw him. Maybe he should at least take the shirt off? Or would that just make it worse? Would he feel like a bigger tit wearing the full bloody costume, or would sitting out here shirtless make him feel all the stupider?

Bowen had just reached for the first button of the top when he heard her call out, "If you laugh at me, I swear to god I'll kill you!"

With that she stepped out of the bathroom, and Bowen . . .

Well, he didn't laugh exactly.

It's just that . . .

"I know," Tamsyn said, throwing up her hands. "They may claim Tywyll House no longer has a ghost, but I sure as shit look like one in this thing."

This thing was a white nightgown that went from her chin to the floor, complete with long sleeves that ended in lacy ruffs where her hands should have been. Her long, dark hair flowed over her shoulders, longer than he'd realized—she usually had it up in a ponytail—and Bowen found he couldn't help but say, "You look like you should be carrying a candelabra and wandering the halls."

Tamsyn lifted one hand, and Bowen assumed she was trying to flip him off, but all that lace obscured whatever rude gesture it was, and she sighed, ineffectually shoving at her sleeves.

"At least it's warm?" she said. "Downstairs was downright balmy with that Yule log, but it's chillier in here, even with that."

She nodded toward the small fireplace where the logs were merely glowing, and Bowen got out of the bed, crossing the slightly threadbare carpet to stand in front of the embers. With a wave of his fingers, he muttered the words that should have made the flames leap up instantly, but they stayed stubbornly smoldering, and he frowned, flexing his fingers again.

"Still no magic?" Tamsyn asked, and Bowen glanced over his shoulder to see her sitting on the edge of the bed, her makeup-free face and all that long loose hair making her look younger, less . . . intimidating.

Which was actually *more* intimidating for some reason, so Bowen turned back to the fireplace, ignoring the growing tightness in both his chest and his pajama pants, and picked up the brass poker.

As he nudged at the sad excuse for a fire, he said, "I haven't done much research on the effects of time travel and magic. It's an elemental thing, magic. Wild and strange. I used to think it was more like science. That's how I treated it, at least. Hypothesize, experiment. Record findings, look for patterns. Try to suss out . . . I don't know, rules, I s'ppose. Like if you could just figure out how it all worked, you could control it. But it doesn't work like that. Read once that magic was like a naked blade. You can hold it, but you damn well better be careful with it, and even if you are, you are probably still going to bleed."

Pausing, Bowen huffed out a breath, shaking his head at himself.

"I know, this kind of thing isn't all that interesting," he said, turning back around.

He expected to see Tamsyn watching him with one of those wry smirks and a smart comment just waiting on those pretty lips. Instead, she was sitting in the middle of that giant bed with its paisley coverlet, her knees pulled up under that tent of a gown, arms wrapped around them.

"Actually, that *is* interesting," she told him, cocking her head to one side. "Maybe just because we're in a castle at night, and there's a fire, and this seems like the kind of place where you should talk about magic, but that was almost like . . ."

She thought it over for a second, and Bowen fought a damn near desperate urge to run the back of his hand down that long fall of brown hair.

"A bedtime story," Tamsyn finally decided, then laughed a little, scooting farther up in the bed. "Speaking of, time travel is exhausting, and we have an awful lot to figure out tomorrow. I'm hitting the . . . I don't even want to say 'hay,' because I feel there's a non-zero chance this thing might actually have hay in it?"

Tamsyn patted the mattress suspiciously, and Bowen huffed out a laugh as he abandoned the fire and crossed to the bed.

"More likely about two centuries of feathers," he told her, reaching down for one of the extra blankets before scooping up a pillow. "Still, you'll be comfortable enough."

Tamsyn had been sliding under the covers, and now she stopped, the duvet still in one hand as she looked over at him. "Don't you mean *we'll* be comfortable?"

Again, Bowen was thankful for his beard, shorter as it was, and the dim light of the room as a red flush spread up his neck. "I was, uh, just gonna sleep on the sofa over there. Or settee. Whatever you call it."

He gestured to the little seat beneath the window. It was covered in navy and gold stripes with a high curving back and rolled arms, and while Bowen wasn't as tall as his brothers, he was fairly sure his legs would have to hang over one of those arms.

Tamsyn sat up now, frowning at the sofa before looking back at him. "Okay, no. You're not spending all night curled up in that thing like a sad urchin. This bed is massive, and we're both adults. I think we can handle sleeping next to each other for a night or two, don't you?"

Bowen did not.

In fact, the idea of sleeping next to her, even with the mattress equivalent of the English Channel between then, still had him hard almost immediately, his mind suddenly flooded with images of sliding those yards of snow-white fabric up her legs, slipping his hand between them, burying his nose in that space between her shoulder and her neck, and just *inhaling* her . . .

"Bowen?" Tamsyn said, still frowning. "Do you want to go down to the kitchen?" she asked, and the change of subject had him blinking and stuttering out, "K-kitchen?"

She nodded. "You just looked like you were starving all of a sudden."

Bloody fucking hell.

Clearing his throat and shaking his head, Bowen reached for another pillow. "No, I'm fine," he replied, and nodded at the sofa. "And I'll be fine over there."

"No, you won't," Tamsyn said firmly, tossing the covers back and giving the absolute acre of mattress a pointed look. "Stop doing whatever this idea of chivalry is and get in the bed, Bowen."

She was right, he knew. The bed was indeed massive, there was no way he was sleeping on that sofa, and the best thing either of them could be was well rested because they were going to need to be sharp if they wanted to figure out a way out of this.

And for fuck's sake, he could handle sleeping next to a woman without wanting to ravish her. He was a grown man fully in control of his body and his thoughts.

With that, Bowen let himself slide into the bed. The mattress was cold and a little lumpy, but the sheets were soft with decades of washing and carried the faint scent of the outdoors on them.

Tamsyn was still sitting up, tugging the extra blanket he'd dropped on the duvet up to wrap around her shoulders. "Can you freeze to death inside?" she asked him, then held up a hand.

"Never mind. It's bedtime, and I don't need twelve examples of when that *did* happen to people."

Chuckling, Bowen got back up and went to one of the massive posts at the foot of the bed. "I can only think of five examples offhand, actually," he told her, then tugged at the velvet cord holding the bed curtain in place.

It gave a soft *whoosh* as it gave way, and Bowen tugged until the panel of fabric made a deep blue wall on his side of the bed. He went around to the other three posts, doing the same, as Tamsyn said, her voice muffled behind the curtains, "And this helps how?"

"Keeps the heat in," he told her, pulling back the velvet on his side and sliding into bed.

The curtain swung into place, leaving them in near total darkness, the only light the dim glow of the embers that occasionally showed through the spaces between the curtains.

It was immediately easier, lying next to her when he couldn't see her. In fact, in the dark, Bowen could almost pretend that he was alone.

That's what he'd do. Lord knew he had plenty of experience with sleeping alone, so he lay on his back, his body still, and closed his eyes.

Right.

Just like back at the cabin. Just him and his bed—cot, really—and no one else for miles and miles—

Tamsyn gave the softest of sighs, and Bowen's eyes shot open, his body immediately aware of her.

The rustle of her nightgown against the sheets, the warmth of her body, the faint smell of woodsmoke that still clung to her hair mingling with the softer, but no less potent, jasmine scent of the soap she must have used in her bath.

"See?" she asked him, her voice drifting through the darkness. "Isn't this nicer than folding yourself in a pretzel on that couch? I bet no one's ever sat on that thing, much less slept on it."

"I've slept on worse," he said, his voice gruff, and she gave one of those low laughs that made him squeeze his eyes tightly shut so that he wouldn't moan.

"Oh, I have no doubt," she said, and he could feel the mattress dip slightly as she turned over, facing him now from the sound of her voice. "You've probably slept . . . I don't know. On the side of an active volcano. Or in some haunted lighthouse in the North Sea. On top of a bear on a glacier."

"Yes, yes, and no, but came close once," he replied, hoping she might laugh that laugh again even though it killed him, and sure enough, she did, and sure enough, he had to close his eyes again and wonder if anyone had ever died from wanting someone like this.

She shifted against the sheets again, still far enough away that even if he stretched out his arm, he wasn't sure he would've been able to touch her.

That was still too close.

"If I had to break my rule about sleeping with clients, I'm glad it was with you," she said, and now Bowen flipped over to his side, facing her even though he couldn't see her.

"This doesn't count," he told her. "Just sleeping, innit? Letter of the law may be broken, but not the spirit."

He could imagine her raising her eyebrows at him as she replied, "I must be rubbing off on you if you're so quick to look for moral loopholes, Bowen."

It was the dark, and the closeness of her without having to look at her, and the insanity of this whole mess they were in, that made him say it.

That and his stupid heart, and his even stupider cock.

"I'm not having us break that rule on a technicality, Tamsyn," he told her, his voice rough. "When we break it, it'll be the real thing, *cariad*."

My love, he'd called her, because she was, fuck him and Saint Bugi and all his parts, but she was.

But Tamsyn didn't speak Welsh, so it was another word she picked up on.

"'When'?" she echoed, sounding breathless, and Bowen thought about playing it off as a mistake, turning it into the kind of teasing flirt Rhys always seemed to be so good at.

But Bowen had never been good at that kind of thing, so all he could do was tell her the truth.

"I think about you all the fucking time," Bowen heard himself say. "Every bloody day, Tamsyn. Your hair. Your skin. The way you laugh. Especially when you're laughing at me."

She gave another one of those breathless sounds, but her voice was wry when she replied, "I do that a lot."

"You do, and it drives me mad in the best way," he told her.

"Just like it drives me mad that I used to go days—hell, *weeks*—without talking to another living soul, and now if I don't talk to you, the day never feels quite right. And . . ." Blowing out a breath, he turned and stared up into the blackness. "Dunno. For me, that feels like a *when* and not an *if,* but maybe it doesn't for you, in which case I'm a sad and delusional bastard, and you're welcome to say so."

Another laugh, softer this time, and then he felt her moving across the mattress, her hand tentatively resting on his chest.

Just that one touch nearly burned him, and it was dark, he was a muddle of a million feelings, and he couldn't help but lift that hand from his chest, kissing one fingertip.

Tamsyn sucked in a breath, and Bowen kissed another finger, then another, slowing making his way down to the pad of her pinkie, hearing her breathing get quicker, her legs moving restlessly against the sheets.

"You're not a sad bastard," she murmured as he laid her hand back on his chest. "I think about you all the time, too. I can't see one interesting thing—not a book or a sunset or a fucking *tree* or some kind of weird crystal—without being like, 'I should show this to Bowen,' and . . ." Her voice trailed off, and she sighed, pulling her hand back. "But I'm serious about not getting involved with anyone I work with. Even incredibly hot men with whom I've somehow magically time traveled."

"I take it there's a story there," he said, and he felt rather than heard her turn her head to look at him.

"No story," she said. "Just self-preservation. I love this job.

Or . . . I love parts of it. Never wanted anything to fuck that up for me."

The sheets rustled again as she turned more fully toward him.

"But *I* take it there's a story with Carys and this dead fiancé of hers. Every time anyone mentioned his name, you looked like you were chewing glass."

The reminder of Carys—of Declan—was what he needed. A metaphorical bucket of ice water before the warm, intimate darkness of this bed made him lose his head altogether. Until Declan was released from the spell that held him in this strange place between life and death, Bowen had no right to be lying here next to a beautiful woman, telling her the kinds of things that became promises in the right light.

"There is," he told Tamsyn now. "But it's . . . it's not a story I can tell. Not yet."

"Not yet," she confirmed, and then sighed.

He sensed her turn again, was fairly certain she was staring up at the canopy, too.

"It sucks," she said. "Being virtuous. Having . . . a code or whatever. Rules. Especially when you're over there, looking like that—not that I can see you, but I see you with my eyes closed every night anyway."

Christ.

Now it was Bowen closing his eyes, and this time, he couldn't bite back the smallest groan.

"Don't fuckin' say things like that," he practically growled. "Don't tell me you think about me at night."

"But I do," she said, her voice low, and it was the darkness again, the way it pulled things out of him, its very own kind of spell.

"And what do you do, Tamsyn?" he asked, his voice not even sounding like his own, his accent thickening, the words rumbling in his chest. "What do you do when you think about me?"

There was a heartbeat, then another. Five in all passed, and Bowen counted every one until her voice drifted out of the gloom.

"Should I show you?"

CHAPTER 13

Tamsyn lay there in the pitch black, the only sounds her heart-beat in her ears and Bowen's rough breathing, and wondered if insanity was a symptom of time travel.

Felt like it must be, but maybe it was just the weirdness of the night, the coziness of the bed, the darkness all around them, and those things Bowen had said—those simple, matter-of-fact, absolutely devastatingly perfect things—that had her already sliding her nightgown up her legs, even as Bowen said, "How can you show me when I can't see you?" his voice gruff, but still somehow gentle. The heat of his body next to her . . .

Once again, a holiday temptation was presenting itself, and once again, Tamsyn found she just couldn't turn it down.

"Well, maybe 'demonstrate' would be a better way of putting it," she told him, and then added, "With description."

Tamsyn could actually hear him swallow, and she smiled in the dark.

"Back home," she said, scooting just the littlest bit closer, "I have all sorts of toys for this."

"Toys," he echoed, his voice like sandpaper, and Tamsyn nodded, her breath speeding up as she slid one hand up her thigh.

"Mmm-hmm. Really good ones, too. And all different types."

"Types?"

He sounded like he was actually choking now, and Tamsyn nearly purred as she curled her toes, sliding her hand away from her leg to cup one breast, her nipple hard against her palm. "You know," she told him, even though she was pretty sure he didn't. "The kind that slides inside. The ones that vibrate. I even have this one shaped like a flower that I sometimes use in the shower."

"Shower," he echoed, and Tamsyn laughed, even though the sound was a little strangled as she tugged at the tip of her breast.

"You just going to repeat everything I say?" she asked, and he shifted closer, his foot nearly brushing hers.

"There's no blood left in my brain, Tamsyn," he told her, and she chuckled.

"And that's a big brain," she answered, letting her hand drift back down her stomach.

"You should see my cock," he replied, and she would've laughed again, except now she was the one whose throat seemed to go tight, her legs clenching together, every part of her lit up with desire.

"I want to do a whole lot more than see it," she told him, finally letting her hand settle between her legs, pressing hard with the heel of her palm. "But I'm the one showing you, remember?"

"Well, hardly seems fair," Bowen said, and she heard him

moving in the darkness, imagined him sliding one of those rough, able hands into the waistband of his pajamas.

He groaned then, and Tamsyn moaned along with him, letting her fingers start to circle. She was wet, wetter than she'd maybe ever been, and the sound would've embarrassed her except for the damn near worshipful sound that came out of Bowen's mouth.

"God in heaven, I'd give anything to taste you right now," he panted, and she could hear his hand moving now, feel the slight shuddering of the mattress.

Closing her eyes, Tamsyn arched her back, her fingers sliding, little cries slipping from her lips, and he was right there with her. She could feel him even though they weren't touching, couldn't even see each other, could only hear and imagine, and holy shit, the things she was imagining.

Bowen's mouth between her legs just like he said, his beard damp with her, his lips and tongue voracious, and her hips bucked against her hand as across the bed, Bowen made a low sound deep in his chest.

He was saying something, something that at first she thought was some kind of spell and had her tipping even closer to the edge—Sex Magic with Bowen was another pretty powerful fantasy of hers—but then she realized he was just saying something in Welsh. She didn't know what it was, but she made out her name.

Tamsyn had heard Bowen say her name a hundred times, but never like this, never in a voice so wrecked, his accent gilding every syllable, and it wasn't just how he said it, but everything she heard behind it.

This gorgeous, powerful man—this literal magical being—was, in this moment, completely in *her* thrall, and that was enough to tip Tamsyn over the edge, her face turning into the pillow as she cried out, her thighs shaking, her fingers soaked, her whole being somehow turned inside out just from her own touch.

She heard Bowen's own cry, low and deep, and it sent another tremor shuddering through her, her breath coming out in gasps now, and she whimpered, letting her hand fall back to the sheets, her chest heaving.

Next to her, Bowen was still breathing like a bellows, and she wanted so much to be able to see him right now, see the darkness of his eyes, the hunger she knew would be in them.

But she was equally glad not to look at him, because she also knew that he'd see what was in her eyes right now, too, and there would be no hiding it with a quick joke, no mask to wear, just the naked vulnerability of how much she liked him—and oh god, she was going to have to admit that this was way bigger than *like* at some point—and Tamsyn wasn't ready for that.

After they got home.

After Y Seren.

Not now.

Now, she turned her head in his direction and said, "So. Do you feel sufficiently educated in what I do when I think about you, Bowen Penhallow?"

He made one of those grunt-huff laughs of his, and Tamsyn's heart swelled in her chest.

"What I feel," he said, sitting up to strip off his pajama top and, Tamsyn assumed, clean himself up, "is the same thing I felt the first night I ever saw you, Tamsyn Bligh."

"Which was?"

Bowen paused, and Tamsyn felt the air move near her face, knew he was reaching for her, but he didn't quite touch her, and she didn't move any closer so that he could, because she knew that whatever he said next was going to go straight to her heart, and it would be that much harder if he were touching her when he said it.

"From the moment you walked into that pub," he said, "I knew you'd be the making and the ruin of me all at once, woman."

And Tamsyn realized she was right—that did go straight to her heart—but wrong at the same time. Because touching her, not touching her, none of it mattered. Bowen didn't have to touch her to make her love him.

She already did.

THE BED CURTAINS were open when Tamsyn woke up the next morning, watery gray light filtering in the thick glass windows, and she sat up, her head immediately swiveling to the other side of the bed.

Bowen was already gone, which was a good thing. She wasn't sure she was ready for waking up beside him, seeing his curls rumpled with sleep, his face soft and relaxed. Last night had been earth-shattering, but she could put it in a box, thinking of it almost like a dream. They hadn't touched each other, hadn't kissed, hadn't fallen asleep with their arms wrapped around each other.

It had been . . . a stress reliever. A fun way to pass the time now that they found themselves in a magical fuckup of pretty serious proportions. Wasn't that normal? Like the way people wanted to have sex after someone died because it reaffirmed life or whatever it was.

Right. That's all last night had been. Orgasms as coping mechanisms.

It was easy to think of last night while she was alone in her— *their*—bedroom, getting ready for the day. In addition to the Haunted Mansion Nightgown, Lady Meredith had sent up a whole heap of outfits, everything from dungarees to evening gowns, and Tamsyn selected a festive red sweater and a pair of tight black trousers before throwing a tweed blazer over the whole thing and, since she was in the Welsh countryside, a pair of dark green wellies.

With the little bit of makeup Lady Meredith had also provided, Tamsyn felt nearly human again as she strode down the stairs of Tywyll House, pausing to give a little salute to the more terrifying-looking Meredith ancestors before moving down the hall to where she remembered the dining room being.

That room was empty, though, the shutters still closed, but Tamsyn could hear sounds farther down the hall, so she followed them until she came to a smaller, brighter room.

There were a few couches scattered about and a wall of windows looked out onto the misty garden. A smaller table had been laid as well as a long buffet against the back wall, and Tamsyn's stomach growled at the scent of food wafting off it. It had been hours—well, decades, literally—since she'd eaten, and she was just about to get a plate when a movement caught her eye, and everything she'd thought about last night—her boxes, her coping mechanisms, her *If a girl can't get herself off next to her crush after breaking the space-time continuum, then honestly, when can she?* justifications—practically exploded in front of her face as she took in Bowen standing by the farthest window, a delicate cup of coffee in one hand, his eyes drinking Tamsyn in like the sun itself had just walked into the room.

She'd told herself she was immune to how handsome he was after all this time, that it was just a fact of him, like how his eyes were brown and he liked talking about elves too much, but like her, he'd attempted to blend in a little today, and the fitted green sweater he was wearing paired with dark gray corduroys made him look less Fearsome Mountain Sorcerer, more the Most Fuckable History Professor Tamsyn had ever seen, and the knowledge that this man could be both had Tamsyn suddenly hungrier for much more than the eggs and bacon that had seemed so tempting before.

He took a step closer to her, and Tamsyn realized they were the only ones in the room, only the judgmental eyes of long-dead Merediths watching them now. Outside, she couldn't even make out the lawns or the maze anymore because the mist outside had gotten so thick, drifting over the glass, eddying over the grass outside as though the entire house were encased in a cloud.

He took another step closer, the cup rattling on its saucer, and Tamsyn wasn't sure what she would have done had Elspeth—Bowen's grandmother, she reminded herself—not swanned into the room with a "Oh, wonderful, another gray day."

It was very hard to remember that this woman would one day birth Bowen's dad, a man she'd heard only ever described as terrifying, because Tamsyn wasn't sure she'd ever seen anyone as beautiful and glamorous as Elspeth Carew. Today, she was wearing a figure-hugging white dress with a cowl collar and fitted sleeves and a pair of low deep green heels, her auburn hair swept back from her face with a pair of tortoiseshell combs.

As she took in the two of them, her red lips curled into a knowing smile. "Am I interrupting something? I certainly hope so. Someone might as well be trysting this weekend now that I'm not going to be a married woman by Yule."

"The only thing you're interrupting is me getting to those sausages," Tamsyn told her, nodding at the buffet. "And that is not a euphemism."

Probably a little risqué for 1957, but Elspeth only laughed, the sound like chiming bells. "Oh, I like you, Mrs. Penhallow," she said.

Tamsyn hated the way that being called that made everything inside her light up, but there it was. In a weird way, nothing that had happened last night had changed anything between her and Bowen, and at the same time, it had changed everything.

Because now she knew. All those times she was lying awake, thinking about him, fantasizing about him, he was thinking about her, too.

Did he have the same fantasies?

Doubtful. Bowen was a smart and creative man, but not the type to gin up Visiting Wizard Must Take Village Maiden as Bride, although if she ever had the chance, she was absolutely going to share that one with him.

But now, she smiled at Elspeth and said, "I like you, too, Miss Carew. A shame we won't be family after all."

Elspeth's expression darkened. "Well," she sniffed, making her way to the sideboard with a flourish of her skirts, "you should talk to Harri about that."

"About what?"

Oh, fabulous, now Harri Penhallow had entered the room, his dark hair messy, his glasses slightly askew, and while he was as handsome as his eventual descendant Rhys Penhallow, he could not have looked more miserable.

"About how your absolute pigheadedness has brought an end to our engagement," Elspeth replied, and Harri's jaw tightened as he stalked to the buffet, filling his plate with roasted tomatoes and sausages robotically.

"There is exactly one person to blame for the dissolution of this engagement, Ellie, and it is you."

"Don't call me 'Ellie' anymore, I don't like it."

"You used to love it," Harri fired back, and then he lowered his voice. "Especially in certain circumstances."

Elspeth straightened up and turned to face him, her chin raised, her expression haughty, but her cheeks rosy pink. "How dare you," she said. "I've taken you for a fool and a . . . a fortune hunter, Henry Penhallow, but never a cad."

"And I took you for a woman worthy of bearing the Penhallow name, but it seems we were both mistaken."

Sidling up to Bowen, Tamsyn picked his coffee cup off his saucer and took a sip before whispering, "I still think your grandparents are hot."

"And I still think you never, ever need to say words like that again," he replied.

Smiling, Tamsyn replaced the cup on the saucer even as she tried very hard not to meet his eyes, because if she did, she couldn't guarantee memories of last night wouldn't have her bursting into flame.

"It's them, though," she went on, nodding at Elspeth and Harri, who were now filling their plates in silence. "They're the reason we're here, I'm sure of it. Something has gone wrong, and now they're not getting married, which means your dad never gets born."

Bowen grunted. "Not sure that's a huge fucking tragedy."

Turning to him, Tamsyn reached up without thinking, taking his face in both her hands. "It is to me if it means you never get born," she said, and oh shit, it was too late now. She was looking in his eyes, and he was looking in hers, and everything that had happened last night in the warm, velvet darkness of that bed—their bed—seemed to fill the space between them.

Tamsyn had slept with her fair share of guys, was no stranger to sex in all its permutations, but nothing had ever been as intimate as those moments with Bowen in the dark, their hands touching their own bodies but not each other's, and yet she'd felt every stroke he'd made, heard every gasp, and she knew he'd felt and heard her, too.

It was too much, too overwhelming, and she looked away, her hands dropping to her sides.

Harri and Elspeth were both sitting at the table now, five chairs between them, but both of them were ignoring their food. Instead, they were watching Bowen and Tamsyn, and they were wearing nearly identical expressions.

Longing.

Envy.

Regret.

Whatever it was that had gone wrong with Harri and Elspeth, it wasn't that they didn't love each other.

Or didn't *want* each other.

And, Tamsyn reasoned, anything that wasn't *that* could be fixed.

Giving one last longing look at the buffet, Tamsyn took the coffee from Bowen's hands, draining the cup and then sitting the cup and the saucer on the table.

"If you'll excuse us," she said to Harri and Elspeth. "We have some work to do."

"Is that what they're calling it these days?" she heard Harri mutter as she dragged Bowen from the room, and Bowen scowled even as he let himself be dragged out into the hallway.

"Stop looking like you want to punch your granddad," Tamsyn said in a low voice, and Bowen glanced down at her.

"Punched my da once," he told her. "And both my brothers. More than once. *Lots* more than once, actually. So a grandda doesn't seem a bridge too far, if I'm being honest."

Tamsyn thought of her own brother, Michael, and tried to imagine punching him, but the image literally wouldn't come. They were as different as night and day—her with this bizarre but adventurous job, no family, no real home, no ties to anything; Michael with his husband, Josh, his insurance business, his condo, and his boat—but she loved him so fiercely that she was pretty sure she'd cut off her own hand before she'd raise it against him.

It was another reminder that she and Bowen were very different, and not just because he was a witch and she wasn't. All the more reason to let things like last night be an anomaly, ne'er to be repeated.

All the more reason to focus on the task ahead.

"We want to get out of here, right?" she asked Bowen, and he stared at her in confusion before saying, "Well, we want to get out of this *time,* the place itself is actually cor—"

Tamsyn clamped a hand over his mouth, trying to ignore how warm his lips were, how his beard was so much softer than she'd remembered. "Fine. We want out of 1957. And I've watched enough time travel movies and TV shows to know that people end up in the past only because they have to fix something that went wrong, something that affects their future. What could affect your future more than your *grandparents breaking up* before they even get married, much less have your father?"

Bowen frowned, that trio of wrinkles appearing over his nose in the way she loved. "Don't disagree, exactly," he said slowly. "But Carys—"

Tamsyn shook her head. "Carys isn't even here. That spell just took *us*. Which means we're here for a reason. And I think I know what it is."

Bowen watched her expectantly, and Tamsyn took a deep breath.

"We have to *Parent Trap* your grandparents."

CHAPTER 14

You need me to explain that reference, don't you?" Tamsyn asked, and Bowen shook his head.

"I know *The Parent Trap,* Tamsyn," he told her. He didn't bother adding that the only reason he knew about it was because in the summer of 2000, Rhys had developed a crush on Lindsay Lohan and forced both his brothers to watch that movie many, many times. Let Tamsyn think he actually knew something about pop culture for once.

"Well, look at you, a part of the twenty-first century after all," Tamsyn replied, slapping his shoulder, and Bowen would've reminded her that that movie—both the remake and the original—had come out in the *twentieth* century, actually, but he was pretty sure that would just get him one of those eye rolls, and besides, he was still trying to right his world on its axis because she'd touched him.

That's where he was now—a slap on the shoulder was enough to have him practically swooning and falling at her feet.

But how could he look at her in her cheerful jumper, her nose adorably wrinkled because she was plotting and she always made that face when she was coming up with a scheme, and not think of last night?

The way those velvet curtains had cocooned them in darkness and warmth, the sounds of her gasps and her moans and her fingers working over her, the smell of her earthy and primal and so fucking *good* he'd come in his own fist like a teenage boy after only a few strokes.

How on the Goddess's great green earth was he supposed to do *anything* now that he had been decimated so thoroughly?

And the worst of it was, she didn't seem to be all that affected by what had happened. Maybe this kind of thing was old hat to her. Maybe she had dozens of lovers, one in every town she'd done a job in.

That was fine. More than fine. Good, really, exactly what a liberated and beautiful woman like Tamsyn *should* do if that's what she wanted, and he was fine with it.

Just . . .

Very, very fine.

Bowen took Tamsyn's elbow and gently steered her farther away from the breakfast room. It was dim in the hallway, the sconces doing nothing against the gloom outside, and it was hard to believe that it was just midmorning. Bowen could smell rain, probably sleet, too, on the air, and hoped there were no more plans for traipsing through the woods tonight as he said to Tamsyn,

"I agree it's worth a shot to see if getting my grandparents over . . . whatever this is gets us back to 2024. But I also think we need to find out a lot more about Y Seren and what powers it might have. Because no matter *why* we're here, that's the thing that sent us back."

"Again, just so many words here in the fifties," Tamsyn mused, then shrugged. "Agreed. No reason not to tackle both the *why* and the *how*. Where do you want to start?"

THREE HOURS LATER, Bowen was greatly regretting his choice.

If they'd stuck with Tamsyn's plan—*Parent Trap* first—they'd be back at the manor house, probably playing a game of sardines or something, anything that gave them an excuse to lock Harri and Elspeth away in a dark room until they remembered they were in love with each other and the wedding was back on.

Instead, Bowen was outside in the rapidly darkening afternoon as a steady drizzle of rain seeped through every item of clothing he was wearing.

And he was riding a fucking *bicycle*.

With a *bell*.

They'd spent over an hour in the dusty library at Tywyll House, a gloomy room with a gallery and a spiral staircase and about a million books, none of which had been opened in decades, if the dust was any indication.

But Bowen had figured it was best to start with books when it came to Y Seren. That's where he always started, after all.

Gather as much basic information as you can, suss out what's good, what's useful, what's interesting but probably not true, and what is utter shite.

Once you had that locked down, *then* you could do the scary part of talking to people. Tamsyn had, of course, wanted to start there, to ask Lady Meredith outright about the jewel, but Bowen pointed out that might raise some suspicions, should the damn thing disappear if they needed it to get back home.

For once, Tamsyn hadn't given him an argument, just a little salute that had been staggeringly erotic for reasons he was not going to look at too closely.

Then they'd searched and read and searched some more, all while Bowen tried to ignore the scent of her perfume, and the nearness of her, and the cozy room with its flickering lamps as the weather outside got nastier.

In the end, the books had yielded exactly one clue about Y Seren: that before the Merediths had purchased it sometime in the last decade, it had belonged to a family named Beddoe.

And then Tamsyn had done that adorable thing with her nose again and said, "Beddoe. That was the name of the pub in the village here. I passed it on my way to Tywyll House. Well, you know, Tywyll House in the future. Or the present as it was at the time." She'd frowned. "God, that makes me sound like you. Anyway, there was a sign over the door that said BEDDOE'S TAVERN, and I remembered it because that's a great last name and one I might use for . . . absolutely legal and non-nefarious purposes."

Bowen had grunted at that, but he'd agreed that this was some-thing, and they could at least go to the village, see if Beddoe's Tavern was still there, and maybe make some discreet inquiries.

Hence the bloody bicycle.

"You're both mad," Emerald had told them as she'd watched them put on coats and wellies at the front door while one of the lads who worked in the gardens brought around the two rickety bicycles. "Going out in this. My gran would say you'd die of the ague, but then my gran died because she accidentally drank poison she'd been meaning to give my papa, so what did she know?"

It might have been the first time in a year that Bowen had ever seen Tamsyn speechless.

But now here they were, mad indeed, pedaling through weather that Bowen was sadly all too familiar with—not hard enough to be rain, too wet to be mist, a miserable kind of thing Declan called "mizzle"—and Bowen squinted against it as he navigated the bike over ruts and puddles on the dirt road that wound through the forest from Tywyll House to the village of Tywyll itself.

He was just thinking he'd never be warm again when he heard a cheerful *brrrng!* and looked over to see Tamsyn ringing the bell on her own bicycle. Her dark hair sparkled with raindrops, and her wellies were splattered with mud, but she was smiling as though this were all just a grand adventure they were having, soaking themselves to the skin in bloody December in 1957.

Goddess, but how he loved her.

Still an awkward thing, that love—still a thing he wasn't sure he was meant to feel, much less talk about it—but there it was, and there was no getting rid of it.

And when she turned and smiled at him, he couldn't feel the cold of the rain at all.

All right, that wasn't entirely true—he was shivering, his beard was dripping, and his cock had retreated so thoroughly that even if Tamsyn had stripped naked right here in the forest, he wasn't sure he'd be able to actually *do* anything about that—but it was the sentiment of the thing, wasn't it? That when he looked at her, life felt . . . easier. Better.

Happier.

Bowen had known people could feel this kind of thing. He hadn't seen it between his parents because he'd been so young when his mam had passed, but he saw it with Rhys and Vivienne. There were times those two were just sitting on the sofa together, Rhys looking at his phone while idly stroking Vivienne's hair with his free hand while she read a book, her own hand resting on Rhys's thigh, and it always looked so . . . nice.

Wells and Gwyn weren't quite so cozy, but they had their moments, too. Like the time Bowen accidentally caught them on the stairs, Gwyn pressed back against the wall, Wells looming over her, not touching her, not kissing her, and yet whatever it was in the air around them had been so electric that Bowen had scurried away, his cheeks hot, like he'd caught them shagging or summat.

Was that what people saw when he and Tamsyn were together? Just last night, Elspeth had told Harri that Bowen and Tamsyn were what two people in love looked like, and the memory warmed him even now.

Or maybe it was just that they were finally rounding the corner onto the village high street, and he could see the pub rising up out of the misty rain like an oasis, the windows glowing, the sign over the door gently swaying.

No TAVERN on the sign in 1957. This just read BEDDOE'S, and Bowen had never been so happy to see a pub in his entire life.

He and Tamsyn wheeled their bicycles to a tall hedge just beside the door, resting them there before hurrying into the pub.

Inside, it was warm, which was a fucking blessing, and a fire crackled merrily in the hearth while the few locals at the bar turned to see the newcomers, judged them not particularly interesting, and then returned to their pints and whatever it was men like these gossiped about seventy years ago. Price of sheep, probably. Weather, always, what with this being Britain.

Next to him, Tamsyn wrinkled her nose. "God, I forgot everybody smoked inside back then. Back . . . now? Anyway."

She rubbed at her reddening eyes, and Bowen glanced around, realizing that there was indeed a sort of cloud hanging about the place, the tips of lit cigarettes glowing in the murkiness, the smell of pipes thick in the air, and Bowen nodded toward the bar. "I'll grab us a couple of pints while you look around, see if there's anyone worth talking to."

"Like a video game," Tamsyn murmured, but when Bowen gave her a questioning look, she just shook him off. "Get me a cider, please," she told him, then, even though her eyes were teary from the smoke, she threw him a quick wink. "Or Rudolph's Rosé, if they have it."

Bowen snorted. "Sip of that would probably kill these people," he said. "They're not ready for what we do to alcohol in the future."

"Fair point," Tamsyn acknowledged, before pointing toward an empty table near the fire. "I'll be over there."

Bowen nodded and moved toward the bar, determined to redeem himself for their first meeting and that first drink, and equally determined to find some casual way of asking if any of the Beddoes were still around.

The bar itself was an ancient piece of oak, scarred up and discolored, and he knew the sight of it would send his brother Wells, who'd once been a publican himself and took great pride in the shininess of his bar—to the point that Rhys had openly wondered if he was overcompensating for something—into conniptions.

The fellow behind the bar was barrel-chested with a steel-gray beard, and he had just turned around when Bowen suddenly felt a tug at his sleeve.

He looked over, then looked down, because the woman at his elbow was tiny. Her face was creased with wrinkles, but her blue eyes were bright and sharp, and Bowen could feel magic rolling off her. No doubt about it, this woman was a witch, and a powerful one at that.

Which was why he wasn't all that surprised when she looked up at him with something near wonder and said, "Oh, *achan*, you are a long way from home."

CHAPTER 15

Tamsyn was sitting by the fire, trying to discreetly rub her itching nose, when Bowen came back to the table, carefully balancing three pints in his hands, while a very tiny, very ancient-looking old lady held on to one of his elbows.

"This is Lowri. She knows we're time travelers."

Glancing around, Tamsyn hissed, "Wanna say that a little louder? Maybe add a nice burning at the stake to this trip?"

Lowri laughed, a sound not unlike someone stepping on a set of bagpipes, and then sat down, wooden beads around her neck rattling. "Oh, darlin', people in Tywyll are used to the strange and unusual. You can't live here and not be. Whole town built on a ley line."

Like Graves Glen, Tamsyn thought, remembering that it was that ley line that powered up the magic in that town, gave the Jones women a lot of their power. Made sense, then, that Tywyll was so weird.

"How did you know?" Tamsyn asked as Bowen took his own seat, passing their drinks around. He and Lowri had something dark and foamy in their glasses, while Tamsyn's was a pale gold that smelled just like walking into an apple orchard.

Lowri took a deep sip of her drink before saying, "Oh, it's all over you. The pair of ya. I felt it as soon as you came in. You both feel . . . well, I don't say this to hurt your feelings, lovies, but you feel as wrong as a snowfall in summer. Or a drought in winter. Or . . . you know when you step into a pond, and the earth beneath you is slimy, and you think, 'That might be the ground itself, but maybe I'm stepping in a nest of eels, and—'"

"Yeah, okay, I think we get the point!" Tamsyn rushed in before Lowri could think of some new horrifying simile. "We feel wrong, and specifically we feel like time travelers."

"Aye," Lowri said with a nod, one gnarled hand playing with the beads around her neck. "Met one years and years ago. Before the war. The first one," she clarified, and Tamsyn tried not to think too hard about how she was sitting across the table from someone who remembered World War I. "He was an odd duck, no idea what became of him."

"Did he get home?" Tamsyn asked, and she noticed the way Bowen leaned forward, his arms folded on the table. For the first time, she noticed his sweater had suede elbow patches, making it a Very Good Sweater Indeed, and great, now she apparently had a new kink.

But lots more important stuff to focus on right now, namely the way Lowri was shaking her head and sighing into her pint.

"No, poor dove never did find out what it was he'd been sent back to do, so he was stuck here. Not in Tywyll—think he eventually moved to London or summat, maybe Cardiff—but out of his own time."

The cider and the fire and Bowen's elbow patches had done a good job of warming Tamsyn up from that freezing ride in the rain, but now a new kind of chill seeped in, one that twisted her stomach.

"He got . . . stuck?" she asked, and Lowri nodded, licking the Guinness mustache from her upper lip.

"Aye. That's the thing with time travel. You only have a certain window to get back." The old woman leaned in closer, smelling like an odd mix of woodsmoke, lavender oil, and mothballs. "When did the two of you arrive?"

"Last night," Bowen answered, his voice rough, and Tamsyn felt that odd, disorienting sensation again, like the ground was sliding out from underneath her.

Less than a day. And yet somehow, everything was different now.

Bowen's eyes briefly met hers, and Tamsyn hoped he thought her cheeks were pink from the fire.

Or from trying not to wheeze to death in all this smoke.

Lowri nodded and said, almost to herself, "Yule, I'd bet. Just a few nights away, and magic loves that kind of deadline. A solstice, a ritual, a moon phase. Yes, if I had to guess, I'd say the two of you need to figure out why you were sent back here lest you want to stay in 1932 forever."

Tamsyn sat up in her chair, the cider suddenly sour in her mouth. "Wait, 1932? I thought this was 1957."

Lowri paused, looking up toward the dim ceiling of the pub before nodding and fiddling with those beads again. "Oh, aye, that's right. I get my years mixed up all the time."

She laughed merrily at that while Tamsyn gave her a kind of sickly smile in return and Bowen scowled into his Guinness.

Great, they'd found one person who might be able to help them with this whole time travel problem, and she *mixed up her years*.

"We were sent back with some kind of spell," Bowen told her. "Or at least we think that's what it was. A witch—one of the Merediths in our time—was wearing a brooch, a piece of jewelry called Y Seren. Do you know anything about that?"

Now it was Lowri's turn to frown. "The Star?" she translated. "No, no, can't say I've ever heard of any jewel like that, but I'll look through my books and such back at the cottage. I live just at the end of the high street in the other direction. Right before you get to the woods. You two come see me in a day or so, I might have something for you then. But for now, Sir Bedivere and I need to be getting home. Gets dark early this time of year, you know."

"Sir Bedivere?" Tamsyn echoed as the old woman got up, and Lowri nodded toward the door of the pub.

It was hard to see through all the smoke, but there, just by the row of pegs where patrons could hang up their coats, was a large basket, and in that basket, a black cat stared back at the three of them with bright yellow-green eyes.

"He's a right love," Lowri told them, "but a devil when he wants to be. Fathered half the cats in this village, I think."

"He doesn't . . . talk, does he?" Bowen asked, and Tamsyn stared at him, because even for Bowen, that was a bizarre question.

But Lowri only laughed again. "Cor, that would be something, wouldn't it? A talking cat! Would love to hear what Sir Bedivere would have to say."

"You wouldn't," Bowen told her, and once again, Tamsyn stared at him, hoping she was telegraphing with her eyes, *Are you having a stroke?*

But Lowri didn't seemed fazed, only shrugged as she set her now empty glass down on the table and made her way to the door. "I mean it," she said, pointing one wizened finger at them. "Figure out why it is you're here, fix it, and do it fast. The solstice is just a few days away, and I'd bet Sir Bedivere himself that's your deadline."

A few days.

A few days to get Harri and Elspeth back together, or she was going to be stuck in the 1950s forever.

With Bowen.

Okay, admittedly, the idea of that wasn't so terrible, but the rest of it? How was she supposed to live in a time when she wouldn't even be able to get a credit card in her own name? Or buy a house? Or be able to watch the next season of *Below Deck*?

No, not happening.

Which meant—

She turned back to Bowen as Lowri was leaving, but he held up a hand. "I know," he said. "*Parent Trap*."

"*Parent Trap*," she confirmed, and, with that, finished off her cider and headed for the door.

Bowen plucked both their jackets off the pegs by the door, and they stepped out into the cold twilight.

She wasn't wearing a watch, but Tamsyn would have guessed it was late afternoon, so it was disorienting to see it already so dark.

"Sun goes down early this time of year in these parts," Bowen told her, flipping up the collar of his coat. It had stopped raining, but it was even colder now, the air biting. "Worst part of winter, if you ask me. Looking up before teatime and seeing the sky already dark."

"Well, the worst part of *this* winter is that our bikes are gone," Tamsyn told him, pointing to the now empty space in front of the hedge.

How were there bike-thieving hooligans in this tiny village in 1957? Wasn't the whole point of the past supposed to be that it was safer and people didn't lock their doors and all that?

Bowen stared at the empty hedge, then heaved a sigh that seemed to come from the bottoms of his feet. "Well, this'll be a pleasant walk," he muttered, and then, hands still shoved in the pockets of his mackintosh, he offered one elbow to Tamsyn.

She took it, giving a sigh of her own, and the two of them headed back up the high street as it turned into the winding road through the forest back toward Tywyll House.

"At least it isn't raining now," she told him, but that was cold comfort—literally—when it was freezing and getting dark, and they were about to walk through an almost certainly Haunted Forest to get back to a house where they had a few days to make two people who were currently fighting like two hissing cats trapped in a burlap sack fall in love.

"Are you all right?" Bowen asked, looking down at her with a concerned frown.

"Why do you ask?"

"Because you were making this . . . whimpering sort of noise?"

Oh.

"Just, you know, not a *huge* fan of the dark. Or the woods. Or walking through the dark woods."

Bowen chuckled, tucking his arm closer to his side and pulling her in so that their hips bumped. "Can't imagine the great Tamsyn Bligh is afraid of much."

"I realize I give that impression, but trust me, terrified of lots of things."

"Such as?"

"Snakes, that's a big one," she said, stepping over a thick root in the path. "And ghosts, we've established that."

"And the dark and the woods and the dark woods," Bowen added, and Tamsyn nodded.

"Those, too. Ooh, and weird dolls. Those scare the shit out of me. What else? Paintings of kids where the eyes are too big. Opening a can of biscuits."

You. How I feel about you. How last night might have ruined me for any other man, and you didn't even touch me.

For once, Tamsyn's inner monologue stayed where it belonged, and she didn't say any of that out loud, but she wondered if he could feel the words hanging there between them, because he didn't say anything for a long time.

Around them, the trees grew thicker, bare branches reaching up into a deepening purple sky that just *looked* cold.

Shivering, Tamsyn tucked herself deeper into her coat and said, "So you think Lowri is right? We have until Yule to get back home?"

"I've learned that when incredibly old witches approach you in a pub and tell you something, you should probably listen," he replied, and she looked up at him even though it was hard to make out his face in the gathering darkness.

"And this happens to you a lot?"

"You'd be surprised."

That made her laugh at least, which kept her mind off the way the wind eerily whistled through the naked trees and how even if there had been a moon, the clouds overhead would have blotted it out. They were mostly making their way by feel now, and once again, she thought of last night, the dark, the bed, Bowen's groan when he came, how wrecked his voice had sounded, how she would've given anything to look at him in that moment and see if what she had been feeling was there in his eyes.

Dangerous thoughts, even if they did do a good job warming her up, so she decided to put her brain back in much less sexy territory. "If Lowri has never heard of Y Seren, maybe it didn't have anything to do with what's happened," Tamsyn said, and Bowen grunted.

"Is that an 'I agree, Tamsyn, you are a genius to point that out' kinda grunt, or is it 'You are a stupid human person who doesn't understand witchy business, of course that ugly piece of jewelry is why we're here' noise? I'm usually good at interpreting, but maybe the time travel fucked with my skills."

Bowen made another sound, this one she had no problem identifying. It was that half laugh thing he did when she'd genuinely amused him.

She loved that one.

"It's neither," he told her now. "It was more 'Not sure I believe it wasn't involved, but more open to the possibility at least, although I still wonder why Carys isn't here, given that she's the one who did the damn spell in the first place.'"

"That is a very verbose grunt, Bowen," she replied, and overhead, an owl hooted.

They walked on in silence for a few more moments, Tamsyn's hand still comfortably tucked into his elbow, and then she said, "Speaking of Carys, we've got a good twenty minutes or so of walking still ahead of us. Is this a good time to ask you about her fiancé? The one who died, I mean, not that Ken doll she was marrying."

Bowen didn't answer for a long time, long enough that Tamsyn was about to rush in and apologize for even asking, when he said, "She was engaged to my best mate, Declan. Met him at university, roomed with him for years."

Again, Tamsyn wished she could see him, but maybe, like last night, the darkness made this easier for him, so she just waited for him to go on even as her chest tightened at the grief in his voice.

"Declan is—was, fuck, I don't even know anymore—a good lad. Best lad, really. Takes the piss out of me all the time. You'd like him."

"I'm sure I would," she said gently, giving his biceps a small squeeze. "But . . . he's . . . he's dead, right?"

"Yes and no," Bowen said with a sigh, and even though he was just a silhouette against the deep purple sky, Tamsyn could see him lift a hand and rub it over his face briefly.

"Back at college, Declan and me . . . we were always looking for arcane spells. The really old, ancient shite no one had messed around with in ages. Mostly we just wanted to study them, see why the witches who invented them came up with them in the first place, figure out if they'd ever worked, if there was any kind of alteration that might make them work now or make them safer. It was supposed to be . . . academic, I guess. Or a way to show off to our teachers at Penhaven."

Tamsyn still couldn't see him, but she could hear a smile in Bowen's voice as he said, "Course, most of our teachers thought we were mad, and it made more than a few of them pretty hacked off that Declan might actually be a more talented witch than any of them."

Tamsyn smiled, too, and rubbed his arm. "Must've been nice for you, having someone just as obsessed with weird old magic as you are."

"It was," he said, and there was a heaviness in his voice now that Tamsyn recognized as grief. "Until I found this one spell. Christ,

I was so proud of the thing. Hunted it down from five different books because the witch who had made it had hidden it like that. Pieces of the spell spread throughout different grimoires from different centuries, nearly impossible to reassemble."

"But you did," Tamsyn said, lulled by his voice and their footsteps. It was full dark now, the clouds parting enough to reveal a smattering of stars overhead.

"I did," Bowen said, and those two words were filled with so much pain that Tamsyn couldn't stop herself from leaning her head against his shoulder, pressing her cheek to the damp fabric of his coat.

She kept her face against him as he continued: "I never meant for anyone to try it. Certainly not Dec, brilliant as he was. We weren't even sure what the damn thing *did*. Declan thought it was some kind of powering up ritual, increasing your natural magic. He was already plenty strong enough—so was I—so I didn't see any reason to attempt it. I just . . . Ah, fuck it, Tamsyn, if I'm honest, I was just showing off. Sticking it to my teachers a bit, maybe proving something to my da, I don't know. I was only twenty-one. Lads are stupid at that age."

"Girls are, too," Tamsyn told him, lifting her cheek from his arm. "I dated a DJ at that age. A *DJ*, Bowen."

He gave that huffing laugh again, then shook his head. "True, suppose lads don't have a monopoly on foolishness in their twenties."

"But my foolishness just resulted in my TV being stolen and

a remix of 'Evil Woman' with my name randomly spliced into it being played at clubs around my college," Tamsyn told him. "Seems like yours went worse."

"Much," he confirmed with a nod. "Declan got nearly obsessed with that fucking spell. Had to try it. Had me sourcing the ingredients, things I'd never even seen used before. Flowers I'd never heard of, water from some river in Norway, grass from a high hill on the Isle of Skye . . . I should never have tracked it down, any of it, but it was like . . . dunno, s'ppose it's like when people get gold fever or summat. Couldn't seem to make myself stop, and we were gassing each other up the whole time, the way lads do, and all the while I was thinking, 'We won't really do it, though. We'll just prove that we could.' And then Declan did the fucking thing."

They turned another bend in the road, and now Tamsyn could see the turrets of Tywyll House against the sky even as the clouds seemed to be moving back in, getting thicker.

"At first, I thought he'd just disappeared. There was this blinding flash of light, a smell like sulfur, and he was gone. Not even a mark on the floor where he'd been. I called his name, and I . . . I think I wanted it all to be some grand joke. That felt like something Dec would've done, you see. Trick me into doing a basic invisibility spell, scare the shit out of me, then reappear laughing his ginger ass off. But it wasn't a joke. He was gone."

"When I asked if he was dead . . ." Tamsyn said, trailing off, and Bowen tipped his head back to look at the sky.

"I said 'yes and no.' And that's the truth of it. Didn't see hide nor hair of him for weeks. His parents were ringing, and I kept making excuses. Told teachers he was sick because I didn't know what else to do. Meanwhile, I was spending every night tearing my bloody hair out trying to learn more about the spell, trying to see if I could bring him back. And then one night, he showed up again, only . . . only he wasn't him. He was like a ghost, but not a ghost. Could talk, could hear me, but you could see right through him. He said he had no memory of what had happened, no idea what he even was anymore."

"Oh, Bowen," Tamsyn said softly, and Bowen scrubbed at his face again.

"Anyway, that's when I got my da involved. I don't know what he told people or who he talked to at Penhaven, but the word got out that Declan had died in a spell gone wrong. A spell he was attempting alone, of course—couldn't let the Penhallow name be attached to a scandal like a boy dying."

There was something darker alongside the grief in his voice now, something Tamsyn suspected was shame, and she murmured, "You were young, Bowen. Practically a kid."

"I know that," he said. "And Saint Bugi knows Declan's reminded me that he was the one who decided to do this of his own free will. But . . ."

He trailed off, and Tamsyn could only nod.

The house was in sight now, lit up and cozy, and seeing it chased some of the lingering sadness from Bowen's story away.

They stopped there at the edge of the drive, and Tamsyn turned to him. "Thank you for telling me," she said, and now there was enough light that she could see his eyes: darker than hers, nearly black, and surrounded by thick lashes, because of course they were. He looked so sad and so handsome, and Tamsyn lifted a hand to his face, his beard damp against her palm.

"Oh, Christ, girl, you can't look at me like that and touch me," he said, his voice raw. "It's fucking hard enough resisting you as it is."

Tamsyn felt her stomach swoop, her heart flutter, and she was leaning in before she could even think, his lips so close, his body radiating heat against the damp chill of the night.

His breath was warm on her face, the soft hair of his beard just brushing her mouth, and in the space of a breath, they'd be kissing, but it was good, holding out like this, letting the moment stretch and heat up between them, breathing each other in until she pressed herself up on her tiptoes, her lips finally touching his . . .

And then, with a crack of thunder that could've brought Tywyll House crumbling to the ground, the skies opened up, and freezing rain poured down, soaking them both.

CHAPTER 16

B owen had never felt a particular need to punch the sky, but as soon as the first fat drops of rain landed on him and Tamsyn and she shrieked, stepping back from what was undoubtedly about to be one hell of a kiss, he was ready to go to war with weather itself.

Or maybe it was for the best, he reasoned, as they made a mad dash for the house, their coats pulled up over their heads, their boots nearly sliding on the slick lawn. Telling her the truth about Declan had cracked him open, left him raw and vulnerable in a way he wasn't used to being, and kissing her would've probably broken him even further, opening up a door he would've had no hope of ever closing.

And he needed it closed.

One of the footmen was there at the door, towels already in hand, and they both took them gratefully as Lady Meredith swanned in wearing tweeds and a worried expression.

"Oh, thank goodness," she said. "When Emerald said the

two of you had headed off to the village, I couldn't believe it. In this weather?"

"It was my fault," Tamsyn said, blotting at her sopping hair. "American."

Bowen wasn't sure what nationality had to do with this, but Lady Meredith's expression immediately cleared as she said, "Ah, yes, of course."

With that, she turned and flicked her fingers in the direction of the upstairs.

"I've started hot baths for each of you," she said, and sure enough, Bowen could hear the distant clanking of ancient pipes.

"That has to be a handy spell in a house like this," Tamsyn commented, and Lady Meredith nodded.

"Yes, it's second only to the spell that alerts me to Madoc digging in the garden the second he starts."

At that very moment, a distant alarm started ringing, and Lady Meredith rolled her eyes.

"That boy, I swear. Emerald! Go get your cousin!" she called out.

"It's raining!" came Emerald's reply, and with one elegant wave, Lady Meredith managed to both send a footman heading out toward the terrace and direct Tamsyn and Bowen up the stairs. "Tamsyn, the en suite in your room is for you. Bowen, your bath is through the hidden door on the right side of the bed. Tap the painting of Saint Cian three times and it'll open."

Together, he and Tamsyn trudged up the stairs and into their bedroom. He couldn't be sure, but Bowen thought Tamsyn's eyes briefly darted to the bed before she opened the door leading to the en suite bathroom, steam billowing out along with the scent of orange blossoms.

"You know, I've always thought magic seemed like more trouble than it's worth, but this? This is amazing." She turned back to him with a grin. "Hope your bath is just as good," she said, and then she shut the door behind her, the steam and scent still lingering.

Bowen crossed the room quickly, because if he spent a second contemplating her getting naked just a few feet away, slipping into hot water with an appreciative groan, her tanned skin going that peachy rose from the heat . . .

Thank sweet fuck Saint Cian was such a grim-faced-looking bastard, because that cooled some of Bowen's desire as he tapped three times on the painting, just as Lady Meredith had suggested, and sure enough, a panel in the wall swung open, revealing a second bathroom.

This one was smaller than the main en suite, but the tub seemed even bigger, a massive claw-footed antique that was nearly filled to the brim with steaming water. No orange blossoms here, but the deeper smell of bergamot mixed with something woodsy.

The room was lined in dark green tile, the fixtures copper, and the only light came from a small lamp on the corner of the sink. A thick pile of towels was stacked next to it, and as Bowen got undressed, he realized there was a full-length mirror in the corner.

He looked like a drowned rat, his long curls still damp as he yanked his jumper over his head, then reached out to turn off the taps.

Sinking into the water was indeed as blissful as he'd hoped, the heat so intense on his chilled skin that it tingled and burned at first before seeping deep into his bones.

With a low sound of pleasure, Bowen sank lower into the water, his arms braced on the sides of the tub as he leaned his head back and closed his eyes. He could've fallen asleep there, and damn near almost did, before he became aware of a small sound at the door.

Tap. Tap. Tap.

Sitting up so fast water sloshed over the curled sides of the tub, Bowen looked in the direction of the door and fully understood that saying he'd heard before, "half agony, half hope," because that's how he felt as the door swung open and Tamsyn stood there.

She was wearing a plush robe in a purple so deep it almost looked black in the dim light of the bathroom. Steam had curled the ends of her long hair, making tendrils of it stick to her flushed cheeks, and for a long while, she just stood there, facing the tub, facing him, her lips parted, the belt at her waist loose enough that the robe gaped open at the top, but not enough, not near enough.

From her vantage point, she probably couldn't see much of his body, concealed as it was by the high sides of the tub and the water cloudy with oil, but she was breathing hard all the same.

Bowen wasn't sure he was breathing at all, and when her hands went to her belt, he felt like his heart had stopped as well.

The velvet slipped from her shoulders, and she stood there

on the tile, naked—gloriously, perfectly naked. Her skin was as lovely, as golden all over, as he'd imagined; her breasts the perfect size for his hands, her nipples hard even in the warm room; and oh, Saint Bugi, Saint Cian, and every other saint he could think of, but he'd forgotten about the mirror in the corner.

Standing where she was, he had a perfect view of all of her, the curve of her hips, the dimples at the base of her spine, and the prettiest, plumpest arse he'd ever had the blessing to look upon.

"You're a wonder," he said to her, the words strangled and rough, but she must have liked them, because those gorgeous lips of hers slowly curled into a sly smile.

"You called me that once before," she told him, taking a step closer and kicking her robe out of the way. "But it was in an email. Have to say, hearing the words come out of your mouth is a very different experience."

"Seeing you like this is a very different experience," he managed to say, and she laughed at that, pushing that long fall of dark hair back off her shoulders.

She kept coming closer, and Bowen's hands instinctively clenched around the rim of the tub, his heart hammering, his cock hard, and every cell of his body aching for her.

"If you're just in here to prove that you're even more gorgeous than I'd thought, you've succeeded," he told her. "But if you don't leave now—"

"I'm not leaving," she said, and she was at the edge of the tub now, her eyes moving over him with unembarrassed, unabashed hunger.

"Your rule," he reminded her, and then she smiled again, lifting one delicate foot and slowly lowering it into the tub.

Her toes brushed his shin, and Rhiannon's tits, just that was enough to have him jumping like he'd been electrocuted.

"Bowen, we're in 1957. There's a chance you might not even be born. There's also a chance we could be stuck here forever. I think my rule should probably get fucked, don't you?"

He didn't answer her.

Not with words.

Instead, he reached out and put both hands on her waist, pulling her into the tub and into his arms.

She gave a spluttering laugh, falling against his wet and naked body a little awkwardly, her knees landing on either side of his thighs, water splashing onto the floor, but then he framed her face with both his hands and kissed her with every bit of longing, every bit of desire, every bit of *love* he'd been trying not to feel since that first night back at the pub in London.

It was probably too much, he told himself. Too fierce, too hungry, too desperate, but he'd wanted her too long to hold back now, and then he realized she was wrapping herself around him, one arm tight around his shoulders, the other hand fisted in his hair, pulling enough for it to hurt, but god, it felt good at the same time, so good that he groaned, or maybe that was her.

Both of them were pressing against each other, their bodies slick from the bath, her mouth almost as hot as the water, her tongue as sweet and perfect as he remembered, and he slid a hand down to cup one of her breasts, his thumb brushing back and forth over her nipple as she made the neediest sounds he'd ever heard.

Her arm still locked around his neck, her mouth still devouring his, Tamsyn took his hand and slid it lower down, his fingers skating over her stomach, her hip, and then he could feel *her,* the soft hair between her legs, the slickness of her sex, the warmth of her body.

She kissed him and held his hand there, moving her hips shamelessly, and he loved that, wanted her to take whatever she wanted from him, wanted to feel her make herself come with his fingers, but he wanted a lot more, too.

It was hard, tearing his mouth from hers, but Bowen did it even as she whimpered in protest, her lips seeking his.

He ducked his head, capturing one nipple between his lips and then his teeth, and Tamsyn gasped, her head falling back, the ends of her hair floating on the water.

Her hand fell away from his to reach up and clutch the side of the tub, but Bowen kept his fingers right where they were.

"Tell me what you want," he ground out against her breast, still touching her, but more gently now, softer.

"You," she gasped, her eyes closed, and Bowen's heart felt like someone had just tightened a fist around it.

"Picked up on that when you walked in here and dropped that robe, love," he said, and she tried to laugh, but he pressed a little harder between her legs just then so it turned into a moan instead. "I mean what you like. How you want me to touch you."

She raised her head and laid a hand on the back of his wet curls again, fingers tightening.

"I want you to fuck me," she told him, breathless, and all the air seemed to leave his lungs, too.

"Ah, *calon bach,*" he muttered before kissing her again, the taste of her every bit as good as he'd remembered.

As he'd dreamed.

"It's been a long time, *cariad,*" he said as his lips slipped down her neck, finding the spots that made her tug his hair even harder. "I want to. Believe me, I do."

"And you seem more than capable of it," she replied, her free hand slipping beneath the water to wrap around his cock in a way that had him dropping his forehead to her collarbone and struggling very hard not to embarrass himself.

"I am that," he said, even as her hand began to move, stripping the last bits of sanity and control from him.

"But . . ."

Lifting his head, he placed one hand on her cheek, loving the way she instinctively bent toward his touch, her whisky-brown eyes hazy and soft, her lips swollen. "Tamsyn, I haven't taken a lass to bed in nigh on five years now."

"You're not taking this lass to bed," she said, and her fingers tightened around him, pumping gently. "You're taking her to bath."

Bowen gave a choked laugh, closing his eyes and reaching down to still her hand. "I just mean . . . I've wanted you since the moment I saw you. I've thought about this a thousand times.

A million even. And I don't know . . . I could be too rough with you. You make me feel . . . Christ, girl, you make me feel wild."

Her eyebrows went up. "And that's a bad thing?"

"You deserve better," Bowen said, and he knew he wasn't just talking about sex now. "Soft sheets and . . . chivalry or summat, I don't know."

The smile on Tamsyn's face was as soft as her skin, as warm as the water surrounding them, and she laid both palms on either side of his face. "Bowen," she said, one cheek dimpling, "please trust me when I say soft sheets and chivalry are the last things on my mind right now. I don't want that. I've *had* that. What I want is you. Wild you. Rough you. All of you."

His hands slid down under the water to cup her arse, and she leaned in close, her teeth nipping his bottom lip.

"And I want it," she practically purred, punctuating the words with another nip that had his fingers flexing on her bottom. "Right. Now."

CHAPTER 17

If you'd asked Tamsyn just a few hours before what she thought about sex in a bathtub, she would've said it was overrated, the kind of thing that looked sexy in movies, but was never as good in real life.

That was before she slid into a bathtub with Bowen Penhallow, though.

She'd thought he might object again, pull that chivalrous card, insist they couldn't do this.

Instead, he took two deep breaths, his eyes never leaving hers, and then he growled—an honest-to-god *growl*—and all Tamsyn could do was hang on for dear life as he pulled her back into his arms and kissed the absolute hell out of her.

He was right—it was rough.

It was wild.

It was perfect.

His tongue tangled with hers, and she slid her hands over his wet biceps, loving the way the muscles bunched there as he held her so tightly, loving it even more when he suddenly sat up, sliding his hands down to her waist and easily lifting her up, turning her until her stomach was pressed against the edge of the tub, her hands braced on the rim as she went up on her knees, thighs spread wide.

Bowen was behind her, moving her hair to kiss the back of her neck, then lower, his lips moving over the knobs at the top of her spine, and when Tamsyn finally felt capable of opening her eyes, she realized why he'd positioned them like this.

The mirror.

She could see herself, wet hair and pink skin, eyes wild and chest heaving while she clutched the edge of the tub, and him behind her, his dark curls slicked back from his face, his beard dripping.

He was up on his knees as well, water spilling onto the floor, and Tamsyn found herself fascinated by the dark hair curling on his chest, the way the small silver medallion he wore caught the light from the lamp, the focused expression on his face as he smoothed a hand around the swell of her hip, his hand sliding forward to touch her exactly where she wanted him to touch her.

His fingers were firm, the pressure perfect, and he might have said it had been a while, but clearly he'd picked up skills somewhere.

Tamsyn wasn't sure whether she wanted to tear that other woman's hair out or send her an Edible Arrangement, but it didn't matter, not when he was touching *her* right now, looking at *her* body like it was some wonderful new magical artifact he'd just discovered.

Using his knee, Bowen spread her legs wider, and his fingers slid deeper, making her shudder and close her eyes.

But then she felt his other hand twist her hair around his fist, gently pulling so that she lifted her head, her eyes opening again.

"Look at yourself," he commanded in a voice straight from her dreams. "Watch how gorgeous you are."

And she was gorgeous. She was wet and her skin was pink and her mouth was open because she was breathing so hard, and her breasts were pressed at an awkward angle against the porcelain, but she'd never felt more beautiful than she did right now with Bowen's eyes meeting hers in the mirror, the serious expression on his face one she'd seen before, but never like this.

Never for her.

And it turned out this whole year of fantasies had been a waste, because nothing—absolutely nothing—could compare to the real thing.

Bowen's hand slid back between her legs, and she didn't close her eyes this time. She watched him and her in the mirror, the way his hand was obscured by the side of the tub, but the flexing of the muscles in his forearm left no doubt to what he was doing to her under the water.

She was close now, so close, but then Bowen groaned, and she could feel him, hard against her backside, and she let her knees spread even wider. "Now," she panted. "Please, Bowen, now."

God love a man who knew how to follow instructions, because he slid inside of her easily, the fullness of him combining with his touch to send her over the edge almost immediately, her cries bouncing off the tile.

Bowen cried out, too, his hands tight on her hips as he thrust, the water rocking around them, and Tamsyn kept her eyes glued on the mirror. He was so beautiful, his face contorted in a pleasure so intense it could've been mistaken for pain, and oh god, she was so in love with him.

So stupidly, crazily, completely in love with him.

And when he met her eyes in the mirror, she realized he might just be in love with her, too, and that was enough to have her shuddering again, her head falling forward so that her hair brushed the puddle of water on the tile as behind her, Bowen gave one last shout before pulling out of her, his hand dropping to his cock, but Tamsyn was already reaching around, taking hold of him and pumping once, twice, then hearing him cry out again as he came, warm wetness spreading over her palm as they both lay there, panting.

Ruined.

Wrecked.

Then, still trying to catch his breath, Bowen asked, "Wild enough for you?"

Tamsyn wanted to make a quip. She probably had a dozen, at least six of them werewolf jokes. But all she could do was croak, "Yup."

His laugh in reply was the best thing she'd ever heard.

"THAT WAS ACTUALLY very annoying," Tamsyn said several minutes later when they were dry and tucked into their massive bed. The fire was higher tonight, but they were both still so warm from the bath—and what had happened in the bath—that they hadn't even bothered with pajamas tonight, lying naked under the sheets.

"That was . . . what?" Bowen asked, turning his head to look at her. His hair had started to dry, curls rioting around his head in a way that was wildly endearing and so cute Tamsyn was fighting the urge to wrap one around her finger.

"Annoying," she repeated with a sigh as she rolled to her back. The sheet slipped down to her waist, but she didn't care, lying there with one hand thrown up by her head, the other flat on the mattress beside her.

"The sex?" Bowen clarified. "The . . . the sex was annoying?"

"Oh, no, the sex was *amazing*," Tamsyn said, shaking her head before turning to look at him. "That's what's annoying. You're already really smart and very handsome, and so being good at sex is, as you Brits like to say, overegging the pudding, frankly."

Bowen rolled onto his side to face her, his head propped on one hand. "I consider myself a fairly smart man, Tamsyn, but talking to you is occasionally like trying to translate . . . I don't know, Greek into Welsh, and then maybe into some dead or dying language. Like Cornish."

"Or summat," she finished for him, and he smiled at her, reaching out to tweak one nipple.

"Glad to see this hasn't changed one thing between us," he said. "You're still going to give me shit no matter what."

"Yup," she confirmed. "Even if we end up stuck in 1957 forever, I'll still be here, making fun of you."

Bowen's expression grew more serious then, his finger coming up to trace the line of her nose. "We're not going to get stuck here," he told her. "If the two of us can find ourselves together, how hard can it be to convince Harri and Elspeth to get *back* together?"

"Maybe we should introduce them to that magical bathroom," Tamsyn suggested, and was delighted by the absolutely horrified look that came over his face. "Bowen, you do realize your grandparents have to have sex for you to exist, right?"

"I can realize that on an intellectual level without ever having to think about it or, Rhiannon forbid, picture it."

"Fine," Tamsyn said, sighing as she slid farther down into the bed. "First thing tomorrow, we come up with a plan to fix their whole deal that *doesn't* involve you having to think about your grandparents doing it."

"Don't say 'doing it.'"

"Shagging."

"Stop it."

"Making the beast with two backs."

"That one is genuinely vile, and I've never understood it."

Grinning, sated, and happy—god, too happy, *scary* happy—Tamsyn reached for him, and it felt so good how easily he slid into her touch, his nose playing along her jaw, his lips and tongue placing a wet, sucking kiss just beneath her ear.

"But that's for tomorrow," she said, already sliding a thigh over his hip. "Now what was it you mentioned earlier about me deserving sex in soft sheets?"

CHAPTER 18

The next morning, Bowen sat at the breakfast table, drinking coffee and staring at his grandparents.

They weren't speaking at the moment, just studiously ignoring each other while they ate their eggs, and he wished Tamsyn would show up already, because she would surely know where to start with this whole "getting these two back together" plan.

Of course, he'd given Tamsyn plenty of reasons to sleep in this morning, he thought, hiding his smirk with his coffee cup. It wasn't like him to smirk—that was more Wells's territory. But he'd spent most of last night making love to the woman of his dreams, so a smirk felt well deserved. His brain was still spooling through images from last night.

Her in the bathtub, her skin wet, the room steamy from more than the water.

Tamsyn in the sheets, uninhibited as anything, her nails scoring his back, her fingers in his hair while he licked and sucked at her, the breathless way she said his name, the way her hips bucked beneath his mouth . . .

Clearing his throat, Bowen distracted himself by refilling his coffee from a silver pot. The last thing he needed was a hard-on while he ate breakfast with his grandparents, even if they didn't *know* they were his grandparents.

His eyes flicked toward the door again, hoping Tamsyn would appear, but no such luck. The only person coming into the breakfast room was Emerald, another one of those velvet ribbons—black this time—holding back her golden hair and yet another book in her hand.

She was so focused on the book she nearly collided with the Ming vase near the doorway, and saved herself only at the last moment with a startled "Oh!" The vase wobbled on its stand, and Emerald reached out with one hand to steady it. As she did, she lowered the hand holding the book, and an entirely separate book slipped out from between its pages, smaller and slighter.

Blushing furiously, the teenager stooped to pick it up, and Bowen pretended not to see. Probably something she wasn't meant to be reading, something "dirty," no doubt—Rhys had had a similar habit of hiding girlie mags in his spellbooks when he was a teenager—and Bowen wasn't about to blow up her spot on that.

Harri and Elspeth didn't seem to notice, and Emerald took her place at the table, reaching for the basket of toast that had been set in the middle of the table. Once she'd slathered a piece with butter and marmalade, she went back to reading, the book in one hand, toast in the other.

"Lady Meredith will have your head if she sees you reading at the table," Elspeth commented, and Emerald shrugged.

"Madoc has locked himself in one of the hidden chambers, and no one can figure out which one. She'll be busy for a while."

"Do you know which one?" Bowen asked, and Emerald looked at him over the top of the book. She had big hazel eyes, and there was no doubt that one day she'd be quite the beauty, but for now, she looked exactly like what she was: a teenager full of attitude and more than a little mischief.

"Maybe," she replied, taking a bite of toast and returning to her book.

Shaking his head, Bowen turned his attention back to Elspeth and Harri and said, "So, Harri, which branch of the Penhallows are you?" as if he didn't already know.

"The useless one," Elspeth answered for him. "The one whose magic has started to fade, which is why they sent him off to woo a powerful witch bride under *false pretenses*."

"False?" Harri echoed, his eyes going wide behind his glasses. "I bloody well loved you, Ellie. That's why I asked you to marry me."

"Huh, and your father's edict had nothing to do with it."

Throwing up his hands, Harri turned in his chair to face his erstwhile fiancée more fully. "Of course my father wanted me to pick a powerful bride. Of course he'd like a strong line of magic reintroduced into the family, especially after Gryffud bugger—" He stopped suddenly, his eyes flicking to Emerald, before amending, "After Gryffud left for America thirty years ago. He was the last Penhallow with any real power."

And he stole most of it from the Jones women there in Graves Glen, Bowen thought, but it was interesting, learning that his family, prior to his da, had been considered less powerful than they'd been. So weak, in fact, that Harri's father had sent him off in search of a bride with enough magic to perk up the bloodline.

For the first time, Bowen looked at these people not as *his* grandparents but as his father's parents. Was this why he was so obsessed with amassing magical power? Had they nearly lost it, only for Elspeth to introduce it back into their DNA?

He could see his father in her, that haughty chin, the high cheekbones, the stubborn set to her mouth, and for the first time in well over a year, he felt . . . wistful, maybe. Sad that Simon had never been the father any of them deserved, and had it all started here? Had the great love story between his grandparents, the one he'd always heard about growing up, actually been something darker, something more businesslike, than he'd been led to believe?

Hell, should these two even be together?

He was still pondering that when Tamsyn appeared in the doorway. She'd put on a black-and-white tartan skirt this morning, nipped in at the waist with a white belt, and paired with a white jumper that clung to curves he now had hands-on—and mouth-on—experience with, and she'd pulled her dark hair back into a low chignon at the base of her neck.

She looked pretty and proper, and he ached to muss up every perfect inch of her.

Her cheeks flushed a bit when she saw him, but then she spotted Harri and Elspeth, and with a bright smile and a cheery "Good morning!" breezed into the room.

After filling her plate at the sideboard, she slid into the seat next to Bowen, her thigh brushing his under the table, and thank god they'd gone with the pretense that they were married, because it meant it was perfectly natural for him to lean over and press his lips to her temple with a murmured *"Bore dai, cariad."*

Tamsyn blushed even more, but played it off with a little laugh as she fluffed her napkin in her lap. "One of these days, I'll learn Welsh so I can know what all you're calling me. *Cariad* could mean *old ball and chain* for all I know."

"It means *my love*," Harri supplied, and Tamsyn turned to Bowen with those eyes of hers filled with almost unbearable softness.

"Oh," she said quietly. "That's . . . well, that's . . . nice, then."

He hoped she didn't remember everything he'd called her last night, because some of those terms were not appropriate for breakfast conversation, especially when the other people at the table were his grandparents and a teenage girl.

"You called me that once," Elspeth said suddenly, turning to Harri. "When you first proposed. I think it was the last time I heard a term of endearment from you."

"Not true," he countered. "I called you *blodyn tatws* all the time."

"That means *potato flower*," Elspeth said dryly. "Not exactly the most romantic description in the world."

"It was what my grandda always called my nan," Harri said softly, and for a moment their eyes met, held.

Bowen found he was holding his breath, and under the table,

Tamsyn clutched his hand. He squeezed back, because he was definitely seeing what she was seeing. There was warmth there. Fondness.

Maybe even love.

Then Elspeth turned back to her plate and shrugged. "Well, that was a pretty piece of manipulation then, wasn't it?"

With a muttered curse, Harri stood up, tossing his napkin onto his chair and storming out of the room.

"So dramatic," Elspeth said to herself, then delicately dabbed her lips with her own napkin before rising and saying, "You see why the idea of marrying that man in two days' time was so abhorrent to me. He never actually loved me, and I deserve better than that. I deserve . . . well, what the two of you have," she said, gesturing between Bowen and Tamsyn.

With that, she also flounced from the room, and Tamsyn sagged back in her chair with a sigh. "Those two are impossible," she said.

Emerald spoke up from the end of the table. "You want the two of them to get back together. Why?"

Startled, Bowen looked over at the girl who was still reading her book while munching her toast. "How did you know that?"

"I've heard you talking about it," she replied, nonchalant. "Yesterday, when you were in the hallway." Then she lifted those big hazel eyes over her book and added, "I hear lots of things."

For a horrified moment, Bowen thought she might be referring to last night. Where in the bloody hell was Emerald's room anyway?

But then she set her book and her toast down, folding her arms delicately on the table, and said, "You two aren't here because you were invited to the wedding and had some kind of magical travel accident. You're from the future. Some spell sent you here, and now you're trying to get back to wherever you come from."

She leaned in closer, the edges of her hair dragging along her toast crumbs.

"Do you live in space where you're from?" she asked in a low voice. "Or have cars that fly? No, wait." Emerald held up a hand. "Don't tell me, I want to find out for myself one day. I plan on living a very long time and being a very frightening old lady."

"You're already a pretty frightening child, so I think you're on the right track," Tamsyn said, and Emerald smiled.

"Thank you. So you need to get Harri and Elspeth married because one of you is related to them, right? I'm guessing you"— she pointed at Bowen—"since you and Harri have the same last name, and you and Elspeth make that same expression all the time, like you just stepped in dog poo."

Bowen scowled. "I don't make that expression."

"You're doing it now," Emerald argued, and Tamsyn leaned over to study him before nodding.

"Yeah, you kind of are." Then she turned her attention back to Emerald. "You're clearly a bright and terrifying person, so do you have any ideas? How do we get those two to realize that they need to be together?"

Emerald screwed up her face, thinking. Then she said, "If I help you with this, will you teach me magic?"

"I'm not a witch," Tamsyn answered, but Emerald shook her head, pointing at Bowen.

"I meant him. Will you teach me some magic?"

Bowen shifted in his seat, stretching his legs out underneath the table. "I can't, love," he told her. "It's not a thing that can be taught. You're either a witch or you're not."

"Has anyone ever become a witch?" she asked. "Like . . . maybe it was inside them the whole time, but no one knew until suddenly they could do magic?"

Tamsyn was right, Emerald was bright and terrifying, but as she looked at Bowen with those big eyes, he was reminded that she was, in fact, a child. That was a child's fantasy, the secret witch taking the place of the hidden princess, a fantasy Bowen could understand but sadly knew was just that—a fantasy.

"Sorry, love," he said again, shaking his head. "And even if such a thing *were* possible, my own magic isn't working at the moment. Time travel apparently fuc—messes those kinds of things up."

"You can say that word in front of me," Emerald said brightly. "I've heard it lots of time, and I also heard the two of you *performing* that word last night."

"Well, if you'll excuse me, I'm going to go throw myself on the Yule log now, be right back," Tamsyn said, standing up from her seat, but Bowen caught the edge of her skirt, tugging her back into her chair.

"It's not polite to eavesdrop, much less bring it up at breakfast," Bowen said, doing his best to channel his da or, at the very least, Wells.

It must've worked, because Emerald looked a little chastened, dropping her head before looking back up and saying, "I apologize. But I'll still help you. Even if you won't teach me magic."

"And how do you plan on doing that?" Tamsyn asked, but before Emerald could answer, there was a high-pitched shriek from somewhere in the house, and Bowen heard Lady Meredith say, "Well, for Rhiannon's sake, Madoc, at some point you have to use your own common sense! Yes, yes, Caradoc, I know he's only four, but that's no excuse! How on earth does one get trapped in a *painting* anyway?"

There was a pause, and then, in an imperious shout that could've brought down the entire castle, Lady Meredith cried, "EMERALD!"

"Neither of you have seen me, and we'll talk later," Emerald said quickly, gathering up her book and rushing from the breakfast room.

For the first time since last night, Bowen was alone with Tamsyn—well, as alone as anyone ever was in a fuck-off big house like this—and he wasn't about to let the opportunity pass him by.

Hooking his ankle around the leg of her chair, he yanked, sending her tumbling against him, and she laughed even as she let herself be pulled onto his lap.

"Someone needs to talk to you about your tendency to manhandle women, Bowen," she said, but since her hands were already moving restlessly over his shoulders, her lower lip tugged between her teeth as she looked at him like perhaps he was the one on the breakfast menu, he didn't think she actually minded all that much.

"Don't manhandle women," he told her, nuzzling the side of her neck, sucking in that scent she wore, the one that smelled like orange and cloves, like she was Yule itself. "Only you."

"Only me," she mused in reply, sitting back to look into his eyes. "Only me for now?"

She was teasing him, or at least trying to, but he saw that flash of vulnerability in her eyes, that real question, so he answered it.

"Only you," he said again, looking into her eyes, making sure she understood what he was saying.

Bowen saw her throat move as she swallowed hard, then she leaned forward, kissing him entirely too filthily for this early in the morning, but not like he gave a single fuck about what was appropriate or proper when it came to this woman.

He was just letting his hands slide up her sides, testing the softness of that white jumper, when he heard a discreet "Ahem" from somewhere near the door.

Pulling himself away, he saw one of those endless servants standing awkwardly in the arch that separated the breakfast room from the hallway, and Tamsyn went to scramble off his lap.

Holding her in place with firm hands, Bowen channeled all the icy arrogance of his ancient bloodline to say, "What is it?"

Tamsyn's hands tightened a bit on his shoulders, so apparently she liked that side of him.

Something he definitely wanted to explore later.

The butler lifted a gloved fist to his mouth, coughed into it, and then said, "There is a visitor asking for you. The both of you."

Tamsyn looked down at Bowen in confusion, but he could only shrug, then gently help her off his lap. Taking her hand, he led her from the room with as much dignity as two people who'd just been caught groping each other before nine A.M. could muster and walked out into the grand foyer.

Upstairs, Madoc was still shrieking, and Lady Meredith was saying, "It's a painted goose, darling, how scary can it possibly be?"

But Bowen was looking toward the front door where Lowri stood, still wearing that same moth-eaten-looking cardigan she'd had on the day before and carrying that basket with that infernal cat, who blinked his eyes slowly at the pair of them.

"Lowri!" Tamsyn cried, dropping Bowen's hand and hurrying to the older woman. "Did you find anything out for us?" she asked, her voice barely a whisper.

Yesterday at the pub, the old woman had seemed cheerful, even amused by their situation, but now she clutched at Tamsyn's hands, her ancient face somehow even more creased with wrinkles.

And worry.

And, Bowen realized with a sinking stomach, fear.

"Oh, darlings," she whispered hoarsely, her eyes darting around as though she were afraid someone might be listening. "Yesterday, after we talked, I went back to my cottage and consulted my books. It took ages—as I said, not a usual type of magic, time travel, and I've only ever known the one—but I fear I gave you some dreadfully bad advice."

"What do you mean?" Tamsyn asked, her hands falling away from Lowri's, and the old woman looked back and forth at them, her lips trembling.

"It's better that I show you. Come with me. Both of you."

CHAPTER 19

The walk to the village was a lot nicer than it had been the day before.

As far as positives went, that was about all Tamsyn had.

Well, that and last night's truly amazing sex, but even that had lost a little of its luster once Tamsyn saw Lowri's worried face. Yesterday, the old woman had seemed so cheerful, so sure that everything would or at least *could* work out.

Now, she was hurrying down the path so quickly that Tamsyn had to run to catch up with her, and the basket at Lowri's hip bounced enough that Tamsyn worried poor Sir Bedivere might go tumbling into the road.

Of all of them, though, he seemed the least concerned, leisurely licking his paws as his owner practically sprinted down the high street.

Now that she wasn't facing freezing rain and stolen bikes, Tamsyn had time to admire the village as they passed. It had been decorated for the holidays, too, pine boughs and garlands strung on windowsills and streetlamps, candles burning in windows even though it was midmorning. The smell of baking bread lingered in the frigid air, and as Tamsyn looked around, she thought that maybe it wouldn't be that bad to be stuck here after all. Ultimate cottagecore.

But then she thought about her little Airstream, about her brother and her family, and no, no matter how quaint and cozy this place was, it wasn't home.

The main road turned slightly, and there, nestled just at the edge of the forest, was a stone cottage, smoke puffing from its chimney. Lowri opened the little gate in the wooden fence that surrounded the home, leading the two of them up a short slate pathway and into her home.

The first thing Tamsyn noticed was the smell, herbal and sharp, and something smoky underneath. Like the village, Lowri's house had been decorated for Yule, and there were pine garlands and candles in her windows, too, which was lovely but also seemed like a fire hazard if you asked Tamsyn.

Speaking of fire, there was one blazing away in the hearth, complete with an iron bar holding an honest-to-god cauldron.

As Lowri put her basket down, Sir Bedivere jumped out and made his way to a pillowy bed just near the fire, settling down with a sigh before closing those bright eyes, and Tamsyn wondered if she should get a cat when she got back home.

If she got back home.

Lowri was at the kitchen table, pushing away herbs and stacks of parchment, fumbling with a heavy leather journal of some kind, and as she flipped through it, Bowen and Tamsyn stepped closer, peering over her shoulder.

"Is this about Y Seren?" Bowen asked, and Lowri waved him off.

"I'm telling you, I've never heard of such a thing. No, this is about you and your predicament. Remember how I told you I'd met that one fellow, how he'd eventually headed out for parts unknown when he got stuck here?"

"Pretty much burned into our brains since you mentioned it," Tamsyn said wryly. "I mean, not exactly something we'd forget."

But Lowri was already shaking her head, white tendrils sticking out of her bun. "I was wrong, though. Look."

She pointed at the book, but all Tamsyn could make out was a lot of heavy calligraphy in a language she couldn't read.

Bowen could, though.

And he was frowning.

"What is it?" Tamsyn asked, and Bowen tapped the page.

"It's a warning against any sort of time magic. It's been done before, and in the fifteenth—no, sixteenth, Rhiannon's tits, this is hard to read—some witches spent real time working on it. And yes, a handful of them managed it and came back, but only once they'd completed whatever it was they went back to do."

"Right," Tamsyn said, resting her hand on the back of one of the cane chairs surrounding the table. "We knew that bit. And the ones that didn't got stuck in whatever time they'd gone back to."

"No," Lowri said, shaking her head. "That's what I was wrong about. They didn't get stuck, they just . . ."

She trailed off, making a sort of poofing motion with her hands, and Tamsyn looked to Bowen. "They just what?" she asked him. "Disappeared?"

"The book says 'ceased to exist,' which is the same thing, I s'ppose."

Maybe so, but it sure as shit sounded a lot scarier to Tamsyn.

"So what?" she asked the pair of witches now, hand still gripping the chair so tight her knuckles were white. "If we don't get your grandparents back together in . . . two nights? We just vanish from the planet? Like we never even existed?"

"That appears to be the long and the short of it," Lowri said, then shook her head, her blue eyes sad. "Oh, that poor lad. All this time I thought he was having a grand old time in the city somewhere. But instead, he'd just . . . poofed."

Something very close to panic started thudding in Tamsyn's chest, cold sweat slicking down her back. "I really don't want to poof," she said. "Firmly anti-poofing."

"We won't," Bowen assured her, reaching out to take her free hand, but his fingers were just as icy as hers, and she hadn't missed the way Lowri kept looking at the both of them with pity, like they were already gone.

Closing her eyes, Tamsyn took a deep breath through her nose.

"Okay," she said. "So the stakes are a little bit higher than we realized. But I thrive under pressure, don't I, Bowen?"

"Better than anyone I know," he replied, and the quickness with which he said it, the absolute conviction shining out of his dark eyes . . . if Tamsyn weren't already in love with him, that would've done it.

"We'll fix this," she said, and wondered how many times she would have to say it before she actually believed it.

"Course you will, dear heart, course you will," Lowri said, but she was already rummaging in yet another basket for something. "But never hurts to have a little extra protection." She handed them both little bundles wrapped in muslin and attached to leather thongs. "Made these myself. Why I wanted you both to come here. Something has always been off with magic around Tywyll House, and I didn't want to risk them getting tainted by the place before you'd had a chance to put them on. Go on, go on," she said, urging them both to put the little packages around their necks.

Tamsyn thought whatever was in hers smelled like mothballs and . . . gin? She took a deeper sniff. Juniper. Maybe some rosemary thrown in. In any case, she'd been in this business long enough to know that when a kindly and ancient witch handed you an amulet of protection, you put the fucking thing on.

So she did, slipping the little bundle underneath her sweater while Bowen did the same with his.

"The solstice is in two days," Lowri said, as if either of them needed reminding. "That'll be the deadline. I'll keep searching here, seeing if I can find anything else that might be of help."

"You've been a tremendous help already, Lowri," Bowen told her, laying one hand on the woman's frail shoulder. "Honestly, we can't thank you enough."

Lowri smiled at that, patting Bowen's hand. "Never let it be said a Jones doesn't do all she can for her fellow witches."

"Jones?" Tamsyn echoed, glancing at Bowen, who met her eyes with a shrug.

"It's a common enough Welsh name, but . . . you don't have any relatives in America, do you, Lowri?"

Lowri beamed. "Indeed, indeed, my cousin Anwyn went years ago. Ended up someplace in the South, I believe. Georgia?"

"Graves Glen," Bowen said, more to himself than to Lowri, but she nodded.

"Aye, that's the place."

It was probably silly that it made Tamsyn feel better, knowing this woman was an ancestor of Vivienne and Gwyn Jones, especially given that she was pretty sure she was never going to be their favorite person, but it did. It felt like a sign, an omen that this would all work out for them in the end.

Somehow.

"Well, if you'll excuse us then," Tamsyn said, letting go of the chair, "it seems like we have some grandparents to trap."

"I have no idea what that means, but I wish you luck all the same!" Lowri replied, and Tamsyn stepped forward, kissing the old woman's cheeks, as wrinkled and soft as old parchment.

"Thank you," she said, and Bowen echoed, gruffly.

"Yes, thank you, Lowri. And if you *do* see something about Y Seren, let me know."

With that, they took their leave, Tamsyn reluctant to step back out into the cold after the cozy warmth of Lowri's cottage.

Or maybe she just didn't want to head back to the house now that she knew failure of their mission wouldn't just result in living in the '50s.

It would mean not living at all.

She didn't say anything as they started the walk back through the village, and neither did Bowen. He did take her hand, though, holding it tight as they passed the pub, the tiny village post office, and the massive Christmas tree put up in the main square.

It wasn't until the village of Tywyll was behind them that Tamsyn finally said, "You're still hung up on Y Seren, huh?"

"Someone was willing to pay a lot of money for it. Carys was holding it when she sent us back here. I don't care that it's nowhere in Lowri's books. It's involved in this somehow."

"Well, maybe you tackle that while I work on getting Harri and Elspeth to get over themselves and *on* each other."

"Please—"

"Don't say that, I know," Tamsyn replied, swinging their joined hands. "Just trying to distract myself from the fact that I might only have forty-eight hours of existence left. You know how it is."

Bowen's grip on her hand tightened, and before Tamsyn knew quite what was happening, he was jerking her off the path and into the woods that surrounded Tywyll House.

"What?" Tamsyn managed, laughing a little as she stumbled along behind him, leaves clinging to her wool stockings, her brogues sliding on the uneven forest floor.

Finally, once they were deep in the trees, Bowen stopped,

and suddenly Tamsyn was whirled around, her back against the trunk of a massive oak, and Bowen's mouth was on hers, hungry and desperate.

He may have caught her by surprise, but it had never taken Tamsyn long to catch up, and she kissed him back just as fiercely, her leg hitching up against his hip.

Bowen caught her underneath her knee, moving against her, and Tamsyn's hips matched his rhythm easily, the cold afternoon no match for the heat kindling between them,

"You've got a hell of a lot more time left than forty-eight hours, Tamsyn Bligh, I fucking swear it to you," Bowen said when he pulled away, his forehead pressed again hers. "I will get us out of this."

"We'll get us out of this," she corrected him, tugging at his hair, and he nodded, kissing her again, not as passionately this time, more like he was sealing a promise.

"We," he agreed, and this time when he kissed her, it was softer, gentler.

It was still enough to have her sighing and reaching for his hand, guiding it underneath her skirt.

When his fingers found her bare, he jerked back, surprised, and Tamsyn smiled at him even as she tilted her hips deeper into his touch, encouraging. "I always thought garter belts must've been a huge pain in the ass, and I'm not going to lie, they kind of are, but then there are some advantages they have over tights. Like easy access."

Bowen's lips quirked in a quick smile. "Unless you're wearing knickers," he reminded her, and she brushed her mouth against his.

"Now why would I do something silly like that?"

Their hands met and fought over his belt briefly, and then he was unbuckled, unbuttoned, shoving his trousers down just enough to free his cock and slide it inside of her.

She was already wet from his touch and the thrill of this, being taken against a tree in the middle of a forest, better than any fantasy she'd ever dreamed up, the sky blue and cold overhead, the bark rough against her back, wreaking hell on her sweater and her hair, probably, but she didn't care. Not when Bowen's lips were on her neck, his breath hot against her ear as he said things in Welsh, things she suspected were filthy as hell and sweet all at the same time.

At least that's how his voice sounded to her, and she hitched her leg higher up against his side, clutching his back, murmuring encouragements—"More," "Harder," "God, right there"—until he grabbed her hip, angled her just right, and her orgasm rushed up from her core, the sounds coming from her mouth primal, wild.

Bowen went to pull out of her, but she held him tight, shaking her head. "IUD," she told him. "I meant to tell you last night, but—"

He cut off her words with another kiss, and then she could feel him coming inside of her, triggering another, smaller orgasm that left her knees trembling, and her entire body feeling limp and sticky and sore and perfect.

They stayed there a long while, Bowen's face buried in her neck, Tamsyn still holding on to him, one leg wrapped around his waist.

"I meant what I said," he told her, his breath still hot on her skin. "We're getting out of this and back to where we belong." Lifting his head, he looked in her eyes and held her face with both hands. "But if somehow we don't . . . if these are the last forty-eight hours of our lives—"

"Don't," Tamsyn said, but Bowen shook his head, stubborn as ever.

"If they are," he repeated, "then I'm disappearing from this earthly plane as happy as I've ever been, *calon bach*."

Tamsyn's throat was suddenly tight, her eyes stinging. "Me, too," she said, and then asked, "What does that one mean, by the way? *Calon bach*?"

"Little heart," Bowen replied, a slight flush staining his cheeks. "You know. On account of you being . . . wee."

"Short," she corrected, even as her heart squeezed tight in her chest. All these beautiful things he had been calling her, all these beautiful things he'd been thinking about her, and she'd never known.

But now that she did, she'd be damned if one little spell gone wrong was going to keep her from hearing and knowing everything he had to say to her for the rest of their lives.

"We need to get back," she told him as they gently disentangled themselves. "Time is running out, and while your grandparents aren't quite as hopeless as I'd originally thought, I'm not sure they can get their shit together in two days."

"Oh, they can," Bowen said. "And they will."

THEY'D MANAGED TO mostly clean themselves up by the time Tywyll House came back into view, although Tamsyn knew she had a hole in the back of one stocking, and while Bowen said he didn't see anything, she was pretty sure there was still a leaf or maybe a piece of bark stuck somewhere in her hair.

As they approached the front steps, the heavy front door creaked open, and Emerald dashed out to meet them, wearing a pair of dungarees and an old sweater, another velvet ribbon—blue now—holding back her hair.

"There you two are!" she said, running up to them only to pull up short. "Were you two shagging in the woods?"

Tamsyn shot Bowen a look, but he was blinking owlishly at Emerald, who rolled her eyes and walked forward, snagging that elusive piece of bark out of Tamsyn's hair.

"Told you so," Tamsyn muttered to Bowen, who only grunted in reply, his face practically scarlet.

"I can't wait to grow up and get married," Emerald said happily as she handed the bark to Tamsyn, who, unsure what exactly she was meant to do with it, shoved it in the pocket of her skirt. "And speaking of," Emerald went on, both hands clasped behind her back as she rocked forward on the balls of her feet, smiling smugly, "I have something to show the pair of you. Come on."

CHAPTER 20

M aybe it's something about this house," Emerald said a few moments later as she, Bowen, and Tamsyn all sat in the little, older kitchen Madoc had shown Bowen and Tamsyn to when they'd first arrived at Tywyll House in their own time.

It was warm and smelled pleasantly of spiced things, but Bowen couldn't appreciate that right now given that he currently had his face pressed to the wood of the table, his eyes shut.

"You did a great job, Emerald," Tamsyn said, and Bowen could hear her pat the younger girl on the back. "I mean . . . very thorough."

"To be fair, they were only kissing when I ran out to get you two," Emerald replied. "I didn't think they'd already be—"

"Stop it," Bowen said, the words muffled by the table.

He wasn't sure how long it might take him to forget the sight of his grandparents . . .

No, he didn't even want to finish that thought.

Not even when Tamsyn laid her hand on his back and said, "Retinal trauma aside, this is a good thing, Bowen! We did it.

Harri and Elspeth are definitely—like, really, *really* definitely—back together."

Bowen grunted.

"How did you manage it?" Tamsyn asked Emerald, and Bowen sat up to see the teenager practically preening as she leaned back in her chair with a steaming teacup.

"Simple, really. Same way I'm always tricking Madoc into hiding in those same passageways. I pretend I've seen something very interesting, I get them to go in with me, and then I lock them in until they start screaming. Or, in Harri and Elspeth's case . . . Well, I suppose that also involved some screaming."

Bowen ground the heels of his hands into his eyes with a sigh. "I'd almost stopped picturing it, I really had."

"Well, we commend your service, Emerald," Tamsyn said, pouring her own cup of tea, "but I really feel the need to reiterate that you're a very frightening child."

"I am!" Emerald said happily, then leaned forward. "So now will you tell me why it was so important you get those two back together? Is it because of something magical?"

"Something like that," Bowen said, and Emerald screwed up her face.

"It's really bloody awful being a non-witch in a family of witches. No one tells you anything interesting about magic because they assume you won't understand it, or they're afraid you'll try it."

Bowen was about to give her some sort of bland comfort, some assurance that just because she didn't have magic, that didn't mean she wasn't important. Look at Tamsyn, the most wonderful woman in the world as far as he was concerned, and *she* couldn't do magic.

But then he stopped, something about her words tickling something in the back of his brain, some memory.

The book she'd been hiding.

He'd assumed it was just a romance novel, something scandalous Lady Meredith might have given her a hard time about reading, but maybe it was something more.

"What was that book you had?" he asked her. "The one you're hiding in a copy of *Rebecca*?"

The guilty expression that flashed across her face told him he was right: this was more than just a filched copy of *Lady Chatterley's Lover* or something similar.

"Just something I found in the library here," Emerald said, reaching into the pocket of her dungarees and pulling out a rolled-up booklet.

Magic and Everyday Spells was written in swirling font on the front, and when Bowen paged through it, he frowned. None of it appeared to be legitimate magic, but there was just enough in there to make him worry. Some of the words, the incantations . . . they weren't right, but they were close enough that in the wrong hands . . .

"Confiscating this for now," he told her, and Emerald gave him such a ferocious scowl he almost sat back in his chair.

"You're not my father," she told him with an imperious lift of her chin. "*And* I just did you a huge favor, so how is it fair to go stealing my things?"

"She's got you there," Tamsyn murmured, sipping her tea, and Bowen glared at her.

"You're supposed to be on my side."

"I am unless you're being high-handed, and you kind of are right now."

St. Bugi's balls, he had sounded a bit like his father. Or Wells. Wasn't sure which was worse, so in the end, he handed Emerald back her book.

"Just don't go around saying any of the spells in there," he said. "No telling where all that was cobbled together from. If you're serious about studying magic, I can talk to someone about sending you to Penhaven in America. It's for witches, mostly, but they have a human side of the school as well, and I'm sure someone knows what to do with a human from a witch family who wants to learn magic."

"Really?" Emerald's eyes were big as saucers, the hero worship in them clear as day, and Bowen was surprised how nice that felt.

"Really," he promised. "But stay out of trouble."

"I will," Emerald said, nodding so hard it was a wonder her head didn't snap clean off.

Then she was up from the table, the chair shrieking over the slate as she shoved it back, and Bowen and Tamsyn watched her vanish into the dark hall.

"You're going to be a good dad someday," Tamsyn said, and the words startled him so much that he almost jumped.

Him, a da.

It was nothing he'd ever thought of before, nothing he'd ever wanted or even thought he could have. Doing archaic magic on a mountain in North Wales didn't exactly lend itself to babies or small children.

But a child.

One with Tamsyn's pretty eyes and smart mouth, someone to teach magic to, a cousin for wee Taran.

Oh, Christ, he suddenly ached for it, but then, as always, he remembered Declan.

He had a duty to fulfill to that man, and until it was done, everything else had to wait.

Even Tamsyn.

He didn't say any of this out loud, but Tamsyn reached over and took his hand before asking gently, "Bowen, has he ever asked you to devote everything to helping him? To put your life on pause until he's back or released or whatever the end of all this is?"

Bowen squeezed her hand, not answering for a long time. No, Declan had never asked it of him. Had only ever blamed himself for the accident, really. He'd been the one to say the words, after all; the one who wanted to try the spell.

But if Bowen had found the right words to stop him, if he hadn't sourced the ingredients . . .

If, if, if.

"That's what you hired me for, isn't it?" she asked. "You're looking for some artifact that will reverse it or bring him back, but you're just throwing spaghetti at the wall right now, and sending me to get the spaghetti." She shrugged before reaching up to pull another little bit of bark from her hair. "Not that I mind being the spaghetti fetcher, but I wish you'd told me that's what I was doing. Maybe I could've helped or asked around a little more specifically."

"Maybe," Bowen acknowledged. "But . . . it's not always easy for me to open up to people."

"This is incredibly shocking news," Tamsyn deadpanned, making him chuckle, and he squeezed her hand again.

"Not like you do a lot of it, either, my girl. I still haven't heard just why you were so adamant about never getting involved with people you work with."

"And you still won't," she said, leaning closer to lift their joined hands off the table to kiss his knuckles. "Saving that one for when we're back home. Which . . ." She looked around the rapidly dimming kitchen. Outside, the sun was setting, and there was a delicate lacing of frost forming on the window. "Shouldn't we . . . I don't know, be poofed back or whatever by now? I mean, if we were sent back to make sure your grandparents get married, mission more than accomplished, right?"

Bowen had been thinking something similar, but didn't mention it because it would mean he'd once again have to talk about what he'd seen in that passageway, and he might never be ready for that.

"Of course, I guess we *did* just see them banging," Tamsyn mused, and yup, there it was again, the Indelible Image of his grandparents shagging against a wall like their lives depended on it. "Maybe they're not *officially* back together yet," Tamsyn went on. "So we don't get to go back until that ring is on that finger, you know?"

"Maybe," Bowen agreed, but it was bothering him a bit, that nothing had changed now that Harri and Elspeth were—graphically—back together.

Unless that was just some sort of Goodbye Shag, and he and Tamsyn still had their work cut out for them.

Or . . .

"You're still thinking about Carys and Y Seren, aren't you?" Tamsyn asked, and Bowen glanced up at her from beneath his brows.

"Hmmph," he said.

"Which means *yes,*" Tamsyn replied, propping her chin on her hand. "I'll find a way to ask Lady Meredith about it provided we don't get poofed back before I have a chance." Then she leaned back, stretching her arms. "But I don't think I have to, because I'm telling you, we're gonna find out it wasn't *just* getting them back together, it was getting them *married*. And that's not until the solstice."

"Which will only give us two more nights to figure out what to do if we're wrong," Bowen reminded her.

Standing up, Tamsyn came around behind his chair to press a kiss on the top of his head. "Don't be such a pessimist. Now come on, let's go get cleaned up."

Tilting his head back, Bowen looked at her gorgeous upside-down face.

"When you say 'cleaned up' . . ."

"I mean I want you to take me back to that big bathtub and fuck me again, yes," she answered.

Bowen shot to his feet so quickly, he nearly clocked Tamsyn on the chin, making her laugh as she gave an exaggerated stumble backward.

Arms around each other's waists, they made their way down the narrow, dark hallways to the main staircase, the smell of candles and evergreen strong, and when Bowen glanced out a nearby window, he saw that a light snow was falling.

"It's really lovely here when there's not a ghost screaming about everything," Tamsyn observed, and Bowen nodded, but he was slightly distracted by the figures coming up the front steps.

It was Harri and Elspeth, Elspeth wearing a long white cape with a fur-trimmed hood, Harri in a dark suit.

"What is it?" Tamsyn asked, but Bowen was already tugging her down the hallway.

They reached the main entrance just as the butler opened the door to a laughing and snow-dusted Harri and Elspeth, who both turned wide smiles on Bowen and Tamsyn when they spotted them.

"Oh, you two! Wonderful, you can be the first to congratulate us!"

"Congratulate?" Bowen echoed, and Elspeth held out her left

hand, now weighed down by the heavy cabochon ruby that all Penhallow brides wore.

Bowen had just seen it on Vivienne's hand a few weeks ago/ several decades from now.

"Harri and I had a little mishap today," Elspeth said, sharing a knowing look at Harri that, had Bowen's entire heart not been sinking somewhere north of his toes, would've made him wish yet again that Bleach for Eyes was a thing one could buy. "And we got to talking, and we realized we've both been so very stupid. Well, mostly me, I have been stupid."

"How dare you talk about my wife that way, pistols at dawn," Harri said to her, making Elspeth throw her head back with laughter as Harri leaned forward to press a kiss to the side of her neck.

"Wife?"

Now it was Tamsyn's turn to repeat things while looking vaguely ill, but luckily Harri and Elspeth were so caught up in each other, they didn't notice.

"Wife," Harri confirmed, pulling Elspeth in front of him and wrapping his arms around his waist. "Once we realized what utter fools we'd been, we didn't want to put off being wed for one more moment. The High Witch who was supposed to come marry us had obviously made other plans when we told him the wedding was off, but luckily, there was a woman in the village who's able to perform weddings, and so she did. Right there in her little cottage with the only witness a big black cat named—"

"Sir Bedivere," Bowen and Tamsyn said as one, and Elspeth laughed again, nodding.

"Oh, so you know her, then! Lovely woman, and so thrilled to marry us. Honestly, I think she may have been more excited than we were!"

Lowri, dear heart she was, would have been thrilled.

She would've thought she was saving us, Bowen thought, and Tamsyn put her hand on his arm, squeezing.

"Now," Harri said, and then stooped to scoop Elspeth into his arms. "If you'll excuse us."

She cried out, still laughing, and clutched at his jacket. "Harri, really," she said, but Harri was already heading for the stairs, practically running, as Elspeth bounced in his arms, and there was a part of Bowen that wanted to be happy for them.

It had been true, after all, in its own unique way. His grandparents *were* a love story, just a little fierier than he'd been led to believe. They'd found their way back to each other, and wasn't that a beautiful thing?

It was.

And so he was happy for them.

Completely happy.

And also totally fucked.

CHAPTER 21

T amsyn had had lots of experience conning people over the years.

And no, she didn't love using that word, because it wasn't exactly a nice thing to do, *conning* a person, but she'd figured out a long time ago that there was no sense in calling ugly things by pretty words just so she could feel better about herself, so she was all for calling it like it was.

Which meant that right now, she was attempting to con the absolute *shit* out of Lady Meredith.

The two of them were sitting in the formal dining room, a pile of evergreen, holly, and copper wires before them. All the women guests at the house with the exception of Elspeth, who was busy enjoying her wedding night—well, wedding *evening*—were at the table, taking the boughs, the berries, and the wire, and twisting them into wreaths. A Yule tradition, Tamsyn had learned, and if she wondered why it was one that only the women seemed to do while the men ran around drinking whisky and shooting things, she reminded herself that it *was* the '50s, after all.

And making wreaths was kind of nice, what with the snow falling outside and candles flickering along the table and on the walls. It reminded Tamsyn of Christmases back home, everyone gathered around, baking, making ornaments, that kind of thing.

Bowen would probably be shocked to learn she'd had such a basic upbringing, given what she did for a living, but that was another story she could tell him once they were home together. She had to keep telling herself that that was going to happen, because otherwise, it made all this—the wreaths, the candles, the quiet gathering of women—feel like the lead-up to her funeral or something, and that made her shiver from a lot more than the cold.

So no, they were getting home. If it hadn't been Harri and Elspeth getting married, then Bowen must've been right all along, and it was Y Seren, and that meant getting some answers from Lady Meredith.

It's why Tamsyn had basically bowled that Lora woman over to be sure she got a seat next to the lady of the house, and why she also kept surreptitiously topping off the little "tipple," as Lady Meredith had called it, from the crystal decanter of gin on the table between them.

"It's so lovely getting to participate in all these Yule traditions, Lady Meredith," Tamsyn said now, shamelessly sucking up. "I really didn't know much about the holiday before Bowen and I were married."

She really did love saying that, which was incredibly stupid, but at this point, she was going to be happy for any little moments of joy she found. That clock was ticking, and if it ran out . . .

Nope, focusing on the task ahead.

"And thank you again for lending me your clothes. I really don't know what I would've done since I don't think nudity is a Yule tradition."

From farther down the table, Lora shot her a scandalized look, but Lady Meredith just laughed merrily, patting her golden hair with one hand. "Well, this Yule it seems to be," she said, throwing Tamsyn a saucy wink. "Two sets of newlyweds in one house, one can practically feel the energy crackling through the place, darling. I'm surprised we haven't all gone up in flames."

Tamsyn laughed, too, even as she blushed, ducking her head a little. She'd spent only a little time with Lady Meredith, but from what she remembered of the older version, the woman had enjoyed being the one to scandalize or shock, so Tamsyn had to be sure to play her part, too, the blushing newlywed who couldn't believe all these daring things a lady of Meredith's standing was saying.

"It's been so kind of you to share so much with us, sincerely," Tamsyn went on. "Your home, your clothes . . . even your jewelry! Those pearl earrings you let me borrow yesterday were so lovely."

Lady Meredith waved one elegant hand carelessly. "Oh, darling, I have more than I could wear in one lifetime. It would be wrong to hoard it all like a dragon. Even if I am Welsh."

She laughed and took another sip of her drink, and Tamsyn seized her opening: "And you have so many gorgeous pieces. That brooch you were wearing the night we first arrived? Stunning. I've really never seen anything like it. Is it a family heirloom?"

"Y Seren?" Lady Meredith asked, and gave a rather unladylike snort. "God, no. That's a piece Caradoc picked up for me from some local family desperate to sell the thing. Tacky, if you ask me, but it is seasonal, and Caradoc loves me in both emeralds and rubies, so I'm always forced to trot it out this time of year."

It wasn't exactly the answer Tamsyn had been hoping for, and she frowned, sucking at her thumb from where a piece of holly had pierced the skin. "Is it . . . It's just that Bowen told me that some pieces of jewelry have spells attached, or are infused with magic. That piece was so striking, I assumed it was something like that."

"Rhiannon's thighs, no!" Lady Meredith said, then gave a little burp she tried to cover with one hand. "It's just an extravagantly ugly piece of decoration that undoubtedly cost some poor sod entirely too much to have made, which is why Caradoc got it for a song." Frowning, she set down her pile of evergreen and holly. "Why is it men take such pleasure in giving you a gift and then telling you how little they paid for it?" Then she shrugged and took another drink. "In any case, if you admire it, you're welcome to wear it tonight when we all go wassailing."

Tamsyn had no idea what "going wassailing" entailed, although she had a vague memory of the concept from some Christmas carol, but it could've meant dashing naked down the high street, and she would've done it happily if it meant Y Seren was in her hands.

"Thank you, Annie," she said, sincerely, and Lady Meredith startled, one hand flying to her impressive bosom before she tilted her head to one side, considering.

"Annie," she mused. "Do you know, no one's ever called me that before, and I should probably rap your knuckles for the informality, my girl, but I rather like it. Annie. Yes."

Half standing out of her chair, Lady Meredith leaned on the table and called down: "Do you hear that? You're all to call me 'Annie' from now on. Well, not you, Lora, but the rest of you who are my friends. Annie." Then she sat back in her seat and reached over, taking Tamsyn's hand. "I don't know why I like you so much, but I do, Tamsyn Penhallow."

Tamsyn almost corrected her without thinking, but then, as the words sank into her bones, warming her as well as any bath she'd ever had—well, maybe not *any* bath—she was glad she hadn't.

If nothing else, if this all went tits up and there was no saving them, at least for the next and maybe last day she'd spend on earth, she'd be Tamsyn Penhallow.

IT WAS PAST ten o'clock that night when they all gathered in the front hallway of Tywyll House, the whole party dressed in evening finery, but covered in long velvet cloaks of the deepest green, each of them wearing a holly crown and holding a lit taper in their hands.

Tamsyn wore an evening gown in a deep, deep scarlet, and sitting heavy over her heart, hidden by her cape, Y Seren glittered.

She hadn't had a chance to talk to Bowen yet. After all the wreath making, she'd been hustled up to her room by one of the maids, who'd actually helped her dress and assured her that Bowen had a valet in a separate room doing the same for him.

So when he joined her in the crowd by the front door, she moved in close, opening her cape just the barest bit so that he could see the brooch.

His eyes went wide, then flew back to hers. "How—" he started, but then Lady Meredith was coming down the stairs, resplendent in gold, holding a thicker candle than the rest of them, and calling, "Beloved guests. Shall we brighten this dark night?"

A cry went up from the group as a footman circulated with a silver tray of tiny crystal glasses filled with a clear liquid, and each guest took one.

Tamsyn threw hers back like she saw everyone else doing and quickly regretted that decision, because whatever was in the glass tasted like someone had managed to distill a Yule log—evergreen and fire and smoke.

Eyes watering, she put her empty glass back on the tray just as Madoc made a jump for his own glass.

The footman skillfully lifted the tray over the little lordling's head, and Madoc's frown was fearsome. "Traditions are traditions!" he insisted. "You cannot wassail without Fire's Draught, and I am lord of this manor! Every tradition has to involve me, because if it doesn't, that's how houses end up *cursed*. In the thirteenth century, a Lord Meredith was denied his Fire's Draught, and that same year, a *dragon descended on the house and ate them all up!*"

"Absolutely none of that happened, Madoc, and you know the rules about Fire's Draught. Not until you're fifteen. Speaking of . . ."

With another one of those graceful gestures, Lady Meredith indicated Emerald should step forward. For once, she was without her velvet ribbon, her hair in a sophisticated updo tonight, her dress black and spangled with silver sparkles.

Eagerly, she took a glass from the tray and sucked it back with the same enthusiasm the adults had, only to immediately turn bright red, her eyes filled with tears. "Oh, that's vile!" she cried, but that only made the other witches laugh, and Caradoc thumped her heartily on the back.

"You'll be glad for it once you're out there for hours, *sosej*," he said, then turned to the assembled crowd. "A happy Yule to all. It has long been Meredith family tradition to greet the dawn of this holiday with a visit to the village, bearing candle, holly, and song. Are we all ready?"

"Are we?" Tamsyn asked Bowen in a low voice, and he nodded at the spot on her dress where Y Seren was hidden by her cloak.

"Here's hoping," he said, and with that, he took her arm, and the party headed out into the winter night.

CHAPTER 22

Bowen's heart pounded as they made their way down the steps, the group ahead of them already launching into "In the Bleak Midwinter" sung in Welsh.

But he kept hold of Tamsyn's arm, holding her back until they were at the very rear of the group, the others a series of bobbing lights headed for the road through the forest.

"They won't notice us missing for a while," he told her in a low voice, trying to lean in close and keep the bloody stupid holly crown on his head at the same time—quite a feat, really.

"So you have a plan?" she whispered.

He did, in a manner of speaking. Basically, it was take Y Seren back into the maze, say some words over it, and hope for the fucking best, but he wasn't sure that's what Tamsyn wanted to hear right now, so he just kissed her temple and murmured, "Of course I do."

They followed the group at a distance, Bowen singing along, Tamsyn humming, until they reached the part of the drive where the road began.

As the others marched on, full of Fire's Draught and caught up in their own merriment, Bowen took hold of Tamsyn's elbow and tugged her onto the lawn and then into the maze.

It was different from how it was in their time, not nearly as tall, and there was no statue of Hecate, but he still knew the way, and Tamsyn followed, the light of her candle flickering, casting the whole scene in a ghostly light.

It had stopped snowing earlier, but now, a few flakes began to drift down again, and as they paused at the part of the maze Bowen remembered from the night they'd come to this time, he took a moment to look at Tamsyn, so lovely in her velvet cape, the snow settling on the hood that covered her dark hair, the candlelight sparkling in her eyes.

"I don't know that this will work," he told her. "I don't even really know what to do, if I'm honest. But we have to try. And . . . and no matter what happens . . . even if we never make it back to 2024, and we blink out of existence . . ."

He didn't know how to finish that statement. There was so much he wanted to tell her, so many things she needed to know, things he should've told her when they had had the time.

But then she leaned forward suddenly, pressing her mouth hard to his, before pulling back and saying, "I trust you, Bowen. More than I've ever trusted anyone. And if this doesn't work, it's not your fault. Just like Declan wasn't your fault. You're the best man I know, Bowen Penhallow, and I'm so glad I broke my rule for you. You were worth it. All of this was worth it."

It felt like a spell, the way those words worked on him.

It felt like magic.

Because it was.

Bowen kissed her back, gently, then reached down and unpinned Y Seren from her dress. The brooch was heavy and cold in his hands, but he couldn't feel any magic in it, and his heart sank even as he kneeled in the frozen grass, holding Y Seren in his cupped hands.

His magic may not be working the way it should while he was here, but wasn't hope its own kind of magic? Wasn't love?

Because both of those things flowed through him as he knelt there on the snowy lawn with Tamsyn in front of him, both their eyes fixed on the brooch.

"Whatever can be undone, so be it," Bowen murmured, repeating Carys's words and hoping—Christ, hoping more desperately than he'd ever hoped for anything before.

But there was no flash of light, no feeling of falling or sliding. The jewels glittered in his hands, but they were cold.

Powerless.

"Let me help," Tamsyn said, resting her hands under his, but he knew it was no use. Whatever had been in Y Seren in the future—in their present—it was gone now.

No, not gone.

Not created yet.

The idea came to Tamsyn at the same time. He could tell from the way her head shot up, her eyes locking on his. "It's not magic now," she said. "But something made it magic in our time. Made it powerful. Maybe something that happened tonight."

His breath was coming fast, and the snow was falling harder now, but Bowen nodded because what she was saying made sense. St. Bugi's balls, that was it. The thing was just a brooch now, an ostentatious bit of sparkle, but at some point, a witch had made it into a powerful artifact.

Had he been that witch?

Taking a deep breath, Bowen closed his eyes, feeling for his magic, but there was nothing there. It just felt . . . cold.

Empty.

Was this what Declan had felt like when that spell had first taken him? When had he realized how badly it had all gone?

Pushing thoughts of Declan away, Bowen concentrated on Y Seren, willing something, *anything,* to happen.

"Are you going back to the future?"

Startled, he glanced up and Tamsyn whirled around, looking over her shoulder to see Emerald emerging from the maze, her hood pushed back, her eyes wide and just the littlest bit glassy.

Fucking Fire's Draught always caught you by surprise the first time.

"That sounds funny," she went on, stumbling a little as she made her way to them. "'Back to the future.'"

"Not as funny as it sounds to us hearing you say it," Tamsyn muttered, almost more to herself, and Emerald frowned in confusion before brushing that away.

"I thought you'd get to go back now that your parents are back together," she said to Bowen.

"Grandparents—how old do you think I am?" Bowen replied,

more than a little offended, but Tamsyn just hit his arm and said, "We did think it was getting them back together that would send us back, yes, but it wasn't. It's something to do with this jewel, but that's not working, either, so you can see where we're a bit stressed at the moment, Emerald."

"This bloody ugly brooch?" Emerald asked, stepping forward. She held out her hands, and Bowen handed it to her without thinking. She might as well look at the thing, it wasn't like there was anything she could—

"Oh! I know what to do!" Emerald cried out, and then took off deeper into the maze at an alarming rate of speed, for a drunken teenager.

For a second, Bowen and Tamsyn were both frozen, kneeling there in the cold grass, stunned into inaction by Emerald's sudden flight.

And then . . .

"Fuck a duck, the book!" Bowen shouted, and jumped to his feet, hauling Tamsyn up with one hand and tearing off in the direction Emerald had run.

His cloak tangled around his legs, though, and Tamsyn was in heels, both of them making awkward progress as they turned this way and that through the hedges, calling Emerald's name, listening for her footsteps, but the snow had muffled everything, and the moon wasn't bright enough.

Bowen slammed into a hedge, cursing as a branch scraped his cheek, then turned, Tamsyn still right behind him, until finally they made another turn, and there she was, Emerald, standing in the middle of an open square in the maze, Y Seren in one hand and that damned booklet in the other.

And she was already saying something.

"Stop!" Bowen shouted.

"I'm helping!" Emerald called back, and the jewel started to glow in her hands.

"Bowen," Tamsyn gasped, clutching his arm. "Maybe—"

There was a sudden flash of light and a sound like a bomb had just gone off, leaving Bowen's ears ringing and Tamsyn wincing as she pressed her face against his biceps, her breath heaving in and out of her lungs.

When the light and the ringing had both faded, they looked to the spot where Emerald had been, but there was nothing there except for Y Seren, lying cold and dead on the grass.

"Where did she go?" Tamsyn asked, her voice hoarse, and Bowen shook his head, despair making him nearly sick as he picked up the brooch.

That fucking spellbook. That nonsense written by a charlatan, with just enough real magic to be dangerous.

Declan all over again.

"Emerald!" he called, hoping against hope.

For a moment, all he could hear was the wind, the gentle whisper of snow falling on the hedges, and then, in the distance, a scream.

No.

A wail.

Coming from the house.

Tamsyn's hand still in his, Bowen started running in that direction, coming out just by the drive.

The front door was still open, light spilling out, and the wailing was louder now, the whole house shaking with it.

He and Tamsyn made their way up the slick stone steps into the castle, and Bowen nearly had to cover his ears against the incessant howling, the shrieking, the clattering of suits of armor from somewhere deeper within the house.

"It's like it was before," Tamsyn said, raising her voice over the cacophony. "When we first got to Tywyll House."

She turned to Bowen, her face pale, her eyes huge and stricken.

"It's Emerald, Bowen. Emerald's the ghost."

CHAPTER 23

Tamsyn had thought it was awful before, hearing those un-earthly wails echoing through Tywyll House, but that had been before she knew the source of those wails was a too-smart teenage girl with big hazel eyes and a love for adventure and the forbidden, a friend who had wanted to help them.

"Don't cry, love, we'll fix this," Bowen said.

Tamsyn hadn't realized she was crying until now, but her cheeks were wet with tears, her eyes stinging.

Emerald.

Oh, Emerald.

"How?" she asked Bowen. "You can't do magic, there's nothing magic *in* the damn brooch, and we don't even know what kind of bullshit spell Emerald did out of that book because the book has vanished, too. We can't fix this just because we want to, Bowen. We need . . . I don't know. We need you to be a witch right now, but you're not."

"Who's not a witch?"

Tamsyn looked up to see Elspeth standing on the stairs, wrapped in a cream silk dressing gown, her long auburn hair loose down her back. Harri was just behind her in a pair of pajamas not unlike those Bowen had worn his first night here, pushing up his glasses with one finger as he studied the scene before him.

"I'm not," Bowen told her. "Or I'm not right now. I'm . . . ah, fuck it. I'm from the future. I was sent back here for Goddess knows why. Thought it was to get you two to realize you should get hitched, but that clearly wasn't it because you're hitched as hitched can be, and I'm still bloody here, aren't I? And Emerald isn't. Or she is, but—"

Another horrible wail filled the air, and Tamsyn saw Bowen slam his eyes shut, a muscle in his jaw twitching.

"She's here, but she's this. And it's my fault. Just like it was with Declan."

"Don't say that," Tamsyn said, taking his hand, but it was no use. The guilt in his face made her stomach hurt, made her wish there were something—anything—she could do to make him stop looking like that.

"Why did you need us to get married?" Elspeth asked, coming down the stairs on bare feet, and then she stopped just on the last step, her eyes searching Bowen's face.

"Oh," she said softly. "You're a Penhallow. You're . . ."

"Your grandson," Bowen said, his voice quiet. "In three years, you'll have a son. You'll call him Simon, and he'll be a right prick most of the time, if I'm being honest. He'll have three sons. Llewellyn, me, and Rhys."

"Not a Henry, then?" Harri asked, and Elspeth shot him a look over her shoulder that had him holding up both hands. "I'm just saying! It's a fine name! Certainly better than Llewellyn. Christ, almost feel sorry for the little bugger. How did I not manage to talk my son out of that?"

He was smiling as he said it, but the longer he looked at Bowen's face, the more that smile faded.

"Because he was born after I died," Harri finally surmised, and Bowen didn't bother to nod.

"And me?" Elspeth asked, her tone light but her eyes sad. "Suppose I wasn't around to talk this Simon out of such a mouthful of a name?"

Again, Bowen didn't answer, and Tamsyn slipped her arm through his, holding him tight.

"If it's any consolation," he said at last, "it's been good getting to know the pair of ye now. I mean, you're both bigger pains in the arse than Da ever let on, but I'm glad I got to know that."

Elspeth laughed at that, but there were tears in her eyes, and when she reached behind her, Harri took her hand and clasped it tightly.

"Well, a good thing we got to meet you, too," Elspeth said, and then she shook her head, brushing away the tears she hadn't let fall. "And a good thing your grandmother—Goddess, that will take some getting used to—is a very powerful witch. Tell me, what has Emerald done?"

Bowen explained the stupid booklet as best he could and Y Seren as well.

"Let me see it," Elspeth said when he was done, and he handed over the brooch. It felt heavier now, colder, and he saw Elspeth shudder as she touched it.

"Ellie," Harri said in a warning tone, but his new wife held up her free hand and said, "This is what you married me for, Harri, so let me do it."

"I actually married you for your amazing tits, but continue."

Elspeth barked out a laugh even as Bowen gritted his teeth and looked briefly heavenward, but Tamsyn just tucked in closer to him and said, "I'm glad you got to see them like this. Young and in love. No matter what happens, Bowen. I'm glad we were here."

He held her hand, looked down at her, and said, simply, "So am I."

She heard everything he was really saying with those three words, and hoped he'd understood what she'd been saying, too. Just in case he hadn't, she raised up on her tiptoes and pressed a kiss to his cheek.

"There is one thing," Elspeth said, studying Y Seren. "I can make this into a very powerful artifact indeed. Powerful enough to bring Emerald back from whatever shadow realm her foolish spell has banished her to. Powerful enough to one day bring the two of you back in time and, one hopes, powerful enough to send you back to where you belong. But there's a chance that a spell this powerful will take just as much as it gives. Harri and I will be safe because of our magic, but the two of you?" She shook her head. "You without your powers, Bowen; you a human, Tamsyn. I am about to infuse this gem with an all-powerful spell, and there is a better than average chance it may drain the life force from one of you. So. Since I'll need to know before I focus my magic, which of you will it be?"

CHAPTER 24

M e," Bowen said so quickly Elspeth had barely finished her sentence.

What other choice was there? Living without Tamsyn? Seeing her sacrifice herself for a mess all of his making? If he hadn't felt so guilty about Declan, if he hadn't been at the wedding in the first place, she wouldn't have been distracted, would've gotten her hands on Y Seren before the first night was out, no doubt.

If anyone was going to lose their life over this, it had to be him.

But then Elspeth said, "And you're sure of that, Tamsyn?"

Bowen looked over, stunned to see Tamsyn at his side, one hand raised.

"One hundred percent," she said, and Bowen shook his head, furious.

"Absolutely not. I said 'me' first."

"I raised my hand before you said that."

"It's my fault we're here."

"It's *my* fault for taking a stupid job just because I wanted enough money not to work for you anymore. And I only wanted not to work for you anymore so I didn't feel guilty about doing all the sex to you, which I've now done anyway. So seriously, this is all on me, and also my vagina."

"Good lord," Harri muttered faintly, but Bowen was focused only on Tamsyn right now.

"I won't let you."

"Will you let Emerald stay trapped like that just because she was trying to help us?"

Bowen wanted to tear his hair out, because good god, he didn't want *any* of this. He wanted Tamsyn home and safe, he wanted Emerald home and safe, and if he had to die to get those things, then so be it.

"Ignore her," he told Elspeth. "If anyone's life force needs to be drained for this spell, it's going to be mine."

"Fuck you, no, it's not!" Tamsyn said, hip-checking him. "I called it first, and that counts for something!"

"If you think I'm letting the woman I love die to fix my own cock-up, you're madder than I ever thought, Tamsyn Bligh. And after you explained the plot of that one movie to me, I already thought you were mad."

"*Midsommar* is a classic, and I'm sorry you don't have taste. But *I* am gonna die for this if anyone has to die. Also . . . did you just call me the woman you love?"

"Yes!" Bowen shouted. Rhiannon's tits, he never shouted, and now he'd done it multiple times in one night. "I love you, of course I do! What kind of idiot would meet the most beautiful, smartest, funniest, sexiest woman on the Goddess's entire fucking green fucking earth and not fall *instantly* in love with her?"

"Well, I love you, too!" she shouted back. "Even when your facial hair is out of control! *Especially* when your facial hair is out of control, which has been really weird for me and made me wonder if I have certain kinks or something! But you're kind and gentle and hot, and oh my god, do you know what a *unicorn* that makes you? And you might *know* actual unicorns, which is a whole other thing I've had to deal with, but here I am! All in love with you and shit!"

By the end of their joint monologues, they were both panting, and if Bowen's grandparents hadn't been standing right there, he was fairly certain he would have swooped Tamsyn into his arms and kissed the bloody hell out of her.

But they were standing there, both of them staring wide-eyed, and finally Elspeth said, "Oh, for the love of all the saints, neither of you are going to *die*. I am an *amazing* witch, I can do this spell in my sleep. I just wanted to make sure you two really cared for each other. And it could not be clearer that you do. Now. Everyone stand back because I'm about to be bloody fantastic."

"Christ, I love you, *blodyn tatws,*" Harri murmured, and Elspeth threw him a fond look over her shoulder before concentrating on Y Seren, indecipherable words falling from her lips.

The wailing faded, and Bowen felt the air begin to shift and change, colder and stiller, as power grew around Elspeth.

"When this spell is over, this brooch will be mightily powerful,"

Elspeth said, taking a deep breath as Y Seren began to glow in her hands. "Promise me you'll use it well, the both of you."

She looked up then, her face slightly hazy as Bowen realized he was fading away.

"My grandson," Elspeth said softly. "*Fy wyr.* Bowen."

Elspeth was growing fainter now, the whole house shimmering around him, and as she stepped close, Bowen tried to reach for her, only to see his hand go through the place where her shoulder should've been.

"I won't see you again if this works," he told her, and she smiled, Rhys suddenly appearing in her face.

"It's going to work. Your bloodline is powerful because of *me*, Bowen Penhallow. Never forget it."

"I won't," he promised, wrapping an arm around Tamsyn's waist and holding her close. "But . . . Elspeth. *Nain.* When you die—"

Elspeth reached out, covering Bowen's lips with one finger even though he couldn't even feel the pressure now. "Are we together?" she asked him. "Me and your *taid*?"

She glanced back at Harri, who still stood on the stairs, one hand on the banister, his expression full of awe for his wife.

"You are," Bowen told her truthfully, and her smile was sad but sweet.

"Then that's all that matters to me. Be well, *fy wyr*. I'm glad I got to know you. And your bride."

"We weren't really—" Tamsyn started to say, but Elspeth just smiled again and shook her head.

"Oh, but you are, *wyres*. Now back you go. To your own time. I have a feeling our Emerald will meet you there."

Bowen wanted to ask what she meant by that, wanted to ask a million things, but that sliding sensation was taking hold again, pulling him in, and with a sudden flash of light, everything went dark.

CHAPTER 25

Oh, I guess I died after all.
   That sucks.

Tamsyn swam up into consciousness slowly with those two thoughts in her mind, even as she began to realize she was freezing and wet, and surely you didn't feel like that if you were dead?

Or maybe you *did,* but only if you—

"You're not dead, *fy ngeneth i,*" a gruff voice said near her ear, and Tamsyn opened her eyes then.

Bowen was leaning over her, his hair wet with rain and dripping onto her face, but his eyes warm as he cupped her face and looked down at her.

Suddenly everything he'd said earlier came back to her, about her being smart and sexy and him being in love with her . . .

"Did I say that stuff out loud again?" she asked, her voice hoarse, and he nodded, his thumb moving briefly over her lips.

"And are we back? Where we should be?"

Bowen lifted his gaze, but just for a second, almost like he couldn't bear to stop looking at her.

She liked that.

"I think so?" he said. "Bit hard to say until we go inside and see for ourselves, but we're back in the clothes we were wearing the night we went back in time."

Tamsyn nodded, or at least she tried to. Her head still felt very . . . spinny.

Still, she had to get up, had to make sure they'd saved Emerald after all, had to know they'd—

"Easy," Bowen said, gently pushing on her shoulder, but she shook him off, rising to her feet on wobbly knees.

"I'm fine," she said. "Just the world's worst jet lag."

"You thought you were dead," he said as he got to his feet, too, and Tamsyn shot him a look.

"Yeah, I think that after long flights, too. Now can we *please* get moving, Mountain Man?"

With that, she took off back toward the entrance of the maze, the ground muddy beneath her heels, slowing her down.

Kicking out one foot and then the other, Tamsyn sent the shoes flying into the hedges with a sound that was suspiciously like one of Bowen's grunts, and then, on bare feet, she jogged out onto Tywyll House's lawn.

"Christ Almighty, how do you move so fast for such a wee woman?" Bowen asked, coming up behind her and sounding slightly out of breath.

"I did track in high school," Tamsyn replied, but she was looking at the drive, her heart pounding as relief flooded through her veins.

"My rental car," she said, pointing to the little red Yaris. "We're back. Elspeth did it, Bowen." Tamsyn couldn't help the laugh that bubbled out of her. "Oh my god, Elspeth really did it. Not that I thought she *wouldn't,* but still."

"She really was that powerful of a witch," Bowen replied, and Tamsyn nodded before that word—*was*—sunk in fully.

Was.

They were gone now, Elspeth and Harri, even though just moments before they'd been standing in front of her and Bowen, young and alive and in love . . .

Tamsyn felt Bowen slide his hand into hers, and she turned to see him looking down at her, his handsome face grave. "I know" was all he said, and Tamsyn squeezed his fingers before sniffling just a little bit and turning resolutely back toward the house.

Elspeth had gotten them back to the right time—now they needed to make sure Emerald had been saved as well.

"Tam—" Bowen started to say, but she was already moving again.

Or at least she was, until her bare feet hit the freezing—and pointy—gravel of the drive.

"Ow!" she cried, wincing as she went to step back onto the grass, and then suddenly she was off her feet altogether, swept up into Bowen's arms.

His tux was as wet as her jumpsuit, but she could still feel the warmth of his body, smell the familiar scent of him that she'd come to think of simply as *home* sometime during the last few days, and as she wrapped her arms around his neck and let him carry her toward the house, Tamsyn looked at that stern jaw, that determined gaze.

"It really is stupid how much I love you," she told him, and he glanced over at her, one corner of his mouth quirking.

"Did you mean to say that out loud?"

"I absolutely did."

"Good," he replied, "because I meant what I said back in 1957. I'm in love with you, have been since that first night."

"It's because you saw me drink out of a twirly straw," she told him. "Men can't resist that."

He gave one of those huffing laughs she loved so much, and Tamsyn held him tighter, snuggled in closer.

"Must've been that," Bowen said, mounting the steps with her still in his arms. "And I was a damn fool not to tell you right then. Damn fool for not telling you a lot of things."

"Like about Declan," Tamsyn guessed softly, and Bowen nodded.

They were at the top of the steps now, and when he paused, Tamsyn maneuvered herself out of his arms and onto her own feet, turning to face him.

"We'll fix it together," she told him, as solemn a promise as she had ever made. "Between the two of us, there has to be something. Some spell you know, some artifact I can acquire . . . whatever we can do to help Declan, Bowen, we'll do."

She saw his throat move with emotion, his eyes bright as he looked down at her, and then, as the door behind her opened, Tamsyn saw those same bright eyes go wide.

"Help Declan with what?" a lilting voice asked, and Tamsyn turned to see a redheaded man in evening wear standing there, amused as he took in the pair of them.

Tamsyn didn't remember seeing him at the party the first time they'd been there, but then, she'd been so focused on Y Seren and everything else that she'd barely noticed anyone.

Confused, she looked to Bowen, who was pale now, his lips slightly parted, and then at the man, who rocked back on both his heels, hands in his trouser pockets.

"If anyone needs help, it appears to be *you,* mate," the man said. "Jesus, what were the pair of you up to out there?" He glanced down at Tamsyn's bare and grassy feet, eyebrows raised, but before Tamsyn could answer, Carys appeared at his side, and Tamsyn caught her breath.

The difference between the woman she'd last seen sobbing her heart out in the maze and the vision now standing before her was so stark it was hard to believe they were the same person. She technically looked the same—same fair hair and dark eyes, same slender frame—but there was a light to her now. She glowed, standing there at the man's side in a deep red gown with a tartan sash, and while rubies sparkled in her ears and at her throat, Y Seren was nowhere to be seen.

"Declan, stop being cheeky and let them in, it's freezing!" Carys said, jokingly shoving at the man, and suddenly Tamsyn understood why Bowen was so pale.

"Declan?" she echoed, and the redheaded man shot her a look of faux hurt as he slipped an arm around Carys's waist.

"Don't tell me you already forgot the name of yer boyfriend's oldest, dearest, and frankly *only* mate, did you?" he asked, and then gestured for both of them to come into the hall.

Tamsyn felt numb from more than just the cold as she moved into the house, the stone floors chilly underneath her bare feet as she took in Declan—handsome, cheerful, and . . .

"Alive," Bowen said, the word so soft that only Tamsyn really heard him.

"What was that?" Declan asked, but instead of answering, Bowen just threw his arms around his friend, damn near lifting him off the ground with the force of his hug.

"Whoa!" Declan exclaimed, still laughing, but he thumped Bowen on the back all the same, his grin never wavering, and suddenly Tamsyn understood just why this man's death—or whatever it had been—had hurt Bowen as badly as it had. Like this version of Carys, there was a light around him, an innate energy, and even though Declan was currently very much alive and standing right in front of her, Tamsyn's heart broke for Bowen all over again.

When he pulled back from the hug, Bowen's eyes were bright again, but some of the color was returning to his face as he gave an almost disbelieving laugh. "Just . . . always good to see you, Dec," he said, and Declan shook his head, bemused.

"Well, remind me to send you off into the maze with your lady love more often," he said, just as Carys suddenly seemed to notice the state of them.

"Oh, you must be freezing! Let me get some towels."

As she scurried off to do that, Tamsyn stared after her, still feeling like the ground was tilting beneath her a little bit.

"What they need is *alcohol,* my darling!" he called, then waved it off before saying, "Wait here."

Tamsyn could hear people talking in the library, but she and Bowen stayed in the front hall as Declan sauntered off.

"That's—" Tamsyn said.

"It is."

"And he's—"

"He is."

"But he's *not*—"

"He's not."

"How?"

In the silence that followed, Tamsyn could hear the ticking of the hall clock, the gentle clinking of ice in glasses, and the murmured lull of several people in low-voiced conversation, but Bowen didn't answer her for the longest time until, finally, he just said, "I don't know."

"Because sometimes," a voice said, and they both turned to see an elegantly dressed elderly woman making her way toward them, "magic finds a way."

CHAPTER 26

H ello, you two."

Bowen stared at the woman in front of him, blinking. She was old, but her hazel eyes were still bright, and if they hadn't given her away, the brilliant green of her dress and the emeralds sparkling in the tiara holding back her white hair would've done it.

"Emerald!" Tamsyn cried, throwing her arms around Emerald, not unlike how Bowen had done so with Declan, albeit a good deal gentler. The girl they'd met at fifteen was in her eighties now, something that was almost impossible to believe, but then Bowen was getting used to believing a lot of impossible things lately.

Time travel was real.

Declan was back.

Tamsyn loved him.

Chuckling, Emerald patted Tamsyn's back as she said, "Actually, I'm Her Grace, the Duchess of Hareford now, but my old friends can always call me Emerald."

"A duchess?" Tamsyn asked, pulling back, her eyes wide. "Does that mean I have to bow to you?"

"No, but Madoc does, and that's very fun," Emerald replied before pounding on the stone floor with the elegant silver—and emerald-crusted, obviously—cane Bowen now saw she held.

"Madoc!" she called, and Bowen turned, half expecting to see that chubby little boy with the curls tearing down the hallway.

Instead, it was the older version who came, if not running, then definitely hurrying, his white tufts of hair bouncing as he made his way from the library to the front hallway.

"Yes, Your Grace?" he asked, his face red from the exertion and also, Bowen guessed, from the very nice glass of whisky he held in his hand, whisky that sloshed as he gave a little bow of his head.

Emerald lifted one shoulder in an elegant shrug. "Never mind. I forget what it was now."

Scowling, he pointed at her with the hand still holding the glass. "You enjoyed that," he told her, and she smiled back at him, serene and unapologetic.

"I did, actually."

Shaking his head, Madoc muttered something in Welsh before looking at Bowen and Tamsyn, his brow wrinkling.

"We met when you arrived, didn't we?" he asked, and Bowen, who had no idea if that were true in this version of things, just nodded.

Madoc nodded as well, thinking it over. "Yes. Yes, I'm sure we did. That's why the two of you look so familiar, no doubt."

"No doubt," Tamsyn echoed, and Madoc nodded again, but looked a little unsure as he headed back to the party, leaving the two of them alone with Emerald.

"Now," Emerald said, turning back to Bowen and Tamsyn. "In answer to your question, namely, *how,* the answer can actually be found in that silly little book of mine. You were right that it wasn't real magic. Or rather it *was,* but it was cobbled together from actual spells, and not exactly the safest spells at that. But there was one thing it said, one thing I always liked, and that was that magic is a wild thing. You can study it, you can learn it, you can attempt to master parts of it, but you'll never really know it, never understand it. The best you can do is try to avoid its risks and be thankful for its gifts."

Stepping forward, she laid one hand on Bowen's cheek. It was the strangest feeling, looking into those eyes he'd last seen in the face of a child and seeing them shining out of the face of the beautiful elderly woman in front of him.

"This was a gift, Bowen Penhallow. Whether it was from Elspeth or the universe or magic herself, it was a gift. One I suggest you be thankful for."

"I am," he told her, then leaned down, pressing a kiss to her wrinkled cheek, the skin there thin but soft and smelling like some expensive perfume. "And I'm so glad you're here, Emerald."

"As am I!" she said with a laugh, patting his shoulder. "The things I would've missed out on if I'd been stuck as a ghost all that time! Finding out I really *did* have powers for one. And my husband for another, but that's . . . well, that's a story for later. After drinks."

She threw him a wink that once again reminded him of the teenage girl she'd been, and Bowen laughed, nodding. "Sounds good."

"Is anything else different?" Tamsyn asked, folding her arms over her chest. "Like, did we alter the future in any ways we might need to know about?"

Emerald shook her head. "No, nothing I can think of. We had always been at war with Mars in 2024, yes?"

When Tamsyn's mouth dropped open, the old woman laughed again, waving a gloved hand.

"Only joking, darlings, couldn't help it. But no, as far as I can tell, things are as they should be."

"And Harri and Elspeth?" Bowen couldn't help asking.

But Emerald only met his gaze, sad but firm. "Things are as they should be," she repeated softly.

Tamsyn stepped close to him, wrapping an arm around his waist and tucking herself tight to his side. "I'm sorry," she said, but he shook his head, remembering what his *nain* had said there on the staircase.

She had been with *Taid* Harri, and that had been what mattered. Maybe if they'd lived, Bowen's father would've been a kinder man, a gentler one, but then Bowen's mother would've died all the same, and that would've changed him. Or maybe he still would've been the same stubborn, self-centered man he'd become no matter what had changed.

That was the past now.

What mattered was the present.

With Tamsyn.

"Oh, by the way," Emerald said, nodding at Tamsyn. "I'll take Y Seren back, if you don't mind."

Tamsyn blinked at her, her face blank for a moment, before

she reached into the pocket of her jumpsuit and slowly pulled out the brooch. She and Bowen both stared at it as it lay in the palm of her hand, the jewels glittering dimly under the chandelier.

"How did it get there?" Tamsyn wondered aloud, but Emerald only snapped a slightly imperious hand at her, making Tamsyn blink again. "Okay, not used to you being older than me," she said, but she handed the jewel over all the same. Even without touching it, Bowen could tell the power it had once held was gone yet again, leaving it nothing more than an ugly piece of jewelry.

And then Emerald looked up at Tamsyn and said, "I assume I can have the reward wired to you?"

Bowen felt Tamsyn startle as she looked up at him and then over at Emerald. "The . . . reward? Wait. *You* placed that listing? I was getting Y Seren for you?"

"I was feeling sentimental," Emerald replied, smiling smugly at them before turning and sauntering away as well as an eighty-two-year-old woman with a cane could saunter. "I'll have the money sent as soon as possible."

They both stood there in stunned silence, watching her walk away, before Tamsyn called out, "How do you have *that* much freaking money?"

"I told you I have some good stories!" Emerald called back, and the laugh that followed sounded much younger than her years.

They were alone again now, and Bowen turned back to Tamsyn, sure he looked just as dumbstruck as she did right now.

"Time travel is really, really weird," she said at last, and he couldn't help but laugh, pulling her in tight, his arms wrapped around her.

"Rhiannon's tits, is it ever," he said, then pulled back to look down at her. "But I'd go anywhere with you. 1957. Mars. That loud bloody pub with its vile bloody drinks."

"America?" she asked, and he heard the real question behind that one.

"Anywhere," he repeated, dipping his head to kiss her.

His lips had only brushed hers when they heard the sound of rushing feet, and they broke apart to see a rather sheepish but grinning Declan and Carys approach, glasses of whisky and towels in hand.

"Sorry, sorry!" Declan said as Carys handed them the towels, her cheeks pink, her eyes shining. "There was, um . . . Well, there was this bit of mistletoe, and we possibly got a little distracted."

"Dangerous thing, mistletoe," Tamsyn said somberly, and Bowen looked at her, this woman he loved so, and then at his best friend, smiling and happy and alive, the woman he loved at his side, and thought how lucky he was, how incredibly, stupidly, unfairly blessed.

"I love you," he told Tamsyn now, not caring that Declan and Carys were standing there. Hell, he would've said it in front of the whole bloody castle full of people if they'd been there. The whole world.

"A Yuletide miracle," Tamsyn mused, her lips curling up in a soft smile that he knew was only his.

Would only be his.

Forever.

And then he kissed her, absolutely no mistletoe required.

EPILOGUE

Next Halloween
Graves Glen

Tamsyn had always loved Halloween. You got candy, you got to be out after dark, you got to dress up . . . zero downsides, in her opinion. In fact, maybe that's what had drawn her to acquiring in the first place. She got to dress up as someone else, she got to go to spooky places, and, sure, she was usually getting something like "Demon's Eyeball Encased in Glass (1702)" as opposed to M&Ms, but the basic joys were the same. So yes, while it now came second to Yule, Halloween had been right up there as a Favorite Holiday.

Until tonight, that was.

Groaning, Tamsyn sat down on the plush sofa in Wells and Gwyn's living room, stretching her aching feet out in front of her as she reached up to pluck the surprisingly heavy plastic crown off her head.

"Is it always like that?" she asked as Gwyn walked over, smirking, and handed her a glass of red wine.

"Pretty much," Gwyn replied, sinking down into a leather armchair across from Tamsyn and kicking her own booted feet up onto the heavy trunk that served as a coffee table. "Last year Wells hid in the storage room at Penhallow's and cried."

"I did not *cry*," Wells countered as he entered the room. Like his girlfriend, he was decked out in long black robes, but unlike Gwyn, he'd skipped the pointy hat, his dark hair slicked back from his face, his beard neat and clipped.

"You did hide, though," Gwyn said, tilting her head to look at him where he stood in the doorway, and Wells nodded.

"Too fucking right I did, it was a madhouse."

Tamsyn could believe that. Tonight, the streets had been full of people in costumes, the local businesses handing out candy and serving Halloween-themed food and drinks, and nowhere had been busier than Something Wicked and Penhallow's. Tamsyn had personally handed out at least a thousand candy bars, she was pretty sure, and Gwyn had completely sold out of nearly every T-shirt Something Wicked had, even the Baby Witches' latest creation, a bright orange shirt that read, "We Have a WITCH-u-ation Here!"

It had been loud and chaotic and fun and a blur of caramel apples and pumpkin spice, and Tamsyn wasn't sure she'd ever been so exhausted in her entire life.

"It's okay if you don't want to marry Bowen now," Gwyn told

her, sinking deeper into her chair. "The beard was already so much to accept, and now Halloween in Graves Glen? How can you ask a woman to bear that, too, Bowen?"

From his spot next to Tamsyn on the sofa, Bowen grunted.

Smiling, Tamsyn turned to look at him. He'd also gone for robes tonight, but his were dark blue with silver thread, an intricate pewter medallion around his neck. It made him look like an ancient sorcerer, and Tamsyn was abso*lute*ly planning on asking him to hold on to this costume. She was definitely planning on keeping hers, a gorgeous purple velvet gown trimmed in ermine, complete with fake jewels sewn onto the low square neckline. She'd been going for a Medieval Princess Thing, a complement to his wizard, and honestly, Tamsyn wondered if it would be weird to use it as her wedding dress in December.

Surely you got to be a little extra when you were marrying a powerful witch?

The emerald, ruby, and diamond ring on her left hand sparkled as she reached over now to squeeze Bowen's leg.

"It would take more than a few hopped up trick-or-treaters to scare me off becoming Mrs. Bowen Penhallow," she told Gwyn, and then she leaned in closer to Bowen, scratching at his beard. "And honestly? This really does it for me."

Bowen grunted again, but he was smiling as he took her hand from his face and brought it to his lips, brushing a kiss over her knuckles.

"I get it," Gwyn said as Wells came over and took the chair

next to her. "Next time we do Girls' Night, I'll tell you about Esquire here and his waistcoats."

Wells waggled his eyebrows at Gwyn, making her laugh, and despite her aching feet, sore head, and the fact that she had somehow ended up with glitter in her hair at some point this evening, Tamsyn felt a glow of happiness settle deep into her bones.

She'd been worried the first time Bowen had brought her to Graves Glen, back at the first of the year, just after they'd gotten back from Tywyll House. Her history with the Jones Witches wasn't great, and they had every reason not to trust her, but to Tamsyn's surprise—and relief—Gwynnevere Jones and Vivienne Jones-Penhallow weren't the kind of women who held grudges.

It probably didn't hurt that Tamsyn had brought a *very* nice bottle of wine and an even better apology that first night all of them had had dinner together here in this very house high in the hills above Graves Glen.

Or maybe it was like Vivi had said when Bowen announced his plans to get a house near town—any woman who made Bowen Penhallow so happy he wanted to settle down was clearly a perfect fit for this misfit family.

It still kind of blew Tamsyn's mind that she had a home now, a real one that wasn't on wheels. The cottage was small—just two bedrooms, one of which Bowen was using as a study—but cozy, and between Bowen's new position at Penhaven College and Tamsyn's job at the local antique store, Haunted Treasures; the Girls' Nights with Gwyn and Vivi; and the ultimately disastrous but still fun First Annual Penhallow Brothers' Bonfire and Barbecue Night, Tamsyn had never felt so ... *wholesome*.

Well, she amended as she looked again at Bowen in his robes and felt a pleasant shiver at the idea of taking them off later this evening, at least *mostly* wholesome.

"Gwynnevere, your mother is a saint!" Rhys announced as he and Vivi entered the room, out of their own witchy costumes and back in jeans and sweaters. "I swear, I only gave Taran one piece of candy, but apparently even that scant amount of sugar was enough to turn him into a whirling dervish of madness."

"You gave him *five* pieces of candy because *you* are a whirling dervish of madness," Vivi corrected, slipping an arm around her husband's waist, her indulgent smile taking any sting out of the words. "Although you're right about Aunt Elaine. Offering to take Taran for tonight should definitely mean even a witch qualifies for sainthood."

Tamsyn smiled again, remembering Taran tearing around Something Wicked, a caramel apple in each hand, one of which had eventually ended up stuck to his honey-blond curls. She'd helped Vivi clean him up, and as Tamsyn had been wiping the last streak of caramel off one chubby cheek, Vivi had said, "Tell Aunt Tamsyn thank you, Taran."

Another reminder of how easily these people had made room for her in their family, and she would never stop being grateful for it.

As Vivi and Rhys filled Gwyn and Wells in on the rest of Taran's Halloween antics, Bowen slid closer to Tamsyn on the sofa, slipping an arm around her hips and pulling her into his side. She went easily, resting her head against his chest as he lowered his voice to ask, "How much longer do we need to stay here and be social?"

Tilting her chin up to look at him, Tamsyn tweaked his beard again. "Until I finish my wine."

"This wine?" Bowen asked, nodding at the glass she'd set on the trunk, and before she could answer, he sat up, picked up the glass, and proceeded to down the entire thing.

"There," he said, sitting the empty glass back down with a decisive thump. "Finished. Guess we should go now."

"Ah, the mountain man returns to his lair," Rhys said, but he was smiling. They all were, Tamsyn realized, looking at both her and Bowen with real fondness, and once again, she thanked whatever quirk of the universe had landed her here in this place with this family.

"Honestly, the fact that he came over at all is a miracle," Gwyn said, then tilted her glass of wine at Tamsyn. "Sure you're not a witch? Because the transformation you've done on this one seems pretty magical to me."

"Nah, I'm just really good in bed," Tamsyn replied, and everyone except Bowen—who was too busy blushing—laughed.

They said their farewells at the door, the women hugging and kissing cheeks, the Penhallow brothers doing their usual thing of vaguely insulting each other before offering claps on the shoulder and handshakes, and as Tamsyn and Bowen stepped out onto the house's front porch, the full moon bathed the surrounding woods in pale silvery light.

It was cool, the air soft and smelling like woodsmoke, and

Tamsyn paused to take a deep breath, tilting her head back to look at the sky.

Behind her, Bowen wrapped his arms around her waist, pulling her in and resting his chin on the top of her head.

"If it weren't for the cars in the driveway, we could be back in 1957," Tamsyn mused. "This place reminds me of Tywyll in a weird way."

"It's the woods," Bowen said, his voice a low grumble. "And the mountains and the magic in the place."

"It is magic," Tamsyn agreed, turning in his arms to face him, her own arms sliding around his neck.

"This," she told him, giving him a light nip to his lower lip that had him sucking in a quick breath, "is where you're supposed to say something like"—she lowered her voice to imitate his growl—"'*You're* magic, *cariad.*'"

Bowen pulled her in closer, their hips flush, and now Tamsyn was the one feeling a little breathless. "You're better than magic," he said.

Simple words, nothing flowery or poetic, but they meant more to her than any sonnet or soliloquy, because coming from this man, it was the most romantic thing anyone had ever said to her.

"I love you kind of a lot, Bowen Penhallow," she said softly, and his teeth glinted in the darkness as he smiled.

"The feeling is mutual, *fy negenth i,*" he told her. "Now let me take you home and prove it."

And he did.

Acknowledgments

As always, I am the luckiest witch in the coven to work with such wonderful people on these books, and for this one especially, I am so grateful!

This book is dedicated to my agent, Holly Root, and my editor, Tessa Woodward, both of whom were endlessly patient and kind during a really difficult period for me and who always valued Me the Person over Me the Writer. That shouldn't be rare in this business, but it is, and I am so thankful for both of them!

Thanks, too, to everyone at Avon who puts so much work into this series, especially Madelyn Blaney, who, like Tessa and Holly, has been such a lovely person to work with even as this book was making me tear my hair out.

Friends and family pulled me through this, and they may be the only people happier than me that I actually managed to cross the finish line!

And most importantly, thank YOU, the readers. I made you wait for this one, and your encouragement and excitement for All Things Graves Glen has meant more than I can ever say. This book truly would not exist without y'all. Love you, witches. XOXO.

About the Author

ERIN STERLING, who also writes as Rachel Hawkins, is the *New York Times* bestselling author of *The Ex Hex* and *The Wife Upstairs*, as well as multiple books for young readers. Her work has been translated in more than a dozen countries. She studied gender and sexuality in Victorian literature at Auburn University and currently lives in Alabama.